T0374180

THE WARRIOR WITHIN

DAVID RAY

WestBow Press books may be ordered through booksellers or by contacting:

WestBow Press
A Division of Thomas Nelson & Zondervan
1663 Liberty Drive
Bloomington, IN 47403
www.westbowpress.com
844-714-3454

ISBN: 978-1-6642-6996-5 (sc)
ISBN: 978-1-6642-6998-9 (hc)
ISBN: 978-1-6642-6997-2 (e)

Library of Congress Control Number: 2022911595

Print information available on the last page.

WestBow Press rev. date: 08/02/2022

For my family: Kay, Josh, and Courtney

For my grandchildren: Benjamin, Shiloh, Micah, and Shelby

And for the wonderful people who worshipped with
us over the years in the congregations we served

the carpenter picks up the saw
and walks toward me again.
i shudder and gasp, “why?
why is he torturing me like this?”
but then, after the blade has done its work,
i realize that in the hands of a master carpenter,
no piece of wood is safe,
from becoming a masterpiece.
—Steven James, *Sailing Between the Stars*

Answer me quickly, O Lord.
My spirit fails.
Do not hide your face from me
Or I will be like those who go down to the pit.
Let the morning bring me word of your unfailing love,
For I have put my trust in you.
Show me the way I should go,
For to you, I lift my soul.
Rescue me from my enemies, O, Lord,
For I hide myself in you.
—Psalm 143:7–9

CHAPTER 1

Intruders

What was that? I wasn't sure what woke me. Was it our new puppy? I grabbed my phone and discovered that it was just after two o'clock in the morning. It seemed like forever as I remained still and listened. The house creaked. Goose, our new puppy, rolled over on her mat near the foot of our bed. I could hear her collar jiggle, but it was obvious she was still asleep. We had been given the black Lab mix almost two months ago from a friend, and like all puppies, she played hard and slept even harder.

I could hear Rebekah's gentle breathing. She swore she didn't snore, as did I, but she did, just very quietly, unlike myself. All seemed in order and at peace, but still I was awake. Something had awoken me. I had heard something. We had planned to drive over to Louisville for the weekend, but the weather forecast of strong winds and possible thunderstorms had made us decide at the last minute to cancel our trip.

Then I heard the noise again. The lock on our back door was being tinkered with. Had we left it unlocked? I continued to lie there listening. Perhaps it was just the wind; maybe the predicted storm had arrived early. No—somebody was attempting to come into our home. I slipped out of bed quietly, trying not to disturb either Rebekah or Goose.

Leading off from our bedroom was a large walk-in closet. On the top shelf was my Glock 19 in a locked case. As quietly as possible, I opened the case, grabbed a loaded clip, and snapped it into place. Then I barefooted my way down the hallway to the top of the stairs. Crouching down, I listened cautiously. The stairs emptied into the front entranceway. To the right was the kitchen and back door; to the left was the great room and fireplace. I heard the faint sound of a footstep. Somebody was inside the house.

A drawer in the kitchen slid open quietly as a dim light flickered from the kitchen area, probably a cell phone. I looked down at the weapon I was holding in the dark. Would I use it? Holding it tightly was one thing, but aiming at a real person and squeezing the trigger was quite another. If I continued down the stairs, I would be forced to make that decision. Did we even have anything in this house for which I was ready to kill in defense? I immediately thought about Rebekah asleep back in our bed; the answer was yes. I examined the Glock and continued to listen.

Another drawer opened. I heard a door slowly creak, perhaps to the pantry. I looked at my phone, which I was still holding. I contemplated calling 911, but that would require an audible voice, even if just a whisper. Such might be heard even from downstairs. I silently punched in the three digits, but I didn't press call. I could hear my heart pounding. Maybe whoever it was would just leave.

Footsteps moved from the kitchen toward the great room, but then they hesitated. Whoever was down there was listening as well. Suddenly, our bedroom door burst open, and light spilled down the hallway. Rebekah leaned out from the bedroom and saw me crouching low at the top of the stairs.

She quietly whispered, "Richard, is something wrong?"

Almost immediately, Goose came charging past Rebekah and bounding toward me. She didn't bark, but the sound of her galloping on the hardwood floor was loud enough to alert our whole neighborhood. Her puppy's heart assumed it was time to play. I punched the call button.

I heard footsteps scurry across the kitchen floor and toward the back door. I also heard a man's voice urge someone else to hurry. Both intruders scrambled out the back door. Goose and I quickly bounded down the stairs. I turned on every light switch that I passed. Just as I entered the kitchen, the 911 operator answered. I quickly gave her the address and explained that we had intruders in the house. She said that the police were on their way and asked if I was positive that no one else remained in our home.

The dispatcher's experienced advice changed my plans. Instead of running out into the backyard to give chase, I conducted a sweep of every downstairs room. There was no one there, as I expected, but my heartbeat continued to pound wildly. Rebekah, wrapped in a white terry cloth robe, holding herself tightly, came down the stairs with a puzzled look on her face. Just as she noticed the Glock in my hand, the doorbell rang. It was the police. They had to have been in the neighborhood to have responded so quickly.

As the two officers stood in the doorway, they suggested that I put away my gun. I hadn't realized that I was waving the Glock around frantically as I told them about the two people breaking into our home. I put the pistol down gently on the fireplace mantel, somewhat relieved that I hadn't needed to pull the trigger.

One of the officers left to survey the outside area. The other officer started asking us questions. Goose was hyped from the excitement, but she obviously just wanted the officer to scratch behind her ears. He obliged her as he noticed the white mark on her chest, which resembled a flying goose against her jet-black fur—thus the explanation for her name. As he continued to investigate us, we heard the back door open. The other officer reentered, having completed his brief search of our property. He reported nothing out of the ordinary.

At the police's urging, we surveyed the downstairs to determine if anything was missing. There didn't seem to be anything out of place, much less gone. The one kitchen drawer that was left open was dusted for fingerprints, but only two sets of prints were found. They would most certainly be Rebekah's and mine. The intruders had obviously worn gloves.

Finally, the police officer said, "This doesn't seem to be a random burglary. The evidence, so far, indicates that the intruders were looking for something specific, not just any type of valuable. Do you have any idea what that might be? Is there anything in your past or present that might explain why you would be the target?"

Rebekah and I looked at each other but decided not to attempt to explain our unbelievable adventure of the past year. We shook our heads, but we both had reservations.

The back door key lock had been picked, as best as the police could tell, but the dead bolt must have been left unlocked. As the officers left, they reminded us to use the dead bolt and explained that we would be contacted by a police detective later in the day.

Standing on the back porch, watching Goose run off her puppy energy in the morning darkness, Rebekah said, "That was unnerving. What could they possibly have been after? I feel violated."

"I don't know. We don't have anything of value here in the house."

We both were disturbed as we personally contemplated our past year and whether there could be any connection to the night's invasion. Rebekah started some coffee, knowing that neither of us were going back to sleep.

I discovered that the fireplace still had some warm coals. After some stoking and an additional log, the flames jumped to life. With our mugs of warm brew in hand, we plopped ourselves down before the fire. Our feet were touching together on the leather footstool. Goose, who evidently didn't have any misgivings about going back to sleep, curled up beside us.

Rebekah said, "This reminds me of our cabin prison on the ranch in Argentina. We were there only ten days or so, but when I think about it, it was one of the most wonderful seasons in my life despite the circumstances. It was just the two of us, and almost every night, this is how we sat in front of that cast-iron potbellied stove. We sat in those old rocking chairs with our feet touching while propped up on a wooden crate we used as a footstool."

"I remember. How could I ever forget? I also recall riding in the back of that truck, wondering what was going to happen to us, and I remember sitting on our church log before our own private waterfall. That was a special moment."

She said with a softer voice, "I recall our wedding in that dark basement, in a cage. You couldn't remember all the words of the wedding vows, but it was sufficient, and it was beautiful." She squeezed my hand.

"I recall the sick feeling I had when I realized that you had been shot." We both sat in silence for several minutes as our memories floated through many more of the details of our year as hostages. I checked my phone for the time. It was approaching five thirty when, unexpectedly, the phone rang. The ringtone startled us as it broke the stillness. I assumed it was the police calling. I was correct—but not for the reason I had anticipated.

The police dispatcher informed me that we needed to come down to the foundation's office. Apparently, it had also been broken into during the night. I could not believe what I was hearing. Were our nightmares of last year beginning again?

Rebekah looked at me, trying to read my face.

I said, "You're not going to believe this. Someone broke into the foundation's office about the same time someone was breaking into our home."

She sat there in shock.

"We need to get dressed and get downtown. The police are waiting for us."

It didn't take us long to get showered and dressed.

As Rebekah finished getting ready, I unloaded the Glock and returned it to its safe, closeted hiding place. I was thankful I had it, but I was also thankful I hadn't had to use it.

As we left the house, we hardly even knew what to say to each other.

Rebekah finally broke the silence as I drove. "There is no way this is a just a coincidence. Somebody thinks we have something they want, but what could it be?"

"I was wondering the same thing."

Even though it was early on a Saturday, I decided to call Mary Ann, my executive assistant. I knew that she would want to be there, and I knew that I needed her there. It wouldn't take her long since she lived in a downtown apartment just a few blocks from the office. I hired her a few days after the foundation came into existence, less than a year ago. *She has been a blessing.*

Our last year's adventure had ended with us finding a huge load of tainted gold. After a quick court decision in Argentina, we were awarded Rebekah's now-deceased husband's ill-gotten loot that he had embezzled from the dark company. We took the haul and created the Polaris Foundation.

The clandestine international organization that had helped secure our escape as hostages was called the Polaris Project, named after the North Star. In honor of the Polaris Project, we decided to name the new foundation following suit. The Polaris Foundation was created to help fund organizations that fight the horror of human trafficking. Managing the investment portfolio and exploring how to award the proceeds to organizations that were involved in this worldwide war was my new job.

As I turned onto Richmond Road toward downtown Lexington, I could see the flash of emergency lights. They were parked in front of the office building where the Polaris Foundation was housed.

Mary Ann was waiting for the two of us at the front door, and a police officer was standing beside her. She looked slightly disheveled, unlike her normal appearance. After introductions were made and our identities confirmed, we were asked to survey the office to check for missing or damaged items.

Our office space consisted of a reception area where Mary

Ann's desk was located, a conference room, and the executive office where my desk was situated. It was noticeable that every file cabinet and desk drawer had been opened and rifled through, but nothing major was missing that we could immediately identify. Significant documents were kept in a wall safe built in between the front office and the conference room. It had not been opened—and it did not even appear to have been discovered.

Mary Ann was still visibly upset, but Rebekah comforted her. It would take some time to clean up this mess, but no serious damage had been done. When the front door had been broken into, a silent alarm had been triggered. The police responded within fifteen minutes, but apparently the intruders were already gone. Again, as at the house, the quickness of the intruder's search indicated that they were looking for something very specific. Did they find it? We didn't know.

When the police realized that Rebekah and I were the same couple whose home had been broken into earlier that morning, they began to question us with more urgency. Did we have any idea who might be behind this? What did we have that these persons wanted? We still couldn't answer their questions. We didn't have a clue, or did we? We had a deep private fear that it might be related to last year's events and the gold fortune we had brought home, but we didn't voice those fears. That information seemed beyond the local police's jurisdiction.

After the officers concluded their investigation and left, Mary Ann said, "Richard, do you think the trouble you and Rebekah were in last year might be connected to this break-in?"

I responded, "I don't see how, but nothing about this makes any sense. Go on back to your apartment and get some rest. We'll get busy cleaning up on Monday morning. Thanks for coming. You know how much we appreciate you."

Rebekah and I went home, ate a snack, and decided to take a nap. We were both exhausted, but neither one of us slept. Our minds were racing through the morning's escapades. That afternoon, we went back up to the foundation and began the process of cleaning up the mess. Mary Ann would need to reorganize our file cabinets, but at least on Monday morning, she would find a floor that wasn't littered with documents.

Rebekah chatted with nervous energy the whole time we picked up papers and file folders, but nothing could be explained. As far as we knew, the evil organization we helped bring down last year no longer existed. We decided that, on Monday, we would call Melinda Thompson at the Polaris Project to check in and see if there were any new developments that might give us a clue. It had been several months since we had been in contact with Melinda. We would let her know about the break-ins and see if she had any idea who might be behind the intrusions.

On Sunday morning, we decided to sleep in. We normally went to church, but we both found ourselves emotionally drained. Eventually, we stirred around and cooked some breakfast. There was a cold drizzle outside as the predicted storm moved on through, but it let up by midmorning. We kept asking ourselves the same questions over and over, but they continued to be unanswerable.

I checked the weather forecast. The chance of additional thunderstorms late this afternoon was mounting. Neither one of us were in the mood to do much, but I wanted to get the garden cleaned up before the next storms, and Rebekah wanted to get in her regular jog. Though it left both of us slightly uncomfortable, on Sunday afternoon, we dressed to pursue our separate interests.

As I began the garden cleanup, I saw a glimpse of Rebekah's head bobbing just over the top of our fence. She was wearing her favorite Boston Red Sox cap and was waving at me over the fence as she jogged past.

If you would have asked me, I would have denied it, but I could almost taste the bitter flavor of worry. Before early yesterday morning, I wouldn't have given it a second thought, but since the double break-ins, I wanted Rebekah beside me. She seemed to be handling everything better than I, but neither of us had any peace.

It had been more than a year since we had been rescued from our "misadventure," and we had done all that we knew to do to disappear back into society and resume normal lives. However, watching her begin her jog into our neighborhood alone left me slightly uneasy.

Sometimes I would join her for her regular jogs, but I really wanted to get our summer garden cleaned up. Last week's freeze had put an end to our vegetable garden, and I wanted to gather the dead and dying plants and haul them to the compost pile. As forecasted, a distant storm was brewing on the horizon, but I felt certain I could finish the garden chore before it moved closer. I hoped that Rebekah was keeping tabs on the encroaching storm as well. If not, she might get drenched.

As I raked the dead tomato, pepper, and squash plants into piles, I thought about last year. Rebekah and I met at a trout fishing lodge in Argentina. At the time, her husband and his brother had been missing for more than four years and were presumed dead. I had lost my wife to cancer about nine months before traveling south to fish.

The trip to Argentina had no specific purpose other than to escape our current situations and perhaps catch a few fish. Neither of us knew what we were looking for. We just needed a time of personal retreat to clear our minds. The concept of meeting someone wasn't in either of our plans, but sometimes plans change.

We spent a marvelous week together fishing the crystal clear waters of Patagonia. It was a week neither one of us wanted to end, and neither of us would ever forget. We were two lonely people in a beautiful foreign land. I found Rebekah to be exciting almost as soon as we met. I think she enjoyed me as well. Her flashing blue eyes and warm smile captivated my heart.

My wondering mind was snapped back to the garden by a quick buzz near my ear. I jumped back in defense and swatted at the buzz so hard that I knocked off my green John Deere cap. Then I spotted the bumblebee hovering over one of the dead vines. A week ago, that bee would have found sweet nectar in the various blooms, but this afternoon, he was coming up empty. Last week's heavy frost had taken care of that. Perhaps his buzz near my ear reflected his frustration that equaled mine. I kept an eye on him as I continued my cleanup chore. Goose was just watching me and didn't seem to be too concerned about the bee or the coming storm.

Following our fishing trip to Argentina, Rebekah and I wanted to make plans to connect, but nothing had been finalized. She lived in Boston, and I lived in Lexington, Kentucky, but the distance hadn't been discussed. I remember the phone call though. It was evident that something had deeply changed in her spirit since we parted at the Bariloche International Airport. I could sense it in her voice. She wanted me to come to Boston so she could show me in person what she had uncovered. Unsure of what I was getting myself into, I still found myself excited to see her again as I disembarked at Logan.

She explained that she had found some peculiar things about her husband after she had returned home from the fishing trip. She had discovered a secret bank account in his name that she had known nothing about previously. It was automatically sending a monthly check to a small town in Argentina and had been doing so for at least four years. She asked me if I would consider going back to Argentina with her to investigate where this money was going—and to whom. I couldn't have said no, even if I had wanted to, which I didn't.

We found the recipient of these monthly distributions, and much more. Without realizing what was happening, we found ourselves in the middle of a dark, cruel organization that ran a monstruous international human trafficking business. We also discovered that Rebekah's husband and brother-in-law had been mixed up with this ugly organization.

She had never trusted her brother-in-law and had always suspected that he had gotten her husband into some sort of trouble. To cripple the organization, her husband had embezzled a chunk of the company's money, which was the gold we eventually discovered. The organization assumed that Rebekah already knew about those funds and had come to Argentina to gather them for herself. Their assumption put the two of us into grave danger.

I refocused on the garden. Working in the dirt in the past had always brought peace to my soul. I enjoyed the feel of moist soil in my hands. I liked to think about the present, past, and future production of good fertile soil, but today, it was just work. Something was unstable inside my spirit.

A lightning bolt struck not too far in the distance as I finished filling the last wheelbarrow load and headed to the compost pile. Dumping the load, I ran back, grabbed the garden tools, and sprinted to the tool shed. The rain began just as Goose and I found shelter under the shed's tin roof. I thought about the bumblebee. Where had he found to protect himself from the encroaching storm?

Small hail began to pound the shed's tin roof, and I cleared off a bench and decided to wait it out. Goose curled up on an old towel beside me. I hoped Rebekah had finished her afternoon jog and wasn't hunkered down under some tree to avoid getting wet or pounded by hail. The cloud had been brewing for some time but had finally moved in rather quickly.

The pounding on the tin roof reminded me of the ten days we spent in that old cabin on the ranch in Argentina. We were told by our captors that we would be spending the winter there unless we told them the whereabouts of the embezzled funds, but we didn't know anything about the money, much less where it was.

Had I been there alone, that season in the old cabin would have been beyond miserable, but together, Rebekah and I found ourselves, and each other. We also rediscovered a faith that we hadn't realized we had lost. We didn't voice it, but we fell deeply in love there in that canyon, backed up into the foothills of the majestic Andes.

I tried to peer through the driving rain to see if I could see lights on in the house, indicating that Rebekah had made it home safely before the storm. I couldn't see any, but I knew that she could take care of herself.

Watching the rain and sleet pepper the stone path leading to the house, I thought about our truck ride across Patagonia loaded with teenagers unaware of what was ahead or where they were being transported. We never saw those kids again. We often wondered what happened to them, though we generally knew what the organization had planned for their futures.

I recalled being on the beach after the long truck ride and the mysterious touch on my shoulder that most definitely kept me from being killed. I remembered the horror of being alone on the oil tanker as it traveled across the Atlantic. At the time, I didn't know where Rebekah had been taken. I didn't know what they intended to do to her, but my vivid imagination had been running in terror mode.

Several of those nights on that tanker had been some of the darkest nights of my life. However, one was the most beautiful. Tears began to well up in my eyes as I thought about that night when I experienced the whisper of God. The rain started to ease up as Goose rubbed against my leg, letting me know she was still there. It appeared the cloud was moving over us, and I prepared to make a quick dash for the back door. Rain was still falling, but I thought I could outrun it.

CHAPTER 2

The Unexpected

Richard went out the back door, as I finished tying up my jogging shoes and headed out the front. I couldn't see Richard over the top of the fence, but I waved as I jogged past. He was working in the garden, but I wanted to get in my daily jog. I ran almost daily during high school and college, but after my first husband failed to come home one day, I just quit. Only in the past few months had I rediscovered the joy of the daily jog.

The year Richard and I spent as hostages obviously didn't allow the time or place for jogging. We swam at least twice a day while we were held prisoners at the mansion in North Africa, but we did more talking with our elbows hooked over the side of the pool than actual swimming.

Richard had suggested that we add a pool to our new house here in Lexington, but we hadn't made any decisions. To be honest, I think the reason Richard learned to appreciate swimming so much were the skimpy swimsuits that our captors had chosen for me to wear. The memory of him peeking to watch me in the leopard skin bikini still makes me blush.

I never run a consistent route through our new neighborhood.

At nearly every intersection, I slow down and decide whether to continue straight or turn left or right. Making the decision to go in any direction is my personal expression of freedom. It's hard to explain, but being robbed of one's liberty, as Richard and I had been, left my soul tied up in knots. Turning left, right, going straight, or even backward shouted to the world and to my own heart that I was now free to choose my own path.

A clap of thunder announced that my jog needed to be cut short, so I reluctantly headed back toward our street. The autumn leaves were just beginning to show their brilliance with the newly turned reds, oranges, and yellows, and it reminded me how much I loved our new home and life. Perhaps that's why the break-ins felt like such a violation. The intruders didn't steal anything, but in a way, they did.

As I turned onto our street, I sensed that the storm was pressing even closer. Another flash much nearer confirmed it. I wondered if Richard had finished his garden project. I started sprinting to our driveway, but just before I turned in, I noticed that Tammy, the across-the-street neighbor, was picking up her mail. She waved while scurrying back to her house, and it dawned on me that we hadn't picked up our mail after all the confusion on Saturday morning.

If I hurried, I could dash down to the centralized mailboxes, grab Saturday's mail, and get back to our front door before the serious rain began. I almost made it before the big drops commenced to fall. A bright flash and instant boom celebrated my arrival.

Picking up our mail didn't really excite me as it once had. In our attempt to disappear off the grid, most of our important mail all went to a mailbox downtown, not far from Richard's office and my new shop. The mail that came to our neighborhood box consisted of mostly grocery flyers, catalogs, and various credit card invitations.

When we gathered our mail, we would typically drop it all into a basket in the hallway leading into the kitchen. Then, once a week, together, we would sort it with most of it going straight to the trash. As I hurriedly dropped the daily pile into the basket, a catalog and a letter fluttered onto the floor, missing the wide-mouthed opening. I scooped up the two wayward pieces of mail, grabbed a bottle of water from the refrigerator, and plopped down into my favorite chair.

The leather recliner faced a big bay window that opened toward our backyard. A magnificent walnut tree dominated the view and certainly predated the house itself. It was raining so hard that the giant tree was barely visible. I could scarcely make out the outline of the garden shed in the corner of the yard, and I wondered if Richard had finished his garden work before the storm moved in. Since the house was quiet, I assumed Richard and Goose were waiting out the storm from inside the shed.

I love him with all my heart, but over the past several months, I have begun wondering about our futures. The year we were held captive left some scars on both of us. Unaware of my own hand movement, my fingers felt under my shirt and found the bullet hole scar. It had healed nicely, but my finger could feel the slight depression just under my collarbone. I didn't know how many times a day my index finger unconsciously felt for that hole.

We were certain that we had discovered proof that my first husband, Gary, had been murdered, but as it turned out, he was very much alive and was instrumental in our being rescued. Unfortunately, he was the only one of our liberators who was fatally wounded in our rescue attempt. He gave his life for ours.

Last week, I was sitting on our back porch as supper cooked. As I relaxed, I remembered the ranch cabin and the odd meals we prepared. I recalled the truck ride across Patagonia. I shuddered as I thought about when Richard and I were split up and the terror of being tortured by being forced to watch video scenes of Richard being abused and then executed. Only later did I discover that all those video scenes had been fabricated just to torture me. It certainly worked. In a heartbeat, I would have given over the exact location of Gary's hidden loot if I had known where to point. My inability to stop Richard's "torture" disturbed me in a manner that I still cannot explain.

I thought about the huge mansion in North Africa and Richard's face when he found me standing at the front door after thinking I had been killed. I also recalled the deep distaste we both had as we were forced to keep the financial books for the human trafficking organization. I could still hear the shots, the breaking of the window, and the thump of the bullet finding my shoulder. Tears started rolling down my face. The memories were still so very vivid, both the good and the bad.

A few weeks ago, I was sorting through some books in our bedroom. In the disorganized pile, I found the green Arabic-covered Bible that Richard had found while we were being held in the desert mansion. Just holding it triggered the emotions that were still attached to it, and I started weeping uncontrollably. I didn't hear Richard slip up behind me.

He wanted to know what was wrong, but I couldn't tell him. Those tears just start rolling from time to time. I know he wants to fix me, to heal my heart, but I don't know what to say; after all, I don't even know what's wrong. I truly was not afraid that the organization still existed and might be looking for us. Even since the two break-ins yesterday morning, I hadn't worried about that, but something inside of me was wounded during our hostage season. Richard has been handling it better than I have—at least I thought so.

The bullet hole healed many months ago, but why I still flinched when I heard a sharp noise made no sense. Even the distant thunder almost made me want to duck and run. I could press on the scar and feel nothing, but other times, it burned like it was on fire without even being touched. I knew Richard was frustrated with me, but it might have been that he was still just scared for me.

As I realized that the rainstorm was beginning to ease up, I glanced at the two pieces of wayward mail that were still in my lap. The catalog was from Bed Bath & Beyond. It could wait. The letter, however, seemed official.

It was addressed to "Mrs. Rebekah Black," which had been my

name a year ago. It was from the Smith, Smith, and Bright law firm in West Plains, Missouri. When I opened it, the formal letter simply said that they had been trying to reach me for several weeks and asked if I would please contact their office when convenient. I read it again, but nothing clarified the purpose of the letter. I had never even heard of West Plains, Missouri.

I heard Richard running onto the back porch and coming in through the washroom. Though he attempted to wait the storm out in the shed, he bolted toward the house too soon. He was soaked to the bone and was shaking like an old, wet dog in the kitchen. Goose was shaking even more than Richard, and I couldn't help but laugh at the sight of the pair of them. He peeled off his wet shirt and jeans and dashed through the den in his boxers, leaving Goose to fend for herself. In a few minutes, he reentered having showered and dressed.

"Richard, do we know anybody from West Plains, Missouri?"

"I don't think so. Why?"

"I got a letter today that came to this address. It's from lawyers in West Plains. They want me to call them."

"What's it about?" he asked.

"It doesn't say. Not even a hint. Just to call."

"At the foundation, we get several letters like that a week. Lawyers represent various people, and they know we give away significant amounts of money to certain organizations. I don't know how they find out about us, but they do. By the way, what's for supper?"

"There are baked potatoes in the oven with pulled pork BBQ that needs heating up," I said.

"Mmm, sounds good."

—

On Monday morning, Richard left for the office early. He and Mary Ann had a busy day ahead of them cleaning up the mess from the intruders. I wanted to stay at home to make the call to the lawyer in West Plains.

I sat down in my favorite chair and set the alarm on my phone to notify me when the law office would open. Goose stretched out beside me and gazed out the window. She was posting guard for squirrels. She hadn't caught one yet, but she enjoyed giving them a worthy pursuit. Comfortable in my leather chair, I dozed off for a few minutes.

My phone rang, startling me from a vivid dream, and it took me several moments to reclaim my bearings and answer. It was a police detective asking if we had anything else to report from the Saturday morning's intrusions. When I told him that, as far as we knew, nothing was missing at either place, he gave me his private number and asked us to call if we discovered anything else of significance. If not, there really wasn't much else the police could do. I assured him that we would call.

I don't dream very often, but when I do, I don't ever seem to remember much about the dream. This dream was different. It was simple, but it was extremely realistic. I decided that I would share it with Richard later in the day to see what he thought.

Checking the time, I made the call to West Plains.

"Good morning, this is Smith, Smith and Bright law firm. How may I direct your call?" said a warm-voiced woman who was probably on up in years.

"I have a letter from your law office asking me to contact you. It doesn't say anything else."

"Ah, you must be Mrs. Rebekah Black," she said.

"I was Rebekah Black before I remarried last year. Now I'm Rebekah Dempsey."

"Mr. James Smith Sr. is expecting your call, Mrs. Dempsey. Let me transfer you to his office," she said still with her cheery spirit.

In a few moments, a voice answered, "Is this Mrs. Rebekah Black, excuse me, Rebekah Dempsey?"

"Yes, it is."

"Mrs. Dempsey, you're not an easy person to locate, but I have some bad news for you. Your uncle, Mr. Billy Bowden, passed away almost a month ago. I'm sorry to be the one bringing you this news, and I'm sorry it has taken us this long to notify you." The older lawyer's voice was precise but gravelly.

I didn't know how to respond, so I didn't.

"I was your uncle's lawyer. I drew up his will about a decade ago. He said that you were the only family he had left, and he wanted you to have his house and farm."

"I don't see how that can be. I only met him once, and that was at my mom's funeral about ten years ago. I vaguely remember him with a round face, red complexion, and almost bald. As soon as the service was over, he scurried out the door. Why would he leave me his house and farm?"

"He had no other family. We have posted a death notification in all the area newspapers and community web pages, which is standard procedure. If there is any other family, or if he has any debts or claims on his estate, they have another month to contact us, but thus far, we've heard nothing."

"I'm still stunned that he wanted me to have it."

"I haven't been out to your uncle's place, but a friend of mine has. He says it's in rough shape. The farm hasn't been cultivated in years, and the house has seen much better days. I suggest that you not get your hopes up too high. It may not be worth very much in its current condition."

"What do I need to do? Do I need to arrange a funeral?"

"No, the county took care of the funeral expenses since we couldn't locate you. It might be appropriate to discuss what they spent with the county commissioner, but there's no rush. When it's convenient for you, why don't you come to West Plains? We can take care of all the necessary paperwork when you're here. Just let me know when you can head this way, and I'll have things arranged. I'm so sorry for your loss, Mrs. Dempsey."

"Thank you. I'll let you know when we can come."

I felt the need to discuss this situation with family, but I no longer had any family—other than Richard. I knew that I had an uncle, but I didn't even know where he lived. I'm not sure Mom knew. She never talked about him. After Mom died and Gary disappeared, I felt so alone.

With Goose's daily needs taken care of, I drove to the shop. When I met Richard on the fishing trip in Argentina, I owned and operated a successful furniture and decorating business in downtown Boston. After we decided to live in Lexington, I sold my Boston store to my partner. After fully recovering from my wound, I bought a store in Lexington and decided to put into practice what I had learned about decorating "wealthy" Bostonian homes. It had been a slow process getting traction, but in the past few months, it had started taking hold. When people are pleased, they tell their friends.

After checking in and discovering that all was well at the Stone Lion: Upscale Furniture and Fine Décor, I walked the two blocks down to the foundation's office. Mary Ann greeted me, but her usual smile was somewhat strained. I didn't blame her. I was still upset myself.

I walked back to the executive office and saw Richard at his desk.

He saw me and started toward me.

"It seems that I had an uncle who lived in West Plains, Missouri."

"Is that what the lawyer's letter was about? I didn't even know you had an uncle."

"He was my mom's brother, older brother, and apparently passed away about a month ago. I remember meeting him at my mom's funeral, and apparently, I'm his only relative. He left me his farm and house."

"That's amazing," Richard said.

"But the lawyer said not to get too excited. He said the place was run down and might not be worth much, but it's all mine. Mr. Smith, the lawyer, suggested that we should come to West Plains whenever we have the time, but there's no hurry. The county paid for his burial expenses, but apparently there are some papers I need to sign."

Mary Ann walked in behind me, holding a note, and said, "Excuse me, Rebekah, I just need him for a moment. I'm sorry, Richard. In all the commotion, I forgot something. You had two calls after you left the office on Friday. One was from Mrs. Gillespie. Her son and her new grandson are going to be in town on Wednesday, so she needs to bow out of the foundation's board meeting. I told her you would certainly understand."

"And the other call?" Richard asked.

"His name was Jerry Jives. He said he went to high school with you and was going to be passing through town. He wanted to stop by and say hello."

"What did you say his name was?"

"Jerry Jives," Mary Ann answered after looking at the note again.

"I don't know a Jerry Jives. I'm sure that I didn't go to high school with anybody by that name. What did you tell him?"

Mary Ann answered, "I explained to him that you were going to be gone for the weekend. He said perhaps he would stop back by on his return trip. I hope I didn't say anything out of place. I didn't know that you and Rebekah had canceled your trip at the last moment."

"I'm sure it will be fine, but I don't know a Jerry Jives."

Mary Ann went back to her office.

Richard said, "What about Wednesday? The foundation's board meets Wednesday morning, but we could drive over to West Plains after it's over. I'm not sure how far it is, but it's about a five-hour drive to St. Louis. I really don't even know where West Plains is. Why don't you call the lawyer back and set up a meeting for Thursday afternoon? We can drive part of the way on Wednesday, spend the night somewhere, and just take it easy. It will be fun to be away together for a few days." He started searching his map app on his phone.

"Are you sure we should be out of town with all that has happened?"

"I think being out of pocket for a few days is just what the doctor ordered. I was counting on our weekend getaway to Louisville. This will make up for that."

I said, "Did the guys who broke into our house think we weren't going to be home? Did they know we changed our plans? I wonder about this mysterious Jerry Jives. Mary Ann told him that we wouldn't be home."

Richard said, "Yeah, I thought about that too. Nobody knew that we changed our plans. The fact is that, in both situations, nothing was taken. That still puzzles me. I suppose their plans were interrupted before they found what they were looking for. We may never know."

Just before five o'clock, I called the law office in West Plains to set up an appointment for Thursday afternoon.

The secretary checked the office calendar and affirmed that Thursday would be acceptable. "And Mr. Smith would like to visit with you for a moment."

Mr. Smith came onto the phone and said, "Mrs. Dempsey, Thursday afternoon at one thirty will be fine, but I have some additional information that you might find interesting. I have been contacted by a prospective buyer for your uncle's property. He didn't mention an actual amount, but I think he was indicating that it might be sizable. We can discuss the details when you're here, but I wanted you to know that an offer might be on the table."

"Well, that was certainly unexpected," I replied. "We can discuss it further on Thursday. Thanks for all you have done."

—

As we washed the supper dishes, I asked, "Did you have a chance to call Melinda Thompson at the Polaris Project today?"

Richard said, "I called, but she wasn't in. Her schedule is hectic, and you never know where she might be. I'm sure she will call back when she has an opportunity."

As we finished putting away the dishes, I said, "Random question. What do you think about dreams?"

He grinned. "Most of my dreams come after I've eaten spicy Mexican food. Why do you ask?"

"Very funny. This morning after you left, Goose and I were relaxing in front of the bay window, and I dozed off and had a dream. The detective called and interrupted it, but the dream was very vivid. I was in a small cave. I was hiding behind a big boulder, holding an old double-barreled shotgun, and pointing at the entrance to the cave.

"A young boy was in my lap. I think he was supposedly my little brother, and I was supposed to protect him. A man with a massive black beard told me to stay out of sight—no matter what I heard—until he came back to get us. He acted like he was our father. The most significant thing about the dream was the dead silence as I listened for whatever was happening outside the cave. Then the phone rang. It was amazingly vivid, but what on earth could it possibly mean?"

Richard laughed and said, "I haven't a clue. Do you have a little brother?"

"I don't think so. At least Mom never mentioned one," I said.

—

A cold chill was in the air, and we decided to build another fire. As we sat down with our feet together, I invited Richard into a thought that I had been contemplating off and on for several weeks. "What if Gary had lived? You don't have to answer this. I'm just thinking out loud. You know I love you, but I wonder what would have happened to us if Gary had survived."

We both watched the fire crackle to life.

Richard finally nodded and said, "There was a movie several years ago about a man who was thought to have died in a plane crash. Somehow, he found his way to a deserted island out in the

Pacific, but his girlfriend, or fiancée, not knowing what happened to him, eventually had to go on with her life. What was the name of that movie? It was a Tom Hanks movie. Anyway, finally he was rescued after several years, I think, only to find out that the love of his life had assumed that he was dead and married her dentist."

"The movie was called *Cast Away.* I started watching it, but when he had to knock out his own tooth with the ice skate, I quit watching. I never did know how or if he was rescued. I didn't know his love interest married her dentist. I guess, in our case, you would be the dentist."

As we both watched the flicker of the flames, I finally asked, "So what happened? What did the guy on the deserted island do when he found out that his lady friend had married her dentist?"

Richard thought for a minute and then said, "He said goodbye, cried, drove away in the rain, went to the Texas Panhandle, and found some lady artist."

"I'm glad I didn't watch it. That's sad."

After a long pause, Richard said, "The what-ifs in life seldom make much sense, but this I know: I love you Mrs. Rebekah Dempsey."

CHAPTER 3

The Mark Twain

On Tuesday, I had lunch plans with Bill Jackson, an old friend from the church I pastored back before I lost my first wife and retired from the congregation. Bill's experience as an investment banker made him one of my first invites when I formed the Polaris Foundation's board.

"What happened Saturday morning?" Bill asked after we had placed our lunch orders.

I tried to explain the two break-ins, but I didn't have any answers to his questions about who, what, or why.

Bill said, "How is Rebekah handling it all? You two have been through a lot."

"Yes, we have, but she appears to be doing fine, at least I think." Bill was one of the few friends in my life who knew the story of my past year. I had shared most of the details with him, but not all. "But to be honest, Bill, Rebekah and I didn't have a regular engagement like most people. We got to know each other under intense pressure and married with the expectation that we were going to be shot by morning."

"Yes, your courtship was far from regular: meeting in Argentina, being held hostage in North Africa, and coming home married," said Bill while smirking and shaking his head.

"You can imagine the look I got from my daughters when we told them our story."

"I would have loved to have seen their faces. By the way, how is the new grandbaby?"

"Oh, he is cute as a button and keeping his mama busy," I said while trying to resist showing the latest photo. "They are all doing well. Once they got to know Rebekah, they loved her. We're planning to spend Christmas together."

"Bill, you know I love Rebekah, and this past year together has been wonderful … except … I don't even know how to explain it. Rebekah has a physical scar on her shoulder where she was shot, but I think we both carry scars deep inside. Occasionally, those wounds raise their ugly faces without warning. Rebekah is as beautiful as ever with her blonde hair and blue eyes, but sometimes I walk in and find her just weeping, and she can't even tell me why. I want to help, but I don't know what to do."

"You two went for some counseling, didn't you?" Bill asked.

"Yes, we went several times, but we couldn't bring ourselves to tell the counselor everything that we had experienced. Some of it was just too personal, and he probably wouldn't have believed it anyway. He helped us some, but in the end, he suggested that we find someone else who might better understand our experiences. Of course, the only other person who understands my experience is Rebekah, and I hers. For the first several months of our marriage, all we talked about was what had happened to us. I think we both just got tired of talking about it. Now, we don't seem to have that much to say to each other."

Bill replied, "I have a college friend who was a marine. He was a good guy, and a good friend, but something happened to him while he was over in the 'sandbox.' He looked the same, sounded the same, but his personality had been altered. He experienced some things that changed him, but he never could talk about it. I don't know how else to describe it, but do you think that something like that could have happened to you two?"

"I don't think so, but maybe."

We concluded our time together talking about tomorrow's board meeting, and I told him about the passing of Rebekah's uncle and our planned trip to Missouri to deal with his estate settlement.

—

After I got back to the office, Mary Ann informed me that Melinda Thompson from the Polaris Project had returned my call and wanted me to call her back. The Polaris Project orchestrated our rescue just before we were to be executed in Sicily. They had also assisted us in recovering the gold along the river in Argentina, which became the seedbed for the foundation. Our newly founded Polaris Foundation was a large financial sponsor of the Polaris Project, and rightly so. We desired to help them deliver as many as possible from the terror of human trafficking.

Melinda answered her phone and said, "Richard, how are you and Rebekah doing? I haven't heard from you in several months."

"We're doing good, but we had a weird event happen to us over the weekend." I told her about the double break-ins and how nothing was missing. "We don't quite know what to think about it. With both our home and office violated on the same night, we were wondering if there might be some connection to the events of last year. We thought it wise to touch base to see what you thought."

"That's unbelievable," she said. "That had to be disturbing for you two after all you have been through. It's obvious they were after something very specific. For them to hit both your home and office at the same time suggests a well-organized group, but as far as the break-ins being connected to the same organization from last year, it's doubtful. We dealt quite a blow to that group. There are other active organizations around the world, but they don't seem to be connected to the one you two brought down. Around our office, we are still very grateful for what you did.

"I had planned to call you, but I wanted to be sure before I did. In the past few days, we have confirmed some rumors that you and Rebekah should be extremely interested in. Gary's brother, Garrett, was one of the few in the organization who slipped through our net. However, he was arrested a few months ago in Morocco for his involvement with human trafficking; apparently, he is now related to another organization. The Moroccan authorities believe in swift justice. There has already been a trial, and he is now serving ten to fifteen years in a Moroccan work prison. I would hate to think about what that would be like. But if, or when, he ever gets out, we'll be notified because we have some pending issues with him as well."

"I can't say that I feel sorry for him," I said. "He had a chance to step away from that ugly business, but he didn't. Now he's getting exactly what he deserves. Rebekah will be delighted to hear this."

Melinda asked, "So, has anything else happened with you guys that might be out of the ordinary?"

"Not really," I said, but I went on and told her about Rebekah's uncle passing and her inheriting the house and farm in West Plains, Missouri. She expressed her sympathies and suggested that I call back after we made our trip west.

"Thanks, Melinda, but before I let you go, I have one other thing that Rebekah and I would like to ask you. We never did get a chance to discuss Gary, Rebekah's husband. We know some of his story, but not all. Rebekah is dealing with so many unanswered questions."

"Sure, if I can. What are her questions?"

"We know he got involved with the organization thinking they were helping lower-income kids find better lives. In his journal that we found, he confessed that he had discovered the real nature of the beast, but he was threatened to keep quiet. Eventually, they sent him to the same ranch house where we had been sent. That's where we found his journal."

"That's right," she said.

"They even threatened to snatch Rebekah in Boston if he started talking. That's when he decided to cut Rebekah out of his life. He did so to protect her. Sometime after that, he started embezzling funds from the company, converting them into gold bullion coins, but after that, we don't know anything. How did he escape from the organization? How did he get connected with you at Polaris?"

She said, "From what he told us, after his embezzlement scheme was discovered, he was tortured to reveal the location of the gold. Eventually, he was taken out to be executed, probably a pattern I am sure you are familiar with, but he bought his way out of it. He evidently didn't bury all the gold, and he knew from experience that crooked people could be bought off. It's amazing how much freedom a two-foot piece of PVC pipe can buy when it's heavily weighted, as you know. It was reported to the company that he had been eliminated, and they had no reason to disbelieve it. Fortunately, he wasn't.

"After he paid off his executioners, he disappeared in Europe. He was still fearful the organization would go after Rebekah, so he stayed below the surface, letting them think he had been eliminated. At some point, he was recognized in Paris by a man who had also once been connected to the company. He too had disassociated himself from the business and was in hiding.

"In their conversation, Gary learned of the Polaris Project and that the human-trafficking organization was squarely in the Polaris crosshairs. Motivated to make his wrongs right, Gary tracked us down while you and Rebekah were in North Africa. We didn't fully trust him, but we agreed to let him join at a basic level. When he found out that Rebekah was involved, he insisted upon being a part, and he volunteered to help with your rescue. We needed a way to get your vehicle stopped at the right location. It was his suggestion for the hay trailer to have a flat tire blocking the road, and it was his idea to ram your vehicle, giving us the jump. He crashed his jeep into you guys much harder than we, or he, had planned. You know the rest of the story."

I said, "He stepped into an organization that was based on lies and deception. Once he realized what he was connected to, he was in too deep. The company was a dark, evil institution. They knew how to mentally torture and manipulate people into compliance. They were professionals at it. I'm glad they're gone."

"I agree, but don't assume the company is gone forever. Big money has a way of resurrecting even the deadest of snakes, and from the bookkeeping you did for the organization, I know you understand the magnitude of the potential for their kind of business. Rumor on the street is that human trafficking has surpassed drug trafficking in profitability for organized crime."

That statement took my breath away. *I know that our work at the foundation is important, but this is staggering.*

Sensing my thoughts, Melinda continued, "Richard, the company, or ones like it, will not stay dead forever. There are people all over the world that want to invest into a business that has a high rate of return. Many times, the individual investors don't even know what the business is where they are investing their money. If healthy dividends are consistently paid, they don't care how corrupt the profits were generated."

"Since starting the foundation, I understand that more than ever. We investigate, in detail, both the projects and organizations we support and the companies with which we invest. Both are critical."

"Yes, I strongly agree. Let me know if you discover anything in Missouri," she said.

I told her that I would.

—

That evening, I told Rebekah all that Melinda had told me about Gary, Garrett, and the company.

She nodded in agreement upon hearing about Garrett, but she was very silent upon hearing about Gary's escape and his decision to continue to cut her off from his life.

After several minutes without comment, she finally blurted out, "Gary bought his way into freedom, and he still didn't try to contact me. He participated in our rescue, which led to his death, but even that seemed to have been motivated by shame. I don't know how I'm supposed to feel about any of that."

I had no idea how to respond. Her reaction caught me off guard. In the silence, I struggled with how overwhelmed I had been upon hearing this information from Melinda. I couldn't imagine how this was affecting Rebekah.

Several more minutes passed before she said, "You would never do that, would you? You would never let me think you were dead—even for my own protection—or would you?"

I put my arms around her and said, "While I was being transported to the mansion in North Africa, they led me to believe that you had already been tortured and killed. They never actually said that, but they were talking about you in past tense. They knew how to threaten, how to manipulate, and how to apply extreme pressure. I don't think I would ever abandon you, but there are phrases in Gary's journal we found that still haunt me. They broke him. I realize now that they came close to breaking me. I know now that I wasn't immune, and that's hard to confess. However, even in Gary's brokenness, he never told them where he hid the gold."

"Yes, I realize that. That gold was more important than I was," she said as she wiped away a tear. "If it's all the same to you, I really don't ever want to talk about Gary again, OK?"

"OK," I said, as I leaned over and kissed the top of her head. She gently pulled away, and I saw the tears streaming down her cheeks.

—

On Wednesday morning, the foundation board met for breakfast. I was blessed to have a solid support group to aid me in evaluating the foundation's giving and investing. We were all like-minded individuals when it came to method and purpose. Having multiple eyes examining the decisions and asking questions was both helpful and healthy. I trusted them, and they trusted me.

After eating and discussing the recent break-ins, we introduced the current business at hand. I shared the information that I had received from Melinda at the Polaris Project. They sat in shock at the thought of human trafficking surpassing drug trafficking in profitability for organized crime. It reiterated the significance of what we were undertaking at the Polaris Foundation.

As we concluded, I shared the news about Rebekah's uncle. They listened with compassion to the story of Billy Bowden of West Plains.

"Share our condolences with Rebekah," said Thomas, a real estate lawyer. "Hopefully, you two can have a wonderful trip together even under these circumstances. Let us know if there is anything we can do to help."

"I certainly will, but it shouldn't be too complicated. From what we know, it's an old farm. Apparently, the house is in poor shape and may need to be demolished before we put it on the market, but we don't really know any details yet."

"May I ask a personal question?" asked Helen, an older but very business-savvy woman who had lost her husband several years back.

"Sure, what's your question?"

"From the beginning, when you established the foundation, we have assisted you and Rebekah to disappear 'somewhat' off the grid. Your house is in the name of the foundation, as are your vehicles. Currently you would be very difficult to locate. Is meeting this lawyer a good idea? Does becoming visible again in selling a farm reestablish a paper trail that could be traced if someone were so inclined? I know that we are assuming the organization you found yourself entangled with last year has been decimated, but do we know that for sure? I just think you need to be careful."

"What are you suggesting, Helen?"

"Why don't you take Rebekah to Disney World, New York, or maybe Paris—or anywhere—and send a lawyer to manage the affairs in Missouri?" She said it with a winsome smile, but she wasn't joking.

I laughed at her suggestion. "Thanks for the warning, but I don't think we'll be exposing ourselves. We'll go and look things over, and if something seems out of sort, we'll come home and send one of our lawyers to take care of the remaining business."

They all nodded in agreement.

—

Shortly after noon, Rebekah and I were driving west. Our friend who had given us Goose had offered to keep her while we were away. I told Rebekah what Helen had said at the board meeting.

She winked at me and said, "I wouldn't mind a trip to New York."

"What do you really know about your uncle?" I asked.

"Hardly anything," she answered. "He was at Mom's funeral, and we shook hands before the service, but he disappeared quickly thereafter. I wanted to visit with him, perhaps get to know him better, but he left. I actually haven't thought about him since."

After several moments of thought, I said, "I guess we have a lot of blanks to fill in. It should be an interesting trip."

As the beautiful fall leaves passed by, Rebekah said, "Melinda's comments about organized crime are troubling. It's hard to believe that human trafficking has surpassed the illegal drug trade in profits."

"It is terrifying."

Rebekah said, "I remember the sick feeling I had when I realized what the coding system we discovered indicated. I think you had already guessed it, but I just assumed that human trafficking was just about selling sex, which is tragic, but that's all I had ever heard about. It never crossed my mind that it really is just out-and-out modern slavery. Some kids are distributed into the sex trade, but many of them are sent into sweat shops or out into the agricultural fields and simply worked to death."

"The truth that disturbs me even more," I added, "is the kids who are sold to the warlords in some parts of the world to be trained as 'boy soldiers.' I've heard that the warlords prefer kids who have been raised playing some of the video games on the market that are particularly violent."

"Don't forget about the 'special' classification that labeled some of the kids by their blood type. It probably is still the smallest percent of kids trafficked, but to think of a child being sold for their organs is beyond belief. It is deeply concerning that there is a growing worldwide market for healthy organs. In some countries, no questions are even asked about the sources for such organs."

Reliving the memories of our encounter with this "horror business" cast a deep darkness over us as we drove. It also triggered a string of memories in both of us, focusing upon our experiences with the underworld.

Rebekah rubbed the bullet hole scar in her shoulder. It was the only physical scar either of us carried, but it wasn't the only wound encountered.

As I drove, Rebekah dozed off. My mind raced back and forth. At times, the events of last year seemed like a decade ago, but at other times, they seemed like yesterday. I glanced over at her. She was indeed a special lady. I was glad that she could get in a nap, and I wondered if she was dreaming again.

The trip west was uneventful. The map app directed us through the full length of Kentucky before crossing the Mississippi River. We ate supper and spent the night in Poplar Bluff.

The next morning, we took it slow and easy, knowing we had plenty of time before we needed to be in West Plains. We began seeing signs for the Mark Twain National Forest not long after leaving Poplar Bluff. There were several places where we pulled over and looked out across the scenic views of forests, rivers, and the Ozark Mountains. The leaves were beginning to be in full fall colors, and we enjoyed the spectacular views. Neither of us had ever been to southern Missouri, and the drive was a new adventure for both of us.

We arrived in West Plains in time for lunch. We chose an old-fashioned café along the main strip, Lucille's Café, and after we had examined the menus and placed our orders, we both had the feeling that we were being very carefully examined. The café was nearly full, and everybody seemed to know each other—and everybody appeared to know that we were strangers. Nobody but the waitress spoke to us, but we had the distinct impression that we were being scrutinized.

I whispered, "Do you get the feeling that this café doesn't see many out-of-towners?"

"Yeah, I sure do. I feel like I have a big bump on my nose that everybody notices, but nobody wants to talk about."

"I promise, you don't have a bump on your nose. I would tell you if you did. This town just doesn't see many beautiful unknown ladies walk into their café," I whispered.

She blushed as her chicken salad was brought to the table.

I had the fried chicken. When in Rome, do as the Romans.

CHAPTER 4

Mint Spring

My chicken salad at Lucille's was very tasty, but Richard's fried chicken looked scrumptious. I almost tested our marriage by making him switch with me, but I didn't want to cause a scene. The good folks of West Plains had already been looking at us like we were from Mars.

Since the lunch crowd was thinning out, we took our time and discussed what we expected at the law office. Richard started making a list of information we needed to find out about my uncle. Since it was only a few blocks down to the lawyer's office, we decided to walk. The air was crisp, but the sun was warm. West Plains had the feel of Americana with small shops and businesses. There were several antique shops that looked interesting.

We snatched up a local newspaper that had been left on a corner bench and scanned it as we strolled. It was obvious that the local high school was planning their homecoming for this weekend, but the football game wasn't going to be played at home. It seemed that the plumbing for the irrigation system had sprung a leak and turned their field into a swamp, so homecoming for the "Zizzers" was going to be an away game. We laughed together at the rather unusual situation.

Promptly on time, we entered the office of Smith, Smith, and Bright: Attorneys-at-Law, and were greeted by the joyful-voiced woman I had visited on the phone. She looked just as she sounded, and we were immediately escorted into a wood-paneled formal conference room. On the conference room wall was a painting of an African lion relaxing on the savanna.

Richard looked over at me to be sure that I saw it too. It wasn't a great work of art, but it reminded us of the stone lion fountain at the mansion in North Africa. That stone lion statue had camouflaged our voices when we didn't want to be overheard, and it symbolized to us that we were not alone. Its presence gave us peace during a difficult season.

An elderly gentleman walked in with a polished hickory cane and introduced himself as Mr. James Smith, attorney-at-law. After we all introduced ourselves, we took our seats around the well-polished walnut conference table. Mr. Smith looked to be the sort of old man who you would be proud to have as your grandfather. His face reflected his many years, yet it still showed considerable warmth and humor. There was a perpetual twinkle in his eyes.

He made small talk by asking about our trip and if we had eaten lunch in his fair city. When he discovered that we had eaten at Lucille's, he wholeheartedly suggested that we would most certainly enjoy the meatloaf on Fridays. He bragged that her world-famous meatloaf was only available on Fridays at lunch. It was clear that he was proud of both Lucille's and the West Plains community.

After the air settled, and we all felt more comfortable, he opened a file. "We're a small town, and we're very informal. We all know each other, but if you don't mind, I will need to see your personal identifications. Driver's licenses will suffice."

Without being asked, I also produced a copy of our marriage license, which reflected that my previous name had been Rebekah Black. "You may need to see this," I said. I winked at Richard as I handed the document to the senior lawyer. The mere mention of that document triggered a series of personal memories for both of us. Our wedding story was unique, unlike anything most had ever heard. We hoped the details wouldn't need to be explained to the lawyer. He glanced at it and handed it back. He seemed satisfied that we were who we had said we were.

"From what you told me over the phone, you and your uncle weren't close," he said.

"No, not at all. He was at my mom's funeral ten years ago, but I barely had a chance to meet him. He seemed like a very quiet man, but I really didn't know him."

The lawyer quickly looked up with a puzzled expression, "Quiet? Your uncle was anything but quiet. When he came to town, he always dropped by several of his favorite hangouts, and you knew when he arrived. His voice would consume an entire room. He loved eating at Lucille's, but when he was there, everybody knew Billy Bowden was on the premises."

We sat and listened.

"I'm assuming that, about the time of your mom's funeral, he came to see me and wanted to update his will. He was exceptionally clear that he wanted everything he had to go to you. He sat in my office and bragged about your success as a home decorator in Boston."

We both nodded.

The lawyer continued, "You were his niece … and his only surviving heir. As such, you are to receive the house, farmland, farm equipment, truck, and anything else that might be determined to be of value."

"Are we sure that my uncle didn't have any other family other than my mom and myself?"

The old lawyer responded, "Apparently so, at least he didn't have any other family according to this document. I think I explained that we have posted legal announcements all over this area. If there are any unknown family members who can prove it, or if Mr. Bowden had any unpaid debts, the interested party has a limited amount of time to contact our office. I doubt that we will hear from anyone, but you never know. That's why there is a law requiring us to post his death announcement."

"What happened?" Richard asked. "How did he die?"

We had both thought it seemed strange that no one had asked for or volunteered that information.

Mr. Smith said, "It appeared that your uncle had a heart attack while driving back to his farm. His old Ford pickup ran off the road at Miller's Orchard. The truck was hidden in the thick trees and undergrowth for a couple of days before one of Don Miller's boys discovered him still sitting in his truck at the wheel. The doctor said that your uncle probably died before leaving the roadway. Since there was no evidence of foul play, the county decided a full autopsy wasn't necessary."

Mr. Smith passed over several documents for me to sign. He explained that this gave me ownership to Billy's bank account and all his property. "I suggest that you go down the street to the West Plains National Bank and visit Mr. Kyle Kirkland. I mentioned to him earlier that you would be in town today and that you would probably be stopping by.

"As I explained over the phone, Howell County paid for your uncle's burial expenses. Mr. Bud Berry, the county commissioner, would like to visit with you. The county would be beholden if you could reimburse those expenses, but it's not required." He handed me a death certificate, offered to produce additional notarized copies if I thought I needed them, and slid over a set of keys. "I assume these keys are to the house and truck, but I don't know what the other keys unlock. As far as I know, your uncle didn't have any life insurance, but when you go through his personal papers, you might want to look for documents of the sort."

As we stood to leave, he repeated what he had said over the phone about the prospective buyer for the farm. "If you are interested in selling, I will get in touch with the gentleman and find out what he is offering. Again, as I said, the farm and house haven't been cared for in years, but it is nearly a hundred acres, and farmland has risen in price over the past few years. A hundred acres may not be that large in some areas of the country, but around here, that's a nice-sized farm. I'll see what the prospective buyer is offering, assuming you are interested in selling."

I said, "We probably will need to sell it, so we're interested in all offers, but we do want to go visit the place and find out for ourselves what's there. We'll let you know. Thanks."

The kindly old man walked us to the front door and pointed his cane in the direction of the bank.

I turned back to the lawyer and said, "I have one more question. You said over the phone that I was a hard person to locate. How did you find me?"

"To be honest, I don't know." He leaned back into the front office and said with some force, "Miss Tyler, how did we track down Mrs. Dempsey?"

The voice from behind the door answered, "We tracked her down through a furniture store in Boston. After repeated attempts, the owner gave us an address in Kentucky. He didn't give us a phone number, or her new name, but the address is where we mailed the letter."

I glanced over at Richard, and he nodded. *Perhaps we need to improve our disappearing act. We weren't that hard to find.*

From the law office, we walked across the street and a block over to the West Plains National Bank. The front door was locked, and a printed sign on the door indicated that the bank lobby closed at 3:00 p.m. We were ten minutes late, but we saw a man hurrying toward us through the glass door.

Mr. Kyle Kirkland unlocked the door and invited us into the lobby and back to his office. He offered condolences for the loss of my uncle and asked if we would like something to drink, but we declined. He was wearing a very nice tweed sport coat with a blue striped tie.

It seemed surreal to think that I was now the owner of someone else's house, farm, and bank account. Everybody we had met seemed to be expecting us to be grieving over our loss, but grief wasn't even in our minds. I didn't know my uncle well enough to grieve.

Once we were all seated, Mr. Kirkland looked at me and said, "So, you are Billy Bowden's niece?" He seemed mildly surprised that Billy had any family at all. "He never mentioned that he had family, but it's good to meet you."

His secretary came in with some paperwork, and they both pointed to the few places where I needed to sign.

After I did so, Mr. Kirkland said, "You are now the one and only signee to your uncle's checking account. We'll honor any checks you write. Have you found his checkbook? If not, we can print you some checks."

I said, "No, we haven't been out to the house yet. We'll probably find it when we do."

Mr. Kirkland said, "I was called last week by a man interested in buying your uncle's farm. He acted as if he was sincerely interested. Have you decided what your plans are for the place?"

I said, "No, we haven't even seen it, but eventually, we probably will sell. Mr. Smith mentioned that someone had contacted him as well. I assume it's the same person."

The banker looked at me with considerable sternness. "I doubt it. The man who called me told me that I would be representing him solely. He wouldn't have called the law office as well, but we'll find out."

Richard asked, "Is the prospective buyer a local person?"

"He informed me that he preferred to stay anonymous. Just let me know what you decide."

From the bank, we walked across the street to the County Courthouse and asked to see the Howell County commissioner, Mr. Bud Berry.

The lady at the front desk told us he wasn't in, but she said that she could probably help us.

I explained, "It's my understanding that the county footed the cost for my uncle's burial. I would like to reimburse the county for those expenses."

She moved to a file cabinet and asked, "What was his name?"

I said, "Billy Bowden."

After several minutes of examining the various files, she extracted one. "We all knew and loved your uncle. He was a fun man to be around, but the county didn't pay for Mr. Bowden's burial. It was paid by an anonymous donor. You owe the county nothing."

I responded, "Who was the donor? I would like to reimburse whoever paid the bill."

The clerk shook her head. "I don't know. The file doesn't say. The Howell County Cemetery Association would have handled that transaction." She gave us directions to the cemetery, and we stepped back outside.

Following her directions, we drove to the edge of town and saw the sign for the West Plains Memorial Cemetery. We went into the office and were greeted by a very plump, but kindly woman in a black pantsuit.

I said, "There are two things we are interested in. First, a month ago, my uncle, Mr. Billy Bowden, was buried here in your cemetery. We would like to see the grave, and two, we understand that the cost of the burial was paid for by an unknown party. We would like to know who that was so we can reimburse those expenses."

She sat down at her desk but made no attempt to look for any information. "I knew your uncle. He will be greatly missed in West Plains. He was in Lucille's feasting on her world-famous meatloaf almost every Friday. I was sorry to hear about his passing."

"Thank you," I said.

Still seated, the lady said, "But he wasn't buried in this cemetery. I'm not even sure where he was laid to rest. Let me see if I can track down that information for you." She fired up her old desktop computer, which seemed to have seen better days, and skimmed through the local newspaper's online obituaries. "Billy Bowden, of Howell County, died August 26. He will be missed by the community that loved him. Burial will be a private graveside ceremony at the Mint Spring Cemetery."

"Mint Spring, where is that?"

She responded, "That's a good question. I've never been out there. I think it's an old pre-Civil War cemetery." She got up from her desk and moved to a large framed map of Howell County on her wall. With a ruler in hand, she looked closely and eventually pointed to a spot in the south section of the county. "Mint Spring Cemetery. It's out in the middle of the national forest, just barely still in the county."

Richard checked his phone app, but he couldn't find Mint Spring. After confirming the location on the county map, he pinned the location in his app, and said, "We should be able to drive to it now."

The clerk said, "Some of our older county cemeteries aren't maintained very well. All the people who cared for them in the past are gone. Be careful out there."

With that, we left and walked back to our car.

On the way, Richard said, "I think we're running out of daylight. We either have time to go out to your uncle's farm or drive out to Mint Spring. I don't think we can do both before it gets dark, and I'm not sure I want to be at either place after sundown."

"Which are you suggesting?" I asked, unsure which I preferred.

Richard said, "The cemetery visit will be the shortest. If we go out to the farm, we will barely get started looking the place over before we lose light. I suggest we find the cemetery and then drive back into town and get a hotel room. I saw several when we drove in this morning."

"To Mint Spring, it is."

To get on the county road we needed, our map app led us through a part of West Plains that we hadn't seen.

Richard said, "What is this?"

Noticing the sign, I said, "That's Missouri State University: West Plains Campus."

He responded, "West Plains has some surprises. I didn't know it was a college town."

After a twenty-minute drive into the forest, we found the road just where we expected from the map. Our GPS informed us that we would no longer be on a paved road, but we discovered that quickly enough without its help. We hoped that we wouldn't need the GPS again, because as we turned, we lost cell service. It was a rough six miles with several ninety-degree turns, but nestled under a stand of oak trees, we stopped beside an ancient wrought iron fence.

There wasn't a sign, but we assumed we had found Mint Spring Cemetery. The gate was wired closed. It appeared to have maybe forty or fifty old graves—at least from what we could tell from the number of headstones—but only a few of them were easily readable. The few dates that we could decipher went back to before the Civil War.

Toward the back of the small cemetery, we noticed the only recent grave. The fresh dirt had been rained on several times, and the oak trees blocked our view. As we walked around the oaks and approached the grave, we hesitated. A new headstone stood over the grave; it was made of polished gray granite and stood about three feet tall.

We still didn't know who had paid for it, but we had assumed there would only be a simple grave marker. The county would not have spent tax money for such an elaborate headstone, but somebody did.

After walking around to the foot of the grave, we read the freshly cut granite: "Billy Jack Bowden," followed by the dates of his birth and death.

"Your uncle was just over eighty years old when he died," Richard said. "He died ten days after his eightieth birthday." Above his name was carved a simple circle, but within the circle was a small etching: "*Dulce et decorum est pro patria mori.*"

"That's Latin, but I don't have a clue as to what it means."

Richard pointed to the last word. "Mori is either death or dying."

We jotted down the phrase and took pictures, but we were both perplexed. It was not the kind of headstone we had expected. Whoever had ordered this expensive memorial stone had it cut and installed rather quickly.

We walked around the small cemetery and looked at several of the old headstones, but many of them had already toppled over. Not one of them was dated after the 1930s except Uncle Billy's, and many more were just too old and weatherworn to read.

We both suddenly realized that all around us, it was absolutely still. There wasn't a breath of wind, not a bird singing, and not a cricket chirping.

After a few minutes, we both felt a cold chill down our backs. It was time to leave.

As we turned back onto the county road, my phone showed that it now had service. I did a quick search to locate the Latin phrase, and it didn't take me long to find a translation. "Apparently it's a famous Latin quote that when roughly translated means, 'It is sweet and proper to die for one's country.'"

As we turned into the Hampton Inn, I said, "That's the kind of quote you would engrave on the tombstone of someone who died defending their country. I wonder why it was put on my uncle's gravestone."

CHAPTER 5

The Old Farm

On Friday morning, we decided to visit Lucille's again for breakfast before exploring the farm. It wasn't quite as crowded as it had been for lunch, but it remained a popular place. As we feasted on our bacon, eggs, and homemade biscuits with gravy, the sheriff entered. He was impressive in size, especially sporting his uniform. His hands looked as if they could crush bowling balls. He visited several tables of West Plains folks before spotting us.

He stopped in front of our table and offered his hand. I shook it, hoping he was not one of those men who liked to demonstrate his manhood with a handshake that made your eyes cross. I was thankful that he wasn't, but he certainly could have been.

Looking at Rebekah, he said, "You must be Billy Bowden's niece, right?"

Rebekah nodded and smiled. We both knew that he was aware of who we were, just like we were sure he knew just about everything that happened in Howell County most of the time before it happened.

"What do you think about that farm of your uncle's? He wasn't one for paint and repairs, but he didn't have a wife to please," he said with eyes dark as coal.

Rebekah responded, "Actually we haven't been out there yet. That's where we're heading as soon as we finish breakfast."

"I understand that you have already sold the old place," he said.

"No, we've heard that there is someone desiring to make an offer, but we haven't decided for sure what we're going to do," Rebekah said.

"I guess I misunderstood, but if I was you, I would seriously consider the offer." He moved on to another table glad-handing several more potential voters and then was handed a coffee-to-go by the cashier. It looked like a well-rehearsed routine.

We were ready to go to see this farm of Billy Bowden's, and we paid for our meal. When we stepped outside, the sheriff was standing just outside the door and visiting with a man who apparently was about to enter. We stepped around the two men and started to our car.

A Marlboro man voice behind us said, "Mr. and Mrs. Dempsey?"

We turned around.

The sheriff said, "I almost forgot to tell you. Danny down at West Plains Garage told me to tell you that he has your uncle's old Ford pickup behind his shop. He told me that you can come by and pick it up anytime."

Rebekah said, "Oh, we hadn't even thought about his truck."

"We had it towed in after Don Miller's boy found it in their orchard. It's an old classic 1968 Ford pickup. Your uncle drove it to town several times per week, so I assume it runs well. We towed it into town because it wouldn't start when we found it, but I think it was just out of gas. You probably will want to go by and check on it."

We thanked him and climbed into our car, but he continued to follow us and knocked on Rebekah's window. We rolled the glass down.

Leaning in, he said, "I strongly suggest you take the offer and sell your uncle's place. You'll probably not get a better deal." His words were a suggestion, but his tone was almost a warning.

The West Plains Garage was near the west edge of town. A man with "Danny" sewed on his shirt pocket came out to meet us. We introduced ourselves, but he knew who we were.

He said, "I thought the world of your uncle. He told the best jokes, not always clean, mind you, but the best. Whatever I can do for you, just let me know. Billy Bowden was a good friend. We'll miss him around here."

We thanked him and followed him to the fenced-in area behind his garage. The pickup showed its years, in that very little of the original blue-green paint clung to the hood. Instinctively, we climbed into the pickup. A roll of worn seat foam was protruding up on the driver's side.

We looked behind and under the seats, not sure what we were expecting to find, and Rebekah finally opened the glove compartment. There was a half-consumed green Gatorade on top and Billy's checkbook below that. A quick glance revealed that it contained one last check. Under that was a suede leather bag. She opened it, and a golden necklace fell out. It was a heavy chain supporting a three-inch golden circle medallion. At first sight, it meant nothing to either one of us. Rebekah handed it to me, and I said, "That's heavy. I'm guessing the chain and circle are both solid gold. That doesn't seem like the kind of thing Uncle Billy would have, much less wear."

Rebekah then pulled out from the glove compartment a leather holster housing a very old, but in excellent condition, Colt revolver. There was also a box of forty-five caliber shells. She said, "My uncle continues to surprise me. Why would he be carrying a gun?"

"I would guess that most farmers carry some kind of firearm for varmints and snakes."

She pulled it from its holster and handed it to me. She held it with both hands like it might bite her.

I checked to be sure it wasn't loaded and replaced it in its holster. "Why don't you put those things in your purse?"

She looked at me like I was out of my mind, but she carefully dropped the gun, the necklace, and the checkbook into her purse, greatly contributing to its weight. She left the partially consumed Gatorade, but she looked around to see if anyone was watching, almost as if she was committing larceny.

"You're not a thief. Those things are yours," I said.

Danny came out the back door of the garage and walked over to us as we were climbing out of the old Ford. He said, "I don't know what you two are planning to do with this old thing, but I have a kid who works for me after school who has his eyes on it. He and his mom live alone just out of town. His dad disappeared several years ago. The kid drools every time he walks past this rusted old Ford. He has asked me every day this past month if the owners have been by yet. What I'm saying is this, if you want to get rid of the truck, I think I can help you with that."

Rebekah smiled and said, "When will your young friend be here so we can meet him?"

Danny said, "He's on the football team, and they have a big game tonight. I think it's homecoming, so he will not be in until the morning."

I said, "Yeah, we heard about homecoming. We've never heard of a homecoming being an away game."

"Yeah, it's a weird situation, but I've heard our football field is a mess. The whole place is a swamp, and there is a hole in one end zone that's big enough to bury this old truck. It probably wouldn't have mattered because our team hasn't needed an end zone very often all season." Danny grinned.

Rebekah said, "We're going out to the old farm now, but we'll be back late this afternoon or maybe in the morning. We don't really have any definite plans."

Danny nodded. "I heard you've already sold Billy's old place for a boatload of money."

Rebekah said, "No, we haven't sold it. We've never even seen it. That's where we're heading now."

As we were leaving town, we decided to stop at the Get-n-Go for gas. While I pumped, Rebekah went inside and loaded up on snacks and lunch options.

As we pulled out of town, Rebekah said, "The older lady who checked me out asked if I was Billy's niece who inherited his farm. It seems that everybody in town knows us—even though we just pulled into town yesterday morning. Why does everybody think we have already sold the place? Let's get out of here."

After sixteen miles east, we turned onto a county road that wound through checkered farmland. Just as the road made a big curve, we saw the rusted sign for "Miller's Orchard." We both grew quiet, and instinctively I slowed out of respect. "Somewhere along this stretch is where your uncle breathed his last." There were several likely places that certainly could hide a pickup, but we didn't see tracks or any other signs indicating the exact location.

The road turned again, and our phones lost service, but after another two miles, we assumed that we had arrived at Billy's. The wire gate was standing open, so we turned onto the narrow lane. A rusted out "No Trespassing" sign laid on the ground next to the fence.

The lane was lined with an ancient, stacked stone fence on both sides with thick trees and vines overhanging. It gave me the feeling of driving down a long, dark tunnel, but it ultimately emptied us into an open, grassy field, and there was the house: a modest but classic two-story wooden-framed house with a big front porch. At one time, it had been painted white, but most of the paint was left to one's imagination now. We eased up to the front without saying much. As we stopped, we both released a soft moan.

Trying to break the somberness, I said, "A real fixer-upper. Chip and Joanna would have a ball."

Rebekah continued in her thoughtful quietness.

Being careful on the steps, I turned back to Rebekah and said, "Watch your step. These porch steps have seen better days. Do you have those keys handy?"

She started digging in her overweighted purse.

"Never mind, the door is open. I wonder if your uncle ever locked it." As I pushed the door inward, a pungent smell emerged. I quickly closed it back.

We both backed away and sat down on the rickety porch steps.

After a few minutes of contemplation, I asked, "What are you thinking?"

"Part of me wants to call the lawyer and tell him to sell it. My uncle didn't have anything but this land. We could spend a lot of time cleaning this house and still not have anything of worth except the land. The potential buyer can deal with that smell. What do you think?"

"The house may well be a train wreck, but just sit here, watch and listen. This is a beautiful place. Look at those trees. You can see a deep green, grassy field beyond. There are two deer staring at us from the tree line. The old red barn may be ready to fall over, but it appears to be like an old classic canvas painting. I think I see a rustic Farmall tractor sitting in front of it."

Rebekah looked at me and said, "I agree. It's beautiful."

We both let the midmorning warm sun embrace us.

Then, with new determination, Rebekah jumped up and said, "OK, let's get to it. Let's see if we can find the source of that rancid smell. Ready?" She offered her hand and helped me to my feet.

With the courage of Don Quixote, I raised my arm and shouted, "Charge!"

Covering our noses, we bolted into Rebekah's new house. Other than the smell, we were pleasantly surprised. It wasn't ready for the Parade of Homes, but it was neat and tidy. The kitchen sink had a few dirty dishes standing in month-old dishwater. *That's one smell that could be eliminated.*

The small bathroom appeared to have been added since the original house had been built. It jutted out where part of the porch originally had been. A mouse had been caught in a trap under the sink, but it was past the point of creating a significant stink.

"Dishes or mouse?" I said with mock gusto.

"I'll take care of the dishes," she said, losing some of her excitement.

By the time I had deposited the mousetrap and its victim into the burn barrel behind the house, Rebekah had drained the nasty water and washed the few dishes. Another load of unrecognizable leftovers from the refrigerator completed the smell eradication. With both front and back doors propped open, a cool breeze removed any other lingering foul aromas.

In the bedroom, the bed was neatly made. There were even a few decorator pillows positioned attractively. Beside the bed was a beat-up rolltop desk. A quick glance suggested that this is where Billy paid his bills and organized his personal business.

Rebekah sat down at the desk and began to review the various piles of unopened mail. She examined each drawer, until the bottom one, which was locked.

I roamed around the downstairs but found nothing of great interest. There didn't seem to be anything in the house less than fifty years old, except a small flat-screen television. A cable box wire was threaded out through the window.

Rebekah was searching in her purse for the keys that the lawyer had given her. "I think it's odd that he didn't lock his gate—or his house—but he locked this bottom drawer. Makes me question what's in there."

"Perhaps we left those keys in the car?" I said. "I'll go look."

"While you do that, I'll prepare us a bite of lunch."

The keys were on the middle console, and I quickly retrieved them. The two deer that had been watching us earlier had moved on. Rebekah had a small ham and cheese sandwich waiting when I came back inside. As we snacked, I said, "What's upstairs?"

"I haven't gone up there yet. I guess we better go check it out," she said as she put away the lunch makings.

We started up the narrow, enclosed staircase. It emptied into a small sitting room, with closed doors going either direction. We opened the first one but didn't get very far.

"Whoa, Uncle Billy was a hoarder," she said with disgust. The door barely would open, revealing stacks of boxes and piles of mail all the way to the ceiling. A narrow trail had once led through, but several boxes had fallen over, blocking any chance of passage.

"What a mess," I said.

"Let's try the other door," Rebekah suggested, and I agreed.

Carefully, we opened the other door only to find the same.

I grabbed the first box that I could reach and dragged it into the sitting room. It was full of paperback books, mostly westerns. I spotted numerous Zane Grey and Louis L'Amour titles. "You have some reading to catch up on," I said with a grin.

"Sorry, not interested."

"Wait just a minute. Here is a real classic." I held up *Jesse James: The Story of His Adventures. A Romance of Terror Vividly Portraying the Daring Deeds of the Most Fearsome and Fearless Bandit Ever Known within the Whole Range of Historical Outlawry.* It was written by I & M Ottenheimer and was published in 1910.

I glanced inside the book. On the first page, printed very carefully in blue ink, it said, "Property of Billy Bowden." It seemed to have been read multiple times and had many dog-eared pages. The complicated title triggered laughter from both of us.

"That must be a real page-turner." She took it from my hand. "*A Romance of Terror?* Wow … I'll let you read it first."

We turned off the lights and stumbled back down the narrow staircase.

I said, "Let's go see the barn. That's probably where the real treasure is stored."

The bottom drawer to the desk was forgotten for a season.

She swung her fist at my chin in a feigned punch and started to the front door. "First one to the red barn wins the prize!" She bolted out the door, down the steps, and took off running. I followed but she had a head start. She also hadn't clarified what prize was being offered.

She made it to the barn first, but only because I stopped at the old tractor. It indeed was a red Farmall, probably from the 1950s.

"Will it run?" she asked, walking back to the tractor without bragging that she had arrived at the barn before I had.

"Probably not. That appears to be the water pump on the seat," I said. "Look at the two old Ford trucks behind it." Brush nearly had them covered, and both were consumed with rust. Neither had their engines.

We stepped into the red barn, but there wasn't much there other than broken farm equipment and some old tools. There were several other outbuildings in various states of ruin around and behind the barn.

I said, "At one time, this seemed to be an active farming operation. They probably raised some milk cows, some chickens, and who knows what else."

"That was probably a long time ago."

Without consciously deciding, we kept walking arm in arm past the barn area into the big grass pasture. On either side, there were thick stands of timber, but straight ahead, there was a rocky outcropping. A faint walking trail beside the trees headed down toward the rocks.

As we neared the rocky point, Rebekah said, "Is that an old cabin?"

"I think it is."

As we got closer, we could see an old square-cut log cabin partly leaning against the rocky bluff. It no longer had a roof, and two medium-sized oak trees were growing up from inside the cabin floor.

"That's interesting," Rebekah said.

"Look at this." I reached down and picked up a piece of a broken cast-iron skillet.

We both examined it.

I said, "I think this place is older than the house and barn, but exactly how old I couldn't say."

We stepped through the doorframe and imagined what it would have looked like when it was first built. The stone chimney was partially toppled over, and another piece of the cast-iron skillet was embedded in the dirt floor.

I took Rebekah's hand and said, "I suspect a young newly married couple started their lives right here in this cabin. They probably raised a couple of kids around this rocky point."

"That would have been a hard life," Rebekah whispered.

Walking past the cabin and along the rocky bluff, the faint trail turned. From there we could see a more modern fence below us. There were four signs attached. One said, "Mark Twain National Forest," and another said, "Irish Wilderness." The third sign said, "No Motorized Vehicles Past this Point."

The last sign faced away from us, so we walked on down to see what it said. Facing the national forest, it said, "Private: No Trespassing." However, there was a worn area where people had been ignoring the sign and jumping the fence. A faint trail led past where we stood and headed to the back side of the rocky outcropping. The trail led toward the entrance to a cave.

I'm not sure why, but the prospect of a cave created some excitement. We both quickened our pace and hurried to the cave entrance. I pulled out my phone and found the flashlight app.

Rebekah said, "You first, I'll be right behind you."

A normal-sized person had to duck down to enter the small entranceway, but once inside, it opened to be much larger. I said, "It looks like it goes back about twenty feet." My flashlight app could just barely highlight the back of the cavern. A drip dropped on my shoulder. "This is exciting."

Rebekah didn't respond.

I turned and discovered that she wasn't even there. I thought she had followed me inside. I quickly emerged from the cave's darkness and saw her standing about twenty feet away. She had a bewildering look on her face.

"What's the matter?" I asked.

She hesitated before whispering, "I've been here before."

"What do you mean?"

"Do you remember that dream I told you about?"

"Yes, the one where you're holding a shotgun with a little brother in your lap."

"That's it ... that's the cave. Go back inside. Toward the back left, you'll find a big boulder that one can hide behind. Near the front there's a spring-fed pool where milk cans could be kept cool."

I stepped back inside. Yes, the boulder was there. A place to hide behind it was there. Near the entrance, there was a damp, mossy soft area that probably once was a spring-fed pool for storing fresh milk cans. I searched the cave but didn't see anything else of interest. Just before exiting, I flashed the light on the rock face above the entrance. There was a carving, a symbol scratched into the rock. It looked to be an anchor, a two-pronged anchor, about ten inches high.

When I stepped back in the sunlight, Rebekah asked, "Did you find the boulder?"

"Yes, it's in there, just as you said."

"And the spring pool?"

"There's a damp, mossy area that might have been a pool once, but it's filled in now."

"I knew it. I could sense it the second I saw the entrance," she said.

"Come look at something. I want you to see this."

"Inside the cave?" she responded with some trepidation.

"In the cave that you dreamed about, was there some kind of symbol above the entrance?"

"I don't think so."

"Come look," I said again.

She seemed very nervous, but she came and stood beside me.

We ducked down together and entered the cave, but with each step, her grip on my arm grew tighter.

Three steps in, she said, "Is this far enough?"

I turned on the app and flashed the light to the rock above the entrance so she could see the symbol.

She took a moment to study it and then bolted back into the sunlight.

I followed her out and joined her as she was heading back toward the house.

A squirrel chattered at us, breaking the silence of the forest, as we passed the old cabin.

When we neared the barn, she said, "Why would there be an anchor out in the middle of Missouri? We're a long way from any ocean."

"I don't know. How could you dream of a cave that you have never been in before?"

"I don't know that either," she said softly.

CHAPTER 6

Neighbors

Back at the old house, we sat down together on the porch steps. Both of us were struggling with what to think about our experience. Richard checked his phone for the first time since our arrival at the farm, but there was no service. There hadn't been phone service since we passed Miller's Orchard. As we were admiring the idyllic view, rain clouds began moving in from the northwest.

"What are our plans?" I finally asked.

Richard was keeping an eye on the cloud formation. "It feels good just to sit here and do nothing, don't you think? We did a lot of that during our year in Argentina and North Africa, just doing nothing except being together. It feels right."

"Our lives have gotten busy since we moved to Lexington. I love our life together, but we are busy, maybe too busy. What are our plans, for tonight?"

"We could go see a homecoming football game that's not at home," Richard said with a smirk. He looked back at the building clouds. "Homecoming may be played on a wet field anyway."

"Other than that?"

"Let's drive home. We could start now and be home around

midnight. In a couple of weeks, we can come back with clearer thoughts about what we should do."

"I'm good with that. Let's go."

As we both nodded in agreement, we heard the faint thump of an engine. At first, we decided that it was a chain saw, but it kept getting closer. Out of the thick timber, a three-wheeler emerged and headed toward us. The driver was wearing dirty denim overalls and waved at us as he killed the engine. Three-wheelers like that hadn't been made in years for safety reasons, and this model seemed to be held together mostly with baling wire and duct tape.

"Hello, new neighbors," the driver said in a deep Ozark slang.

"Hello," we returned in unison.

"I'm Henry, Henry Smally. I'm your neighbor to the west. I assume that you are Billy's niece and the new owner of his farm."

"I am. I'm Rebekah Dempsey, and this is my husband, Richard. It's good to meet you, Henry."

"My wife told me she thought she heard a car pull in earlier. We had heard that you were in West Plains, and I just wanted to slip over and say hello. Your uncle and I were good friends. There's an old logging road concealed in the timber that connects our places. Most of the time, we don't even close the gate."

"How long have you lived here?" Richard asked.

"My grandpappy lived here for many years. After my daddy didn't come back from the army, me and my two older brothers moved in with him, so I guess I could say that I've lived here most of my whole life." His Ozark slang became even more pronounced the longer he spoke.

"We would like to talk to you sometime when we have more time. We're very interested in learning more about this area," I said.

"Sure, anytime. Just let me know when. For years, I would come over and visit with your uncle, usually about once a week. I used to come over and plow his field and plant soybeans, but he decided to stop that several years ago. He told me he needed that lower field left in grass."

"We were wondering why Billy quit farming the place," Richard said.

"He never talked about that, but everybody in West Plains knew when his high-powered friends came to town," he said.

"What do you mean, Henry?" I asked.

"Well, as I said, he never talked to me about them, but about twice a year, fancy cars would come through West Plains and head out here to Billy's farm. Our little county road never sees much traffic, but twice a year, we would start seeing Billy's friends arriving. More than once, a car has pulled down our lane by mistake and ended up having to ask for directions."

"Who were they?" I asked.

"I don't know. It's the great secret. They have been coming out here for several decades, and everybody in town knows when they arrive, but the visitors are all tight-lipped. They stop and eat, get gas, and then they come out here for the weekend to do whatever it is they do."

"And you don't know what it is they do?" I asked.

Appearing to be a bit embarrassed, Henry said, "Once, many years ago now, I walked over and peered through the trees one Friday night after his friends arrived. I was spying, and I'm not proud of that, but there were several dozen tents set up in that lower pasture with a bonfire in the middle. I decided to not get any closer.

"Sometime the next week, Billy came over to the house. Somehow, he seemed to know that I had been watching them from over there in the trees, and he asked me not to come back during those weekends. I promised him, and I never have since. We can see the glow from their fire from our house, but I don't know what they do. I know that, by Sunday afternoon, all is quiet again."

"And you don't know who they are?" I asked.

"No, but most of them seem to be big-city Easterners. Others talk funny, like they're from France or Germany, or some foreign place. Their license plates seem to be from just about everywhere. Once there were two guys dressed up in Arab pajamas, whatever they call those clothes. People in West Plains tend to pay close attention to foreigners in case you haven't noticed, but these people have never caused any problems, and so around here, nobody really cares. The sheriff knows all about them."

"And they come twice a year?" Richard asked.

"Yep, like clockwork, the first of April and usually the end of October. I could always tell because Billy would spend at least a week cleaning up the place. Now that he's gone, and you are the new owners, I guess you'll need to clean up the place before they come. Usually, your uncle would ask me to bring over a case of my wife's special medicine," he said with some hopefulness.

"This is the first we've heard of this," Richard said.

"By the way, I don't know what your plans are, but in town, I heard that you have already sold the place. I was hoping that I might get in a bid on it before you sold it."

I said, "Mr. Smith, the lawyer, told us that he had a potential buyer who was ready to make an offer, but then Mr. Kirkland, at the bank, told us the same thing. We don't know if it is the same person of if there are two possible offers; regardless, we haven't made any decisions."

"Well, I probably can't pay what some folks are willing to fork over, but I would take care of this place if I owned it. It's sad to watch it run down. Just let me know before you make any decisions."

"I'm just wondering about something, Henry. If you were able to purchase this place, would you allow this group to continue using it?" I asked.

"Are you kidding me? Of course not! That secret group wouldn't be welcome anymore. Are you going to let them come while you own it?"

We looked at each other. That was a question we needed to address.

"Just remember me before you sell it."

Richard said, "We will, Henry. It's good to meet you. By the way, who owns the property to our east?"

"Everything to the east is the Mark Twain. It's not wilderness, but it is federal land. People go in there to hunt deer or squirrel during season. Some hike through it to get to the Jacks Fork River or the Eleven Point."

"So, we have the Irish Wilderness to the south, your place is to the west, the Mark Twain National Forest to the east, and the back end of Miller's Orchard to the north across the road." Richard pointed out the four directions.

"That's why I would like to buy it. None of that federal land will ever be up for sale."

"Just curious ... what kind of medicine did Billy want you to bring over for his guests?" I asked, even though I had an educated guess.

"Oh, my wife and I whip up a batch of corn squeezing a couple of times per year. She needs it for her rheumatism, but Billy's guests enjoyed it for other reasons I suspect. Let me know if you need a case or two, and I can bring it over. Twelve quarts is the standing order."

"Thanks for stopping by," I said.

With that, the battered three-wheeler fired up and roared back into the timberline.

—

In fifteen minutes, we were driving east. We decided to go a different route than we came in on, and the first town we entered was named Wilderness. It had a cool name and obviously had been named after the nearby forested areas, but there didn't seem to be much left there today. Next, we saw William's Grocery. We stopped and walked around the old general store. Near the front door was a display with free brochures advertising the various things to see and do in southeastern Missouri.

I picked up a couple of brochures, and we settled back in the car with ice-cream bars.

As Richard drove, I started reading about the Mark Twain, and especially the Irish Wilderness. After skimming the material, I asked if he wanted the long version or the condensed version.

"You decide. I like hearing your voice either way."

"Great, get ready. First, the Irish Wilderness is a section within the Mark Twain National Forest, and thus the two signs on the farm's back fence. The wilderness consists of 16,500 acres of the 1.5 million acres that make up the Mark Twain. The Irish Wilderness has its roots in Ireland."

"Thus, the name, 'Irish' Wilderness," Richard said, being sarcastic.

I continued, "In the 1840s, a blight attacked the potato crops in Ireland. At that time, many of the Irish lived in destitute poverty. They depended upon those potatoes, and without their primary food source, more than a million Irish died of starvation in a single year. Another two million left Ireland, scattering wherever, and at least a million of those immigrated to the United States.

"Many of them found that they weren't welcome in the States, and they scattered all around the country, seeking to find work and the potential for a better life. One such group of misplaced Irish landed in a neighborhood in St. Louis, nearly doubling the size of the city. It wasn't a pleasant place to begin with, but it quickly degenerated into a dark and very dangerous slum. Most of the women could get jobs doing washing and ironing, but the men had to leave town to work on the railroad. It was very difficult on families, especially the children.

"A local Catholic priest had a creative dream. He rounded up a group of Irish families from this desperate neighborhood and moved them to southeastern Missouri. He had purchased a large section of unsettled land in the Ozarks, paying twelve cents per acre. Father Hogan became quite the hero, and he and his horse, John the Baptist, were known everywhere from St. Louis to the Ozarks."

"John the Baptist? That's an interesting name for a Catholic priest's horse," Richard said.

"It says that he bought it from a Baptist preacher in St. Louis. For several years, the new colony flourished. A grist mill and a sawmill were started. They built a school and a church. They cleared land for fields and gardens. Father John Hogan's community found a measure of prosperity, but most of all, they found a home. Life wasn't easy, but compared to where they came from, they were content. However, their little piece of heaven was short-lived." I paused and watched the fall foliage pass as Richard continued driving.

"Don't leave me hanging. What happened?"

I smiled at his eagerness. "Remember your American history?"

"What year did they start this new colony?" Richard asked.

"The first of the Irish came in 1859."

"Didn't the Civil War erupt in 1861?" Richard asked.

"Exactly. The Civil War started, and much of Missouri became a no-man's land between the North and the South. The new Irish colonists didn't fit in with the money of the North and didn't own slaves with the Southerners. It just wasn't their war. They wanted to be left alone, but such wasn't going to happen.

"First, the North came and confiscated their cattle and sheep to feed their troops. Then a few months later, the South came and took everything else. Nobody really knows for sure all that happened, but after the Civil War, the colony of Irish had vanished. One group of Union troops coming home from the war said that the wilderness area was picked so clean that they were obliged to carry feed for their own horses."

"Are you sure we're talking about the same place? Look how thick it is now." Richard pointed to the timber.

"Yes, this is the same place. The new community of Irish immigrants simply disappeared. It is one of the great mysteries of the Ozarks. Even Father Hogan, in his personal journal, said he never heard what had happened to his friends. Following the war, this area became home to outlaws and deserters. Southern sympathizers, called bushwhackers, camped in the region, making raids upon the North well after the war was over. For more than a decade, it was a very dangerous place for any outsiders.

"Then, at the turn of the century, timber barons set their sights on the old-growth oaks, hickories, and yellow pines. They stripped the area, shipping the lumber by train to build homes and buildings in the growing cites back East and for the railroad out West. By the end of World War I, it was reported that not a usable tree was still standing in the Ozarks. The entire region had been reduced to a field of stumps.

"With nothing left to harvest, the wilderness started reasserting itself, but it was a tangle of wild vegetation with thickets of scrub brush. Some trees were replanted by the Civilian Conservation Corp in the 1930s, and the wilderness began the long, slow process of restoration.

"In 1984, the area was given 'wilderness status,' forever named after the mysterious disappearance of the Irish immigrants. They say that remnants of the old colony are scattered throughout the present wilderness area. There's a big iron paddle wheel still standing in a creek. There are foundations to ruined houses. There is at least one cemetery."

Richard responded, "Your uncle's farm borders the Irish. I suspect that cabin and cave date back to Father Hogan's colony."

"Yes, I expect so. I would like to hike through the wilderness to see what is still there."

"It's an amazing story. It's also a sad story. Can you imagine what it would have been like to have been a child nearly starving to death back in Ireland—and then caught up in the middle of the Civil War after immigrating?"

I said, "And hiding in a cave, holding a shotgun and listening for your dad's voice, but only hearing silence. Yes, I can imagine that. I *definitely* can imagine that."

Richard said, "You were nervous about entering that cave. I have never seen you that anxious. We faced sheer terror in Argentina and North Africa, but you were never that tense."

"I know. I can't explain it." I felt my eyes growing heavy. "Wake me up if you need me to drive."

—

Richard's phone told him that we were less than seven hours from home, so he drove, drank some coffee, and thought about all that had happened. I tried to sleep, but I couldn't get it all processed. Before our walk down to the national forest boundary fence, I would have been ready to sell the place to the first bidder. Now I was interested, very interested, in the farm, but why did Sheriff Nelson seem to care what we did with it?

Henry, the neighbor, had given us more questions than answers. *Who are these people who use Uncle Billy's farm twice a year? What do they do when they came? If they come in April and the end of October, then they will be coming in a few weeks. Today is October 1. Perhaps that's why anonymous buyers are already making offers.* I knew that Richard thought I was sound asleep, and maybe I did doze off once or twice, but my mind was racing. Finally, I sat up and looked outside, but it was too dark to see much.

"You couldn't sleep?"

"No, the conversation with our new neighbor has me thinking. The group has been coming to the farm for more than twenty years. All of West Plains knows about them, but nobody seems to know anything specific about their group. Even the sheriff knows. I wonder what he would tell us?"

"Do you really want to ask him?"

"Not really. He's doesn't appear to be one who would break open secrets easily, but I would like to try. He did seem intent on convincing us to sell."

Richard kept driving, and we found ourselves pulling into our driveway not long after midnight. It was comforting to find the doors all locked and the new alarm system still actively on alert. We hadn't had any more home intruders during our trip west.

We slept in on Saturday morning—or at least Richard did. I got up before he did and went to pick up Goose from down the street.

When we returned to the house, Goose immediately searched and found Richard still in bed. She was wildly excited to have her family restored. Any thought of another hour of sleep for Richard was out of the question.

Just before lunch, Richard FaceTimed his daughter, Micah. Her new baby was rolling over and scooting around. It was a joy to see his grandbaby laughing and giggling. It was even more of a joy seeing his daughter and son-in-law's faces filled with pride. As the call came to an end, Micah asked if we had spoken to Lisa yet, Richard's other daughter. She encouraged us to do so "immediately." From the tone of her voice and the expression on her face, we suspected that sometime next year Richard was going to be a granddad twice over. He quickly made the second call to Lisa, and she confirmed our guess with her joyful news.

Richard and I went to worship on Sunday morning. It was good to see many of our friends and to see many new faces. The preacher's sermon was on the passage in Acts where Paul was traveling from town to town sharing the good news. When he finished in one town, he looked at his map to see where to go next, but one night, Paul had a dream. It was a vision of a man begging him to come to his city across the sea.

The next morning, Paul told his traveling companions about the dream. They decided they were going to skip over the next several villages and sail to the city of the man who had called to him in the vision. I wasn't sure what the preacher's point was, but for the rest of the day, I thought about the concept of dreams and visions. Did God still direct us in that way? I thought about my dream and wondered what it meant—if anything.

—

On Sunday evening, I attempted to share with Richard how I felt as I stood in front of the cave at the farm. "In my dream, there were at least three major points, I think. First, there was the silence. I was listening for my dad's voice, but I could hear absolutely nothing. I never realized how 'loud' silence could be.

"Second, holding the shotgun was out of character for me. When I handed you Uncle Billy's revolver from his glove compartment, that was the first time I'd ever actually held any type of firearm. In the dream, I had to hold the shotgun and decide whether I could pull the trigger if someone came into the cave. Holding the little boy, and the shotgun, meant I was responsible."

Richard said, "I had that same thought when I realized we had intruders in our house last Saturday morning. Pulling the trigger on any firearm is a serious decision."

I continued, "And third, holding the shotgun tells me that I'm called to defend Uncle Billy's farm now. I'm not sure how or why, but I'm holding a shotgun and I'm ready to defend it."

"Wow," Richard said. "I just thought you were afraid of going into caves."

"I may be, but there's more to it than that."

CHAPTER 7

The Double J

On Monday, we both played catch-up at work. Rebekah had several new clients who were interested in updating their homes. She made the calls and set up appointments. I dealt with the business at hand at the foundation.

That evening, I cooked supper for us, grilling steaks and veggies on the outside grill. My plan was to relax and watch *Monday Night Football* after we had eaten. When I turned on the television, I realized it already was a blowout in the second quarter involving two teams I didn't even care about. At halftime, I started surfing for something else to watch.

Sensing that football was no longer the focus, Rebekah came into the den to join me. I had stopped my surfing on the History Channel where an archaeologist was talking to a reporter about the famous outlaw Jesse James. They were exploring in western Missouri using a metal detector to locate treasure that Jesse James supposedly buried.

From what the archaeologist was saying, Jesse often used glass Mason jars that he would fill with gold and silver coins from his most recent plunder. He would then bury the jars and mark the area with symbols to indicate their various locations. Over the years, many of these Mason jar caches had been discovered, but they were guessing that there were many more.

Rebekah and I casually watched and listened.

Rebekah said, "Uncle Billy must have been very interested in Jesse James. In that box you pulled out, there were at least a dozen old books about the outlaw—not to mention that classic that you found on top. Did we leave that book at the house?"

"I think so. I certainly had no plans to read it," I responded. "What? Look at that!"

The archeologist on the documentary had led the investigative reporter to a cliffside that was covered in graffiti. He pointed out some Native American pictographs, probably Sioux, and then he pointed out some names and dates that were probably early settlers passing through Missouri on their way west.

When the archeologist pointed to a two-pronged anchor, Rebekah and I jumped up so fast that we scared Goose. *It's the symbol from the cave.*

The archeologist asked the reporter what he thought the anchor symbolized. He offered several wild suggestions, in the same way we had ourselves, but the archeologist stopped him before he made a total fool of himself.

"That's the double J. The first is a J, and the second is a J in reverse." He traced it out with his finger. "That's the personal brand of Jesse James. Everywhere we find the double J, we know that Jesse James has been there."

They resumed their hunt with their metal detectors, but I backed up the program and proceeded to watch it again. The double J was Jesse James's brand carved into the stone. We watched them dig up several "hits" from their metal detectors, but they only found a few worthless individual coins and several rusted Mason jar lids.

"That would be exciting to run a metal detector around that old cabin and cave area," I said.

Rebekah nodded, but she lacked the enthusiasm that I felt.

"Have I ever mentioned my college roommate from Boston College?" she asked.

"I don't think so. What was her name?"

"Phillis Morgan. I roomed with her my freshman year. We became good friends, but we haven't kept up with each other. Now she is Dr. Phillis Morgan. She was a history major and now teaches at Transylvania. I feel the need to sit down with a history professor. Want to join me?"

"Are you talking about the Transylvania over in Romania, home to Count Dracula?" I asked facetiously.

"Of course not, I'm talking about Transylvania University, right here in Lexington."

"I was just making sure. I've driven past Transylvania University many times. It's a beautiful campus from what you can see from the road, but I'll let you visit with your friend. If she say's anything significant, you can fill me in later. I assume that you are comfortable going by yourself."

"I assume you are comfortable in letting me go by myself."

I squeezed her hand. I still found myself slightly paranoid when we weren't together since the break-ins, but we needed to move on and live our lives without fear.

Rebekah said, "I think I'll call her tomorrow and see if she has any time for an old friend."

—

On Tuesday, I left the foundation during lunch and walked down Richmond Road to a pawnshop that I had shopped in before. I was looking for something specific. When we returned to the farm, I wanted to take a metal detector.

The salesman took me behind the shop and demonstrated how to use it. He put a gold coin, a copper button, and an iron nail under a piece of cardboard and demonstrated how the impressive machine sounded with the various metals.

I was excited to use it, and I quickly made the purchase. I did feel somewhat self-conscious walking back down Richmond Road with the metal detector. People who passed probably thought I was searching for spare change on the sidewalk.

That evening, after supper, Rebekah and I sat down in front of the fireplace. Goose wanted to snuggle in between us. Rebekah told me that she had talked to her old college roommate, the history professor, and they were planning on having lunch tomorrow.

I told Rebekah about my new toy, and we compared our calendars and decided that we both wanted to go back to the farm for the weekend. There was no reason to wait, and we decided to leave on Friday morning.

With our feet being warmed by the fire, Rebekah said, "On my way home this afternoon, I had the radio on a Christian station. A Kentucky mountain preacher was giving a five-minute devotional. I can't remember his name, but in essence, he said, 'In life, we never need to worry because everything that happens is in God's will. We just need to trust him.' Do you believe that?"

"Do I believe that we should trust God?" I asked.

"No, do you believe that everything that happens is God's will?"

"I know that some Christians believe that everything that happens is God's will, but I don't. I know that I have done some things in the past that were wrong. God did not want me to sin, and He did not plan for me to sin. What I did was not in His will, and apart from the forgiveness that I found in Christ, those sins would have had a terrible consequence on my life and future."

"What about us? Do you think it was God's will for us to be captured and held hostage for a year?"

"I believe that God used those evil circumstances and twisted them around for our good, but the circumstances were still evil, very evil. Those kids on the truck with us across Argentina were eventually sold into slavery. They faced horrors most can't even imagine. That was not God's will for their lives."

"No, it wasn't. I can't imagine God wanted those kids to be in slavery. He wouldn't be 'good' if that was the case. He wouldn't be a God that I would, or could, worship," she said with some conviction.

I said, "When Jesus's disciples asked Jesus to teach them to pray, he gave them a model prayer. Most of us call it the Lord's Prayer. In it, he says that we should pray for God's will to be done. If he's instructing us to pray for God's will to be done, then the clear implication is that God's will isn't being done now—at least not in fullness. But I don't want to sound like an old preacher."

"There are no easy answers to these questions, are there?"

"When I first started studying for the ministry, a tornado struck several counties over. It was devastating for one little town, but the tornado was odd in its destruction. There was one neighborhood of houses where approximately every third house was left standing while all the others were flattened to the ground.

"A news reporter was interviewing a woman whose house was essentially untouched. She was exuberant with joy that God had delivered her house. She said it four or five times loudly that God had saved her. 'Praise God!' she shouted over and over, but just over her shoulder was her neighbor, a little old woman. She was bending over a pile of rubble that once had been her home. That woman could hear her neighbor praising God. She turned to look, but then she just lowered her head, turned away, and resumed digging into her own pile of trash. It broke my heart, and I decided there and then that I never wanted my praise to God to be a source of pain for another."

"I guess I have had similar thoughts. Do you remember the young man who was shot in the back of the head there in Patagonia, right in front of us?"

"How could I ever forget? We never did hear who he was or why he was killed," I said.

"That could have been us."

"I know. They wanted us to realize that possibility. That's why they did it right in front of us. They wanted us to see what they were capable of doing."

"You went through a personal period of doubt, didn't you?" she said.

"Yes, after my first wife died of cancer and I resigned from the church, I went into a season of intense confusion. Some of the answers I thought I knew, just didn't make sense any longer."

"That's one of the things that I love about you. You're honest about your faith. You never cover up or pretend to believe when you have serious questions and doubts. Thank you for your honesty."

"There is one passage in Luke that helps me. It doesn't explain everything; it just helps me. Jesus said it right after John the Baptist sent out questions to him. John wanted to know for sure. Are you really the Messiah? Are you the One?"

"Yes, I think I remember that passage. John the Baptist was in prison, wasn't he?"

"Yes, John was in prison. He was facing his own execution. From his perspective, things weren't making much sense. If Jesus was really the One, then why did he feel forgotten—and why was he still in prison? Why could he hear his captors sharpening their ax? I suspect that the disciples had the same question. If Jesus didn't do something to help John the Baptist now—His cousin, the prophet—then should they expect that He would do something for them if they were in the same predicament?

"But then Jesus said, 'Blessed is the man who does not fall away on account of me.' That means, at least to me, that Jesus may not do everything that I want, or expect, or hope. He may disappoint me, but even if He does, I will not fall away."

"Wow, I don't remember reading that statement before, but perhaps we need to back up a bit. What were your sins that you were referring to earlier?" she said with a wink and a smile.

I softly said, "I can't remember," and then I leaned over and kissed her.

CHAPTER 8

Circulo Dorado

On Wednesday, I met my former college roommate at a sandwich shop not far from her campus. Richard decided not to join us. When I had called, she said that Wednesday was the only day she had free, but she was excited to see me. When I walked into the sandwich shop, Phillis stood to greet me. "It's been too long!"

"I haven't seen you since you received your doctorate. Congratulations, Dr. Phillis Morgan, my friend."

We ordered our sandwiches, and she shared the highlights of her life since our university days. "Enough about me. What about you?"

I decided not to mention my year as a hostage; that story would dominate our entire conversation, and I had some other topics I wanted to discuss with a history professor. "My uncle died and left me his small farm in Missouri."

"I'm sorry for your loss," she said.

"I didn't really know him, so it was a surprise to find out that he wanted me to inherit his farm. In exploring his old place, we found an interesting carving in a cave. It looked like a two-pronged anchor, but on the History Channel, we saw the same symbol on a show about Jesse James. They proclaimed that the anchor was a 'double J,' and it was Jesse James's personal brand. Have you ever heard of such a thing?"

"Yes, one of my graduate students actually wrote a paper on Jesse James, and he had quite a bit of proof that the 'double J' was indeed connected to Jesse James. You found it in a cave on your uncle's farm?"

I nodded.

"Is there anything else there?" she asked.

"The place backs up to the Irish Wilderness."

"The Irish? That's a wild place." She proceeded to tell the story I had read from the brochure.

"And there are no hints as to what happened to the Irish colony?" I asked.

Phillis said, "I personally think they attempted to defend themselves and lost. Since they didn't support the North or the South, neither side trusted them. We don't know which side did the deed, but one or the other destroyed their colony. The historians don't believe anyone survived.

"A group of captives from southern Missouri were loaded onto a train and shipped to a prison camp just before the war was over. Some scholars have tried to compare the names of the captives on that train with Father Hogan's list of the colonists, but the names don't match. The only reason that would explain why they weren't on that train is because none of them were still alive. I think that is probably true. Have you hiked around in the Irish Wilderness?"

"No, Richard and I would like to, but we haven't yet."

"You will find it interesting. There are still multiple ruins and the big iron paddle wheel they used to turn their grist mill is still standing in a creek."

"Was Jesse James connected to the Irish?" I asked.

"Probably not. He may have been in and out of the area after the colony disappeared, but it's hard to track him down."

"What do we actually know about Jesse James?"

"Not nearly as much as many believe. It is thought that no one has had more legends created about them than Jesse James. Dozens of books have been written about the famous outlaw, mostly by people who didn't know him, and people bought the books.

"It's odd how Americans are attracted to outlaws, and it's more than just here in America. When Japanese tourists come to the United States, there are two absolute musts on their bucket list: the Grand Canyon and the grave of Billy the Kid in New Mexico. Jesse James's grave isn't far behind.

"But the truth is, Jesse James had good PR. Any time there was a bank robbery, or train holdup, for at least twenty years, somebody would claim to have recognized the James brothers as being involved. Sometimes, Jesse was seen in Texas and in Missouri on the exact same day. And now, after more than a hundred years, it's very difficult to know what all he did, or didn't do."

I said, "Do we know why Jesse got so actively involved?"

"The Civil War was a confusing time for our country, especially in places like Clay County, Missouri, Jesse's hometown. Clay County residents were mostly transplants from Kentucky and Tennessee. Sometimes the area was referred to as 'Little Dixie.' Many of them were slave owners. They officially supported the North, yet they were strongly against the North's war effort. They referred to themselves as 'Peace Democrats,' and they refused to support the North or the South. Their neighbors to the north called them 'Copperheads' after the poisonous snake, but Clay County took pride in the name, pointing to Lady Liberty on the back of a copper penny.

"Though families in Clay County sent men to fight for either side, when the war broke out, Frank James, Jesse's older brother, enlisted with the South. We're not sure what happened, but apparently, he fell ill and came home to recover. After he healed, he decided that the South was losing and thought he would better serve the South by joining Quantrill's Raiders. They fought the North with guerrilla tactics, not like a real army. They were ruthless and often even executed their prisoners. They would attack with ferocity and then disappear back into the Wilderness.

"We think that a company of Northern militia came to Clay County attempting to locate the whereabouts of Frank and his bushwhacker friends. They believed his family knew his camp's location. Jesse's father had been killed in California, but his mother, Zerelda, had remarried. In hopes of prying information from Zerelda, they lynched her new husband, Reuben Samuel, in their front yard—but after a few seconds, they let him live. The story is that they then tied thirteen-year-old Jesse to a tree and whipped him severely. Regardless, Frank's location wasn't disclosed."

"That's horrible," I said. "Thirteen years old? That would have emotionally damaged a kid."

"It bred a deep-seated hatred for the North in Jesse. About the time the war was over, Jesse was old enough to join Frank and the bushwhackers. That's when they were probably in and out of the Irish Wilderness area.

"After Lee surrendered in 1865, several groups of bushwhackers refused to give up and continued to battle. Eventually, Frank and Jesse started their own gang. The two brothers had always been close. Their dad had been a slave-owning Baptist preacher, and out of respect for their dad, neither Frank nor Jesse ever used curse words. They were ruthless killers, but they didn't swear. It's been said that Jesse accidently shot off the tip of his own finger and jumped around the room shouting, 'Dod-dingus.' From that point on, Frank always referred to his little brother as 'Dingus.'

Later, the two brothers joined the two Younger brothers, and that's when the myths really started flying. For twenty years, the James-Younger gang raided banks, trains, and Northern businesses. In 1882, Jesse was the most wanted man in the United States, and he was chased by the famous Chicago detective agency, the Pinkertons.

"In the minds of the defeated South, Jesse became a 'Robin Hood' type of character, but there's no indication that he ever helped the poor. That's part of his mystique. But there's also no evidence he ever spent any of the loot on himself. Jesse's Mason jars have been located over a wide area, but nowhere near all of the loot has been found."

"I have another question. What do you know about the Knights of the Golden Circle?"

She said, "That's a different animal. We have more historical facts about them. They were mostly Southern businessmen and politicians who started meeting before the Civil War, but they weren't all Southerners. Their founder was actually from Cincinnati, Ohio.

"It's hard to know how many members the KGC had, but we know what they were planning to do. They wanted to start an alternative country—a pro-slavery country named Circulo Dorado. They thought they could pull together Florida, the Gulf States, Southern Texas, the eastern section of Mexico, and most of the Caribbean, which is roughly a circle shape around the Gulf of Mexico. They were planning to make Havana, Cuba, their capital city.

"They thought that if they could get Mexico to join them, then the Civil War might be averted. Obviously, that didn't happen because Mexico refused to participate. There were numerous myths that floated around about the KGC. Except for a few, the membership was largely secret, but names like John Wilkes Boothe and Jesse James have been connected to the KGC by many. Some say that they can prove that Jesse James was raising funds for the KGC through his robberies, but that has been difficult to establish.

"As an organization, the KGC ceased to exist not long after the Civil War was over, but there have been local pockets of people who have attempted to resurrect the movement since. None of them have been successful, as far as I know. The last reported KGC activity that I am aware of was in a small town in Missouri, probably not far from the Irish Wilderness."

I felt a sinking feeling in my chest. "What town would that be?"

"West Plains," she said. "I think it was back in 1903 that the local KGC in West Plains ran off the entire black population with threats of violence. That event really happened, but no one is positive now that the KGC was behind it. Have you been to West Plains?"

Somewhat in shock, I said, "Yes, we have, just last weekend. Ironically, my uncle's farm is near West Plains. Do you have any knowledge of modern KGC groups?"

She responded, "No, nothing recent. I will be anxious to hear what you find out about your uncle, but I have a class coming up. I need to run, but it has been so good to see you."

—

That night, I told Richard everything my friend had shared with me. We both were unsure what this new information meant for us, but we knew that we would have a difficult time seeing West Plains in the same light.

—

On Thursday afternoon, I got free early and went home. Richard was already home. He didn't hear me pull up, but I saw him in the backyard. He had his new metal detector fired up and was 'sweeping' the backyard under the walnut tree. It was amusing to spy on him. I slipped up behind him and startled him. He was slightly embarrassed, but just then, his new toy started chirping.

I said, "You found something! In our yard!"

He reached down and picked up a quarter. "Of course I did. I hid it there. I just wanted to practice."

"You have the fever, don't you?"

"Yep, no denying it. I can't wait to get to the farm and fire up this bad boy."

CHAPTER 9

Treasure

We got an early start on Friday after dropping off Goose again at our friends' house. She seemed to understand this time that we were leaving her, but we hugged her, and she went off to play happily with her sister. She really was a good dog.

We made good time driving through Kentucky. The leaves were in full autumn mode, and we enjoyed the drive. Our plan was to slip in from the back side and not even go through West Plains, but as we were nearing our turn into the Mark Twain, Rebekah jumped up and said, "We forgot about the truck. We were going to go by the garage last Saturday and see about selling it to the kid who works for Danny. We simply forgot."

"We'll go by and find him in the morning and apologize. I expect that he has a football game tonight, but I suspect he will still be interested in buying the truck."

"Perhaps we should just give the truck to him," she said.

"I appreciate your heart. I really do, but may I offer a suggestion?"

She nodded in agreement.

"A schoolkid getting his first vehicle shouldn't have it just given to him. You could give him a great deal, but there ought to be a price.

If you just give it to him, you will endanger his spirit. He may not fully appreciate what he has if it comes too easily. However, it's your uncle's truck, which is now your truck, so you decide what's best."

She looked me with a frown and then turned away. "Okay, we can wait until morning. Are we ever going to be in West Plains for lunch on a Friday? I would like to try Lucille's world-famous meatloaf."

I smiled and said, "Someday, we will make it happen. I enjoy meatloaf too."

As we turned into Uncle Billy's lane, the wire gate was open again.

"I know I closed it when we left last week," I said. "Somebody has been here. I brought a lock and chain to put on it this time."

We drove down the lane, half expecting to see another vehicle in front of the house, but there wasn't. Other than the gate being opened, we couldn't see anything out of place.

After checking the house, I said, "Do you know what I want to do?"

"Yes, I do. Get your new toy and go find Jesse James's million dollars," she said as she pushed me out the front door. "I'm going to go investigate that locked bottom drawer in Uncle Billy's desk, and then I'll go upstairs and poke around. Have fun."

Securing the metal detector, my small shovel, and a warm jacket, I started down the path to the cabin and cave. At the cabin, I anxiously fired up my new toy, and it immediately started beeping and squawking. Like a mad dog digging for a bone, I dropped to my knees and started shoveling dirt. My first find was a nail. My second great find was another nail and then another. After a dozen nails, the excitement started wearing thin.

Sweeping through the old cabin, I found another piece of the broken skillet, a button, and six more nails. Down by the cave entrance, there were two cigarette butts on the ground. Somebody had been here since last week, but the metal detector remained silent.

I walked on down to the national forest fence and started west.

I decided to just walk the edge of the property to see what I could find. A hundred yards from the cave entrance, I noticed a slight impression in the grass. Walking around it, I realized that I was standing on the ruined foundation of some type of structure. Most of the wood had deteriorated, but it clearly was a rectangular frame.

Now that I knew what I was looking for, I found several more collapsed foundations hidden in the deep grass. There were at least three or four more that I could make out on the Irish Wilderness side of the fence, but the most complete frame was on our side. It was standing the thickness of at least three logs high.

From there, I turned on the metal detector and just started walking. To have done it in a grid pattern would have been smarter, but I didn't have the time or patience. I was tired of finding nails, but about forty feet from the last of the ruins, the detector jumped to life like a swarm of bees.

I grabbed my shovel and started digging. Six inches deep, I saw the corner of an object. As my heart raced, I dug and pried until the earth released its hold. It was a hard wooden box wrapped with iron straps, like the strongboxes they carried on stagecoaches in old western movies. A rusted padlock had it locked up tight. I shook it but heard nothing. *Why would an empty box be locked?*

With the new find under one arm and the metal detector slung over my shoulder, I proceeded west. My plan was to follow the fence until I found the corner, which would indicate the beginning to Henry's farm. It couldn't be that far, but the farther I went, the rougher it became. Trees were blown down and had to be either crawled over or ducked under. When I found the fenced corner, I decided it was time for a break.

In the stillness of the timber, I started noticing how thick the trees were, but not one of them was much more than eight or ten inches in diameter. The largest might have been twelve inches. There were stumps everywhere, some of them massive in size. I remembered what Rebekah had read about the clear-cutting of the Ozarks at the turn of the century. I guess I really didn't imagine that to be completely true until that moment when I saw all the giant stumps.

As I continued resting, a squirrel began to scold me for being too close to his tree. As I stood and reloaded my gear and loot, I noticed what appeared to be a pipe sticking from the ground next to one of the larger stumps. It wouldn't budge, so I dug down a foot and finally forced it loose. I immediately knew what it was.

It was the barrel to a shotgun. The wooden stock had completely rotted away, but the works and barrel were intact. I stopped listening to the pesky squirrel and loaded up all my findings, including the newly acquired shotgun. I followed the old fence until I found the faint logging road that Henry had mentioned. The tracks of his three-wheeler were evident. It led me straight to the house.

I stomped around on the porch, ridding my boots of the dirt and mud.

After hearing the commotion, Rebekah came to the door to see if I had been successful.

I revealed each "prize" like a kid at school during show-and-tell.

She didn't fully appreciate the nails or the old shotgun, but she was very curious about the strongbox. "What's in it?"

"Sounds like air," I said as I shook the box. "I'm going to go down to the barn and see if I can find some tools to open it. I can't imagine that someone would bother to lock an empty strongbox. What did you find around here?"

She grinned and laughed. "Some interesting things—but nothing as intriguing as a locked strongbox. Let's go open the box first, and then I will show what I found."

No argument came from me. In the barn, I found two or three hammers that might have worked, but one swift strike on the padlock was all that was needed. The rust-encrusted lock gave way.

With great anticipation and our heads together like a couple of kids, we slowly forced open the lid. Our heart immediately sank. The box appeared to be empty.

Rebekah ran her hand along the bottom and felt something stuck in a corner. "Wait, what is this?"

Another gentle tap with the hammer loosened it. It was a coin. I grabbed a dirty rag and rubbed off most of the grime. It was gold. With additional cleaning, we could tell that it was an 1871 twenty-dollar Liberty gold piece. Neither of us knew what the coin was worth, but that didn't really matter. We had found gold.

The sun was dipping down behind the tree line as we walked back to the house.

I said, "Now show me what you found."

Rebekah walked me into the bedroom and pointed to the bottom drawer, which was now open and empty. "One of the keys on that ring opened it." She had all the goods from the bottom drawer spread across the bedspread.

The first item I saw was a roll of silver dollars in a plastic storage tube that held twenty coins. They were all 1986 silver Eagles and looked to be uncirculated. "Very nice," I said.

Next was a thick gold ribbon with a Golden Circle medallion threaded on it. It was a larger version of the one we had found in Billy's glove compartment, but it too felt like it was solid gold. I also saw a stack of paper brochures, four pages each, stapled together: *History of the Knights of the Golden Circle.* "That should be interesting reading," I quipped.

She held up the sash and the attached golden circle "The KGC—the Knights of the Golden Circle. I guess that could explain the circle on his gravestone. Perhaps it even explains the Latin quote and the use of a Civil War cemetery?"

"And it probably also explains who will be planning to come visit us in a few weeks," I said, mostly to myself.

The next item was a guest registration book. It didn't specify what people were registering for, but it had dates that went back ten years with between twenty and forty names at each event.

"I presume we now have the names of the KGC participants," I said as I thumbed through the various signed pages.

"Look on the last page from April's event," Rebekah said.

"What am I looking for?" I asked.

"Look four lines from the bottom."

"Jerry Jives! Are you kidding me!"

"That's your old high school buddy … the one who called the foundation several weeks ago and wanted to visit you."

I reread the names on the page. "I still don't know a Jerry Jives."

"It's a unique name, but it's the same name that Mary Ann said called, and it's the same name that was told that we were out of town just before somebody broke into our house and office."

"I'm telling you, I don't know a Jerry Jives," I insisted.

"But he seems to know you, and it appears he was here at the farm in April!"

The last item on the bed was a leather-bound King James Bible. The leather was starting to show significant wear, making it feel almost like suede. I tenderly cracked it open and realized that it had been used extensively. There were notes and underlines throughout. Before I closed it, I scanned the title page. There was the name "Billy Bowden" in blue ink, just like in the old Jesse James book.

In all the excitement, it had gotten dark outside. The lights of the house weren't bright, but they were on. We had brought a few groceries, and I asked Rebekah if she was hungry.

She admitted that she was, but she wasn't sure what we should do.

I said, "Are you interested in driving back into town for supper and a hotel—or do you want us to prepare supper and spend the night here in Billy's house?"

Rebekah said, "I brought clean sheets for the bed and some towels, but to be honest, I'm not sure that I feel comfortable out here—at least not yet. That gate was left open. Somebody has been out here since last week."

I thought about the cigarette butts down by the cave, but I didn't mention them.

"It was probably just a group of teenagers who knew Billy was gone," I said, trying to calm her concerns. "They probably came out to party and drink. I doubt they present any danger, but I'm game to drive into town for dinner and a hotel bed. We can meet the kid about the truck in the morning."

"That suits me fine," said Rebekah.

We loaded the gold coin and the roll of silver dollars into the strongbox and moved it to the car. I picked up the Bible and carefully wrapped it in a black trash bag to protect it along with the stack of KGC documents.

We made it to Lucille's by eight o'clock. There was obviously another out-of-town football game going on because West Plains was almost deserted. There were a few folks in Lucille's for supper, but not many.

When the waitress came over, I said, "We have heard from several sources that your meatloaf is world-famous, but that it is only served on Fridays at lunch. We couldn't get here by lunch. Is there any chance that there might be some meatloaf leftovers back in the kitchen?"

The waitress looked around as if she was about to tell a state secret and then whispered, "I'll go find out. If there is, do both of you want some?"

We both nodded.

—

On the way to the hotel, Rebekah said, "I wouldn't travel around the world for that meatloaf, but it was good, very tasty. I'm glad we got to experience it."

I said, "I enjoyed it too. I wonder if Lucille gives out her recipe?"

"You can ask, but I bet her recipe is treated like a state secret."

—

The next morning, we snacked at the hotel hot breakfast bar, eating an omelet that resembled a Frisbee in taste and texture, and then drove down to Danny's garage. He told us that the kid was still interested and should be there at any moment. He almost never was tardy—even after a late-night football game.

A well-driven Honda Accord pulled up beside the garage, and a tall, lanky kid with bushy red hair jumped out. As the car pulled away—driven by his mom, we assumed—he walked over and introduced himself.

"I'm Dennis Duggins."

"We're the Dempseys, Richard and Rebekah. Billy was my uncle. We understand that you're interested in owning a well-used Ford pickup."

"Yes, ma'am, I certainly am. Are you interested in selling it?"

"We are. Are you interesting in buying?"

"I am. I am very interested," he said with a grin.

"What do you think it's worth?' she asked.

"I'm not sure," he said. His face showed some uncertainty.

"How about four hundred dollars," she said.

His smile remained, but his face turned slightly downcast. It was obvious that he didn't have four hundred dollars.

"How about forty dollars a month for the next ten months? Would that work?"

His face lit up. He didn't have four hundred dollars, but he knew that he could pay forty dollars a month. "Oh, yes, ma'am, that would be perfect." He whipped out his wallet and pulled out two twenties. It looked like there might have been another ten in the wallet—but not much more.

She took the money and said, "My uncle took care of that truck. Will you promise to take care of it?"

"Yes, ma'am. I certainly will."

"I found the vehicle registration in my uncle's desk. Let me sign it, and then you can take it to the county courthouse on Monday and change the registration into your name. Here's the key. We don't need a loan agreement; a handshake is more than enough. Here is my address where you can send the payments." She handed him her business card.

He looked like a little kid in a candy store.

As we climbed into our car, Danny waved and nodded at us.

Rebekah said, "It wouldn't have been the same if we had just given it to him, would it?"

I smiled back at her.

"Are we in a rush?" Rebekah asked.

"No, I don't think so."

"A couple of blocks from Lucille's, there is an old classic brick building. I don't know what it once was, but it appears to be an antique shop. I would like to check it out," she said.

"Let's go. Show me which way."

We pulled up at the Downtown Antique Mall, which was a three-story building with "1914" engraved over the door.

Rebekah looked like she had just won the lottery as we entered. There were books, guns, furniture, old pictures, and so much more. I was happy when I saw the coffee shop. I decided to have a cup of coffee while Rebekah took her time perusing through the store and its wealth of artifacts. In some way, it appeared to be more like a museum than a retail store.

While I sipped my coffee, an older woman sat down at the other end of the table. She said, "I bet I know who you are. You and your wife are Billy Bowden's relatives. You two inherited his farm."

I nodded and took another sip of my medium roast.

"What kind of shape is Billy's old house in?"

"It needs some paint, but it's not too bad. We haven't tried to spend the night out there yet, but maybe tonight."

"Did Billy have any antiques in his house?"

I said, "Not really. Actually, there's not much furniture at all."

"Being next to the old Irish Wilderness community, I thought maybe Billy would have found some interesting artifacts over the years."

"We found an old cast-iron skillet that was broken into pieces, but that's about all." I didn't think she needed to know about the strongbox and the gold coin. "Have you lived in West Plains all your life?"

"No, I was raised out at Wilderness, but I graduated from high school here in West Plains and attended college right here at MSU."

"Can I ask you some questions about the area?"

"Sure, I know everybody in Howell County—or at least something about them."

"Uncle Billy apparently was a member of the Knights of the Golden Circle. Do you know anything about that group?"

"There was a group of the Knights back in the 1950s in West Plains. Several of them had been KKK members before that, but my understanding is that they disbanded when the Lion's Club came to town. The Lions took over the need that some men have for a social club without women, and of course, we have the Masons here as well. They have a big lodge a few blocks over, but I don't think there are any Knights still around. Are you sure Billy was a Knight of the Golden Circle?"

"We're not sure of anything, but we have found some KGC materials at his house."

"That may explain something. Twice a year, Billy hosts a big campout and barbecue out at his farm. People come from all over, and maybe they call themselves the KGC. Sometimes they stop here and shop for antiques, but I've never heard them refer to themselves as Knights. They all have a wad of money, and they never try to argue on a price. If they want it and it will fit into their car, they buy it—and nearly always with cash. We like Billy's friends here at the Antique Mall. They're good for business."

Rebekah walked over with an old walnut fruit bowl.

The woman said, "You have great taste. That walnut came straight out of the Irish Wilderness and dates to the 1900s. It's a fine piece of old Ozark handiwork."

We paid for the bowl and stepped outside. A nice bench was positioned in the sun, and since it was just warming up from the morning chill, we sat down to enjoy the sunshine. Beside the bench, there was a rack with real estate advertisements. I started thumbing through one.

On an inside page, it listed the average price for farmland in the area at $4,200 per acre, but I quickly realized that wasn't reliable. The price per acre depended largely on the house, barns, and other improvements that came with the land. One listing of a hundred-acre farm was priced at $450,000, but the photo revealed a very nice home and barn. Another was listed at $325,000 but didn't mention a house or any structure. Neither of them said anything about being on the border of a national forest. I wondered whether the national forest and wilderness border would hurt or help the listing price.

"What are you discovering?" asked Rebekah.

"It's hard to know what you're looking at from these listings. There are so many variables involved, such as houses, barns, water, and location. If we get ready to sell, we will definitely need to visit with a Realtor who knows the area."

"What about national forest and wilderness borders?" she asked.

"I don't know."

As I continued to scan the listings, I saw Mr. Kirkland from the bank walking toward us.

"Mr. and Mrs. Dempsey, I was hoping I would bump into you this weekend."

Rebekah and I stood and greeted him.

"I have some information that I think you will appreciate. I told you that I had been contacted by a party interested in buying the old Bowden place. He called yesterday and told me that he was ready to make an offer. Are you interested in hearing about it?"

"We'll listen, but we haven't decided what our plans are," said Rebekah.

"He told me that if he could remain anonymous, and if I could handle the transaction, that he would be ready to hand over a cashier's check for $1.5 million."

We looked at each other, somewhat amazed.

"That's a generous offer, but as I said, we haven't decided what we're going to do." I was still holding the real estate newspaper.

"What would it take for you to decide?" he said with some

firmness. "I think this buyer might be open to raise his price a little more, that is, if you would be willing to sell in the next few days."

"Why does he want it? Has he even seen it?" asked Rebekah.

"I haven't asked those questions. I'm just representing him in his attempt to purchase it. What his plans are, I couldn't say."

"Is your potential buyer a member of the Knights of the Golden Circle?" I asked.

His face turned slightly red. "What? I don't know what that is."

We had the distinct feeling that we had caught him off guard with that question. It was clear that he wanted us to sell the property to whomever he was representing, but it was also clear that he didn't want to pursue the present conversation any further. He handed me his business card and said, "Let me know, but I don't how long this offer will be on the table." With that, he turned and briskly walked away.

"I think we aggravated him," said Rebekah.

"Yes, I think so too. He didn't expect that question about the KGC."

CHAPTER 10

Almost Lost

"What are you thinking about the farm?" Richard asked.

"Do you think there is treasure buried out there?" I asked.

"I have found something to dig up nearly every time I turn on that 'magic stick.' I think a person could spend a lifetime digging up nails, buttons, musket balls, and broken pieces of cast-iron, but I don't expect there's a load of treasure out there. It's fun to search, but the real treasure source we probably just aggravated." Richard glanced in the direction of the banker.

"I understand," I said.

"Are you ready to pursue selling the farm?" Richard asked.

I nodded, but I wasn't certain what specifically he was suggesting.

He opened his wallet and found the business card from the lawyer. He punched in the personal number and waited with the speaker turned on.

A woman answered, "This is the James Smith residence."

"This is Richard Dempsey. My wife and I have talked to Mr. Smith about selling some acreage of property. He told us to call if we had any questions."

In a moment, the lawyer's gravelly voice said, "Mr. Dempsey, has your wife made up her mind about selling the farm?"

I said, "We would like to visit with you about it."

"Hello, Rebekah. I didn't know both of you were on the line. Where are you two now?"

"Currently, we are sitting on a bench in front of the Downtown Antique Mall," I answered.

"I live two blocks from there. Would you like to come by here—or would you prefer me to meet you there?"

"We can come to your house. We'll be there in a few minutes."

He gave us his address, and we started walking the two blocks.

His home was about what we expected, maybe more. The beautiful plantation-style home was very nicely landscaped.

A maid met us at the front door and ushered us into a wonderful den with wood-paneled walls that were full of loaded bookshelves.

Mr. Smith rose from behind his cluttered desk and came around to greet us.

I took charge, not giving the lawyer a chance to initiate the conversation. "We have a question," I said. "Is your potential buyer for my uncle's farm a member of Knights of the Golden Circle?"

Mr. Smith didn't seem uncomfortable with the question. "Yes, he is, but it's probably not what you think it is."

We both waited for him to continue.

"Whatever the KGC may have been in the past, today, it's just an investors' club. People meet and discuss the newest stock recommendations, IPOs, or the next exciting business venture. That's all it is. Your uncle was a member because they enjoyed meeting out at his place and have been doing so for many years."

"Are you a member of the KGC?' I asked somewhat bluntly.

He relaxed with a smile and said, "I used to be, but I don't attend any longer. Camping out is not my cup of tea at this time of my life, and I'm past my prime when it comes to aggressive investing. Most of the members don't even live in this area anymore—other than your uncle. With him gone, they may not even be interested in coming back."

"Then why does a KGC member want to buy my uncle's property?" I asked.

"I can tell you why, though I'm not sure I should. He didn't insist that I hide anything. He wants to remain anonymous, but why he desires to purchase it isn't a secret. He has been going out to Billy's farm for at least twenty years, and I know he has been going more often than just the twice-a-year official outing. I think he likes to hunt squirrels, but other than that, he and your uncle were good friends. I assume that you have seen the Double J engraving in that little cave, and I assume you have made the Jesse James connection."

We nodded and waited for him to continue.

He buzzed an intercom and asked his maid to bring us all some hot tea. "This prospective buyer thinks he is related to Jesse James. And he may be, but I don't have any way of knowing that one way or the other. He thinks Zerelda James, Jesse's mother, was his great-grandmother. He has spent considerable time attempting to connect the dots. The gentleman told me that he just feels connected to his family heritage when he's out at your uncle's place. He did well when he sold his business in Chicago and is now ready and willing to pay you a handsome sum to keep his access open to the old farm. Does that answer your question?"

"Partly," I said.

"He hasn't told me for sure, but it wouldn't surprise me—if he is able to buy the farm—for him to bulldoze the old house and build a very nice home on the same lot. It is a beautiful place, at least I've been told, and my guess is that he wants to live there."

"What is his offer?" I asked.

The maid carried in a silver tray with three china teacups. She poured the tea and then left.

"He said he was willing to offer two million for the whole place."

We drank our tea and told him that we would let him know. It was a very generous offer.

We left the lawyer's home and started walking back to the Downtown Antique Mall to get our car.

I said, "I believe him. He didn't seem flustered by my question about the KGC. He was quite open about the connection."

"No, he didn't get flustered, but he is a lawyer," said Richard.

"That's not a nice thing to say," I said.

He squeezed my hand and kept walking.

—

When we arrived back at the farm, it was one of those beautiful autumn days. It was still crisp in the shade, but the sky was a deep blue. The leaves seemed to have intensified in colors since last week.

The thought of working in the house just didn't seem appealing.

Richard said, "Before we start the upstairs trash removal, let's just soak in the warmth. Let's go for a walk. There's one area on the farm that neither of us has explored."

We started down toward the barn.

Richard said, "Everybody seems to think that Billy's guests pitch tents and have a bonfire when they come. There's only one place where that could happen. Let's go find it."

We passed through the first tree line and entered the large grassy pasture where Henry said he used to plow and plant soybeans.

About halfway across the field, we found it. It clearly was the spot where repeated bonfires had burned. There was even a small pile of firewood stacked nearby."

According to Henry, this is where he saw the tents," Richard said.

"So, whatever the KGC does, they do it here—or at least they plan it here," I said.

We looked around, but we couldn't find a shred of evidence of camping activity other than the bonfire.

Richard said, "Either they clean up after themselves, or they pay Billy to clean up their mess. If they are planning to come back here in a few weeks, you would think they would have contacted us by now. Surely, they know of Billy's death."

"I think they assume that one of their members will own the farm by then," I said.

For the rest of the afternoon, we hauled boxes from the upstairs of the old house to the front porch. From there, after a brief perusal, I would declare the value of the contents.

Most were marked for the burn barrel. Rather than hauling the boxes around the house to the barrel, Richard pushed the barrel over and rolled it around to the front. The first box of junk mail was great kindling to get it started. From then on, box after box slowly added to the hot blaze.

As Richard carried each box to the burning barrel, he reminded me of a story he remembered about a woman who lived in one of the small towns where he lived before moving to Lexington. "She was a talkative old woman and would talk your ear off if given a chance. She was always either at the local museum or the Dairy Queen. One day, she dropped dead at the Dairy Queen.

"Since there were no relatives, the county took it upon themselves to pay for her burial and dispense with her belongings. She lived several miles out of town, and no one had personally been to her house in many years. They discovered that she had been a hoarder, even worse than your Uncle Billy. Her entire house was loaded with junk mail, and she had cats, multiple cats.

"The smell in her house was overwhelming, and no one volunteered to clean it out. Now I understand why. Finally, the county decided to dig a big hole behind the house, and just push the house into it and bury it. The cats were given a chance to escape, and the whole thing was buried. A historical marker was erected on the spot in honor of the woman's work at the museum."

We both laughed at that story as we continued to carry Uncle Billy's boxes.

One box was full of credit card offers. As Richard eased it over the edge of the barrel, I heard him say, "Why would he keep this stuff?" Several more boxes were packed with tractor supply catalogs, seed catalogs, cattle auction announcements, operating manuals, and a dozen more boxes of miscellaneous junk.

It seemed like forever, but eventually we could see the end of one side of the upstairs. As Richard carried down one of the remaining boxes, he tried to read to whom this stack of letters was addressed. The letters were official mailings from an organization named "SHSMO." He had to open a letter to decipher the meaning of that abbreviation: "The State Historical Society of Missouri."

After skimming several of the letters, he read part of one out loud for me. The third paragraph read: "Your request for permission to excavate the restricted area is denied. As we have clearly indicated in previous correspondence, it would be a serious violation of at least eight state and federal regulations to remove any artifact, excavate, or employ the use of a metal detector within one hundred feet of the National Forest/Irish Wilderness boundary line. We understand that said property is under your ownership, but the people of the state of Missouri have the right for their cultural heritage sites to be preserved."

I started laughing. "You're a felon! I'm married to a felon!" Still laughing, I tried to pop him with a dish towel, but he blocked it and chased me around the kitchen table. I didn't try very hard to keep him from catching me. It was time for a break.

—

After grilled cheese sandwiches for supper, we resumed our work to reverse Uncle Billy's hoarding tendency.

"What should we do with all those letters back and forth from SHSMO?" Richard asked.

"Burn 'em, you felon," I growled.

"By the amount of correspondence in this box alone, your uncle felt certain he was right. It was his land, and nobody should be able to tell him what he can or can't do on his own property."

"You sound like a true southerner. By the way, I'm curious. How far away were you from the fence when you found that strongbox that is sitting in the back seat of the Lexus?" I asked while still giggling.

"I didn't have a measuring tape with me, but I eyeballed it as one hundred and one feet," he said.

I grinned and muttered to myself, "I'll come visit you in prison."

He carried the box with the "SHSMO" correspondence to the barrel containing the flames of hell. I wondered if he was contemplating if ignorance would be an acceptable defense in a Missouri courtroom.

Back inside, we sat down at the kitchen table.

Richard picked up one of the brochures I had found in the bottom drawer of Uncle Billy's desk: "The History of the Knights of the Golden Circle." He didn't read it word for word, but after a brief survey, it told me that the KGC didn't believe that the federal government ought to be able to dictate the rights of any one state. Though it wasn't as clear in the brochure, the concept of a new country was suggested. It would be a country where states could decide for themselves what was best for their own citizens.

He said, "Listen to the next-to-last paragraph. It reads, 'While slavery may not be a healthy institution for a culture, or God's perfect will for a people, in the present environment, it would be cruel to turn all current slaves into society when they are neither equipped nor qualified to handle such freedom. For the best interest of the enslaved and of their families, the institution of slavery offers a better way of life. Immediate freedom for most slaves would lead to starvation, prison, or death. Perhaps in the future there will be a better world, but for now, we strongly advocate maintaining the status quo.'"

"When do you think that was written?" I asked.

"I assume it was a pre-Civil War sentiment," he said. "The language feels old, but the paper feels like it came off of a modern copier just last week."

"Maybe, but have things really changed?" I asked. "Prior to the Civil War, most slaves were owned by plantation owners, but today, much of the black population is 'owned' by the federal government and liberal politicians. In many of our large cities today, the black populations have been trained to be dependent upon food stamps, welfare, and affirmative action in the same way their ancestors were dependent upon the plantation owners. Being owned is still being owned."

"Whoa, that's a strong statement," Richard said.

"I realize that, but exchanging one type of slavery for another isn't the answer," I said.

Richard started surveying Uncle Billy's Bible. As I looked over his shoulder, it was interesting to see what Billy underlined and the various notes he had written in the margins. I wanted to look at it more carefully in the future.

I found a booklet about the Irish Wilderness on Billy's bookshelf. "Listen to what Father Hogan wrote in his journal about the Irish Wilderness: 'Nowhere could the human soul so profoundly worship as in the depths of that leafy forest, beneath the swaying branches of the lofty oaks and pines, where solitude and the heart of man united in praise and wonder of the Great Creator.'"

Richard said, "He was quite the wordsmith, but from what I read, he really wanted some of the fertile farmland in central Missouri to start his colony, but that land was too expensive. The wilderness area was thought to be worthless as farmland, but it was all he could afford. I guess the wilderness grew on him."

"Do you realize that tomorrow is Sunday?" I asked.

"Yes, what are you thinking?" Richard asked.

"Let's follow Father Hogan's sentiment and go to church. Let's go visit the wilderness. I've been wanting to hike in the Irish ever since we first heard about it."

"I'm game. Do you want to jump our back fence and start hiking there—or do you want to drive around the thirty miles to the main trailhead?"

"I want to be legal. I don't want to jump the back fence and then have to explain to a ranger that we considered ourselves above the law," I said.

"Then, in the morning, let's get up early and drive around to the trailhead. We can stop somewhere along the way for breakfast. I too have been wanting to experience the Irish Wilderness ever since we saw the first sign." He added a log to our fireplace.

I continued to read about the Wilderness. After a few minutes, I said, "I think I spoke too quickly. There is a trailhead parking area, but there is no ranger station or place to check in. From what I can gather people, can enter the wilderness from any number of locations. We might as well jump our own fence."

"That's fine by me. I'm assuming that you are good with spending the night out here at the farm?" Richard asked.

"I think so. The fireplace is warm."

—

The next morning, we were dressed and ready for a hike before sunrise. The October air was chilly, but the sky was clear. The forecast suggested no worries. Twilight stars helped lead us past the barn, the old log cabin, and the cave entrance. We helped each other climb over the fence.

"The one thing that I read about the trails in the Irish is that the path isn't always easy to follow," I said.

"Are you suggesting that we might get lost?" Richard responded.

I grinned and said, "You never get lost, so I'm not worried," and I kept walking.

Our unspoken plan was to walk straight into the wilderness until we found the main trail that made the eighteen-mile circle through the Irish. We had no illusion of covering the full eighteen miles, but we wanted to see as much as we could.

About a mile in, we thought we had found the main trail, the White Creek Trail, but it wasn't clearly marked. The ground was blanketed in dead leaves, essentially burying any walking paths.

After climbing down and back up two steep hollows and crossing dry creeks, we couldn't find anything that resembled a trail. Unsure of which direction to go, we followed the edge of one hill to a rocky point. From there, we could see a river down below several miles away.

"In the brochure you picked up, there is a photo that resembles this scene. I think that's the Eleven Point River," Richard said.

"It's beautiful. Let's follow Father Hogan's advice and spend some time in the quietness," I whispered.

We found a fallen log and made ourselves comfortable with a view down to the river. It was amazingly quiet. It reminded us of our "church log" facing the waterfall behind the old cabin in Argentina. We enjoyed the stillness for nearly half an hour before we heard rustling behind us. It was a deer, a nice buck, moving quickly down the slope. Occasionally, the buck would slow and glance behind him, but he didn't seem to notice us.

After he was out of sight, I said, "It's not hunting season, is it?"

"I'm fairly certain it's not gun season, but I think it is bow season. There probably are bowhunters out and about."

"That deer seemed to be watching for something. Perhaps we need to find our way out. I don't want an arrow to find my backside," I said.

With that thought, we scurried around and started back. It had taken us about two hours to find our log with a view, but attempting to follow our own tracks backward proved to be difficult.

We never used the term "lost," but we never once recognized a location we had seen before. What took us two hours to get in took us four hours to get out, and then it was only because Richard turned around to say something and accidently caught a view through the trees revealing the top of the rocky bluff that was on the farm above the cave. We could have walked past it just as easily. We were both glad to see the fence and Uncle Billy's "No Trespassing" sign.

Helping each other over the fence brought a sigh of relief from both of us.

"You don't have blisters, do you?" Richard asked.

"No, I do not," I said. I knew he was referring to the blister I developed on our hike in Argentina. "But if I did, I wouldn't mind you treating it. I understand you're quite good at treating blisters." I leaned over and kissed him.

CHAPTER 11

Cannonball

"Shall we attempt to revisit your cave?" I asked.

Having just completed our wilderness hike, we were near the cave entrance.

"Yes, I think I need to. I didn't spend much time in it the other day." Without saying another word, Rebekah took my hand and led the way to the cave opening.

We both ducked down and stepped into the darkness.

I pulled out my phone and prepared to switch on the flashlight app, but Rebekah said, "Wait. I want to see it as it was in my dream." She walked to the back and stepped behind the boulder. I just watched from near the entrance as her head disappeared into the hiding place.

"This is almost exactly how I remembered it in my dream. I held the shotgun resting on the boulder like this. Just inside, where the sunlight stops, there was a clear pool about two feet deep. Its sides were covered in green moss, but above the entrance, where the 'double J' brand is now, it would have been almost impossible to see with just the natural cave lighting."

I switched on the app and illuminated the double J.

"Jesse James's personal brand," she whispered.

"You weren't nearly as nervous about entering the cave today as you were the first time," I said as we started back to the house.

She didn't respond.

We sat down on the porch steps and just let the late-afternoon sun soak over us.

"I don't know about you, but I'm tired. That was more hiking than I'm accustomed to," I said.

She stared up at the blue October sky. She was obviously tired as well, but she didn't want me to know it.

"We haven't discussed our schedule," I said.

"I need to get home tomorrow afternoon. We have some orders at the shop that should be arriving Tuesday morning. I'll have a busy week," she said.

In the distance, we could hear the familiar thump of Henry's three-wheeler. We waited until we saw him emerge from the timber and waved while we continued to relax on the porch steps.

He said, "It's a beautiful day. I was just wondering what you have decided. You haven't sold the place yet, have you?"

"No, we haven't," said Rebekah.

Neither of us wanted to tell him about the high-dollar offers.

"Don't forget about me," he said.

We promised him that we wouldn't, and then I said, "Henry, what about cell phone service out here?"

"Billy never had a cell phone, so he never cared about service. My wife and I have one, but it's broken right now. We don't use it very often anyway, but I'll let you in on a secret. There is cell service about halfway to Miller's Orchard going that way." He pointed northeast. "But if you drive west about a mile, there's a high spot on the road. Right on top of that hill, you can usually get a good signal."

We thanked him again.

He cranked up his "thunder machine" and was gone.

We went back inside and turned on the TV to check the weather forecast. The Weather Channel told us a storm would pass through northern Missouri tonight, but their map indicated that we would miss the brunt of it. Perhaps there might be some wind, but the ice and snow would all be north of us.

I started carrying down boxes from the other upstairs room. The first several were more paperback novels, mostly westerns and thrillers, but then I lifted a box that felt different. I opened it while still upstairs.

It was full of artifacts. Billy clearly had not been totally obedient to the SHSMO regulations. There were more than a dozen musket balls, three rusty plates, a metal mug, and several broken pieces of a cast-iron stove. There also were half a dozen old tools and an ax-head. I hadn't seen a metal detector in Billy's house or barn, so I assumed these were all found without the aid of such.

The next box contained bank statements. Most of them were unopened.

Rebekah emptied them out onto the kitchen table and started sorting them by the most recent.

I continued hauling boxes, and as I passed by with a load, I asked, "Have you discovered anything of interest?"

"It is interesting," she said. "Billy received his monthly Social Security check, but he also must have worked for the railroad at some time because he has been getting a small monthly pension from the Union Pacific Railroad."

"Was that the total of his income?"

"No, he gets a $1,200 monthly check from … guess who?" she looked at me as if I should know the answer, but I didn't.

"The KGC."

"You're pulling my leg," I said.

"No, right there it is." She pointed to an entry on the bank statement. "It comes the first of every month—plus a bonus check twice a year of thirty thousand dollars. Guess which two months?"

"April and October," I said.

"Close enough. Actually, the bonus comes the first of May and the first of November."

"I guess that means your uncle worked in some capacity for the KGC—or at least he leased his property to them for two weekends out of the year."

Rebekah continued opening bank statements from previous years to see how far back this relationship went.

Suddenly, both the television and the lights went dark.

We stepped out onto the porch, and I said, "Maybe we have thrown a breaker." I walked around to the back of the house where I had seen the breaker box. It didn't appear to have any thrown switches, but even after I switched them all off and back on, the house was still lifeless.

"What do we need to do?" asked Rebekah.

"Let's drive past Henry's and find that high spot so we can call the power company."

As we drove past Henry's road, the next thing we saw was something we hadn't even thought about. There were four rusty mailboxes lined up in a row. All four of them had multiple gunshot holes from target-practicing teens. The last box had "Billy Bowden" painted on the side. We backed up, and Rebekah reached inside. The letter on top was from the Howell-Oregon County Electric Coop, Inc.

"I suspect Billy hasn't paid his electric bill for this month."

We both shook our heads in dismay. Why hadn't we thought about that?

A mile later, we found the hill, and our phones registered service. I called the emergency number that was on the power company invoice and was told that a technician would be out within the hour, assuming that we would have a check ready for the delinquent payment. We agreed and turned around.

Back at the house, Rebekah sorted the month's mail. We were somewhat surprised that only the power had been turned off. She said, "We'll need to take care of several of these unpaid bills unless we decide to sell in the next day or so." Without thinking, she leaned over and flipped the light switch. She hoped I hadn't seen her. I was glad that she hadn't noticed that I had already done the same thing twice.

As we sat on the steps waiting for the power company rep, we were being watched by a pair of deer along the tree line. We heard a wild turkey's gobble coming from the direction of the national forest.

After an hour of enjoying the beauty and stillness, we heard the truck. A woman in the power company's uniform climbed out and apologized for the mix-up. "We didn't know anyone was living here since Mr. Bowden's death."

Rebekah explained our situation and handed her a check. She drove off, and in less than five minutes, the power returned.

"She may be the only one in Howell County who didn't already know everything about us," I said.

"I'm hungry," said Rebekah. "And we don't have any groceries for supper. How about pizza?"

"Pizza? That sounds great. Shall we drive into town and see if we can find a good pizza?"

"I already know where to go. While you were checking on farm prices in Howell County, I noticed an ad on the back of that newspaper: 'For the best pizza in West Plains, come to Ozark Pizza and Bread.' I've been thinking about pizza ever since."

"Honey, you're on a roll. I like your style. I guess we better get our shoes on."

As we passed Miller's Orchard, I said, "I have a strange feeling in my gut. We know of at least two people who are ready and willing to pay a substantial amount of money over the average listing price per acre for the county. What do they know that we don't?"

"What do you mean?" she asked.

"There is a strange little parable that Jesus shared about a man who found a treasure in a field. It wasn't his field, so he hid the treasure again, and then he sold everything he had to put together the funds to purchase the plot of land. He bought it, and then he owned both the field and the hidden treasure."

"What's your point?"

"I think that Jesus was trying to convince us that the kingdom of God is worth all we have, and I certainly agree, but think about the ethics of this little story. The man was digging around in a field that wasn't his, and then he bought the field without telling the owner what he had discovered. Was he obligated to? What if the owner hadn't wanted to sell the land? That would have fouled up Jesus's parable. But what if the owner had seen him digging in his field and went out and dug up the treasure himself? When the man who sold everything came with funds to buy the field, would the owner be obligated to tell him that he personally had found and removed the treasure? I don't know the answer to any of these questions, but one knew more than the other."

"You make things complicated," she said.

"Maybe, but why does it seem that everybody wants your uncle's farm? What have they found that we haven't? Is it just a strange family relationship some guy has with a long-dead outlaw?"

Rebekah turned to me and said, "I don't know what they think they have found, but I've been thinking. In my dream, I felt like holding the shotgun meant I was supposed to protect something. With that as the context, I want to offer a suggestion."

"I'm all ears."

"What if we carve off the hundred feet next to the wilderness, and then we sell it to the US Forest Service or just give it to them, and then let's ask Mr. Smith to notify everybody interested in buying the property and have a sealed bid auction to sell the remainder of the farm? That way, we wash our hands of the place, but we also protect the section that was probably part of the Irish colony anyway. What do you think about that idea?"

"Wow, I think that's a great idea. How did you come up that? That's wonderful."

"On the back wall of the Antique Mall, while you were talking to the older storekeeper, I saw an old etching from *Harper's*. It showed Union forces requisitioning livestock from a family living in a square-cut log cabin, like the one down by the cave. Supposedly, the old etching illustrated the beginning of the Civil War when the Union forces seized the livestock of an Irish Wilderness family. The menfolk were already beaten and on the ground. The mom, standing at the cabin's door, was shielding her eyes as the troops were chasing her ducks, chickens, and turkeys. A little girl was watching the chaos from a window while her dog was barking at the soldiers. The chaotic scene captivated my heart. That little girl deserves to have some peace—even if a century and a half have already passed."

"I think I understand," I said.

—

With our craving for pizza satisfied by a surprisingly good supreme, we snuggled up in front of the fireplace. We both felt at peace. We had a plan, a workable plan, and it felt right. Cutting off the back strip of the property might weed out some of the high-dollar offers, but it still felt like what we ought to do.

"Do you think there is treasure buried here on this property?" she asked.

"No, I have no delusion that there is any hidden treasure, but in a way, it has already produced within us a joy and a sense of adventure that has been worth more than money."

She squeezed my hand. She felt the same way I did.

"Let's pack up in the morning and drive back to West Plains and visit with Mr. Smith, the lawyer. Do you think he will agree to be our bid collector?"

"I think he will be more than willing, but he may not like the concept of cutting off the back hundred feet. The buyer he represents will not like the thought of not owning the cave with its iconic brand."

"There is one thing I forgot to mention to you. I discovered it just before the power went out," she said.

"What's that?" I asked.

"I found Billy's life insurance policy."

"Are you serious?"

"Yes. It's a half a million-dollar policy, but there is one catch. Billy quit paying the premiums about twenty years ago."

"So, I will need to fire up the burn barrel again," I said.

We both giggled at the thought.

The next morning, I got up early. In my mind, I was thinking about Jesus' parable of the field with the treasure. I knew it would be at least an hour before we needed to leave, so I grabbed the metal detector and started out across the farm. I turned the setting to the ultimate. It shouldn't chirp at anything unless there was something substantial. I didn't want any more nails or buttons.

I started at the top of the grass pasture and proceeded straight to the bonfire area. From there, I turned straight west and continued toward Henry's farm. Then I lined myself up with about where I had found the strongbox with the gold coin. About twenty steps following that path, the beeping started. There was no mistake. About six inches deep, I saw it. I didn't recognize it at first, but I saw it. I had to dig around it to break it lose. It was a cannonball, a twelve-pound cast-iron cannonball.

As I held it in my hands, I thought about what it would have been like to have had that fired in your direction. I sat down and continued to clean off the dirt from the old projectile. A somber spirit engulfed me. Americans died right here. Brothers fought against brothers. Father Hogan's Irish colony simply disappeared. A ball like this fired at your enemy would snap off legs or arms. It would take a life in an instance. I carried the cannonball back to the house, but I wasn't as proud of the find as I thought I would be. It was a serious killing machine in its time.

When I got back to the house, Rebekah had our suitcases on the porch. I washed up, and the half-hour drive put us at Lucille's in time for breakfast—just before the law firm would open.

We enjoyed our breakfast and entered the law office five minutes after the door was unlocked. We had not called for an appointment and were surprised to find that the senior Mr. Smith wasn't in town. We were told he was out of town on business, but Mr. Scott Bright was available to see us if that would suffice.

In the same conference room where we had met Mr. Smith, Mr. Bright joined us. We mutually nodded at the African lion painting and took our seats. Mr. Bright was a much younger lawyer than the senior Mr. Smith, but he still had a warm smile and a gentle spirit. He was aware of Billy's death and our situation as the new owners to his property, but he did not know about a potential buyer.

We explained our decision, and he thought the concept of cutting off the back hundred feet and adding that to the official wilderness designation was a fantastic idea. He said it was a wise and generous offer. We had assumed that Mr. Smith would have challenged us on that concept, but Mr. Bright was directly the opposite. He and Mr. Smith could have their discussion later.

With a warm smile, he agreed to receive the sealed bids. He suggested that we also send the letter of invitation to the three major real estate businesses in West Plains, and we wholeheartedly agreed. His only other concern was the quickness of the deadline, but we held to our decision and left it for next Thursday afternoon. Without voicing it, we wanted the deal to be over before having to face the KGC's routine visit.

Since we had the wording for the letters thought out in our minds, Mr. Bright invited his legal secretary into the room. In just a few minutes, she left with her notes, and in just a few minutes more, she had returned with typed letters ready for mailing. Mr. Smith's letter would be left on his desk. Mr. Kirkland would have his letter hand-delivered at the bank within the hour. Mr. Henry Smally would have his in a day or so, assuming he checked his mailbox.

Knowing what we knew about West Plains, we assumed that all the other West Plains citizens would know of the plan before we left the city limits. We told him that we would be in contact with the National Forest Service to pursue the transfer of the hundred-foot strip.

Believing our business was complete, Rebekah said, "I have another question. Do you know anything about an organization called the Knights of the Golden Circle?"

He laughed in a very disarming matter, and then he asked how we had heard of the Knights of the Golden Circle.

Rebekah said, "We have found evidence that my uncle was associated with them. We've been led to believe that some of the KGC members are extremely interested in purchasing my uncle's farm. Mr. Smith told us that at least one of the members of the KGC wanted him to represent his interest in the purchase."

"James hasn't mentioned that to me, and we talk about nearly everything. I think Mr. Smith was a member of that organization many years ago, but I haven't heard anything about it in several years—other than the group that visits your uncle a couple of times a year."

Rebekah said, "In your opinion, what is the KGC? And is it wise for us to sell the farm to an existing member?"

"Are you familiar with the Freemasons?" he asked.

We both nodded that we had at least heard of the Masons.

"The Knights of the Golden Circle is a fraternal group like the Masons. They have private meetings from time to time, but generally they are quite harmless, I think. I'm not sure if anyone from West Plains is still a member, especially now that your uncle has passed. In a previous generation, they were certainly more active. I know that your uncle has hosted those gatherings of the KGC for a long time."

"So, you don't have any qualms with us selling the property to a KGC member?" she asked.

"I don't think so. I don't know much about their history, but they haven't caused any trouble around here, and no one ever seems to be upset when they come," the young lawyer explained.

We thanked him and said goodbye to West Plains.

CHAPTER 12

Clear Streams

As Richard drove, I thought about lions. A quick scan of the Bible verses that mentioned lions indicated what I expected. They were the apex predators, the king of the jungle. If a person met a hungry lion, it would be terrifying. Samson met one and killed it with his bare hands to protect himself. Daniel was thrown into a den of lions as a means of execution, but God closed their mouths. Benaiah faced one on a snowy day. But then suddenly Jesus was referred to as the Lion of Judah.

"Richard, why is Jesus referred to as a lion?" I asked, breaking the silence of the drive. "It seems strange to me. Lions are terrifying animals. Is Jesus terrifying?"

He responded, "Jesus is named the Lion of Judah in Revelation. It's only fitting that the king of the jungle symbolizes the King of kings."

"But doesn't Peter say that the devil goes around like a roaring lion?" I asked.

"You're right. He does, but the devil is 'like' a lion. He is a 'pretend' lion, a 'fake lion.' Jesus is the true Lion."

"That makes sense," I said. "Why has the symbol of the lion become so important to you?"

"Have you ever read the Chronicles of Narnia?" Richard asked.

"I read the first one years ago, but that's all."

"In the Chronicles, C.S. Lewis used the lion image as a symbol for Jesus. When the kids in the story hear this, they had the same question you're asking. They wanted to know if they should be terrified if they meet him. The response they got was that the lion could indeed be terrifying, but he was caring.

"I remember that scene. The kids were talking to a talking animal if I recall," I said.

"Yes, but there is another scene that I appreciate even more. A little girl is thirsty, but the only water she can discover is a stream. However, the lion seems to be guarding the stream. She was terrified and asked the lion if it was safe for her to approach. The lion didn't deny his terror, but he invited her to have a drink anyway. That scene still speaks to me."

"I need to read all seven of the Chronicles. I want a painting of a lion for our house to hang over the fireplace mantel. The lion symbol meant a lot to us during our year as hostages."

"Yes, it did. At the fishing lodge in Argentina, above my bed, there was an impressive painting of a lion. I liked that painting," he said.

"I don't remember seeing it."

"That's because you were never in my bedroom," he said with a glint in his eye.

"No, I wasn't, and you weren't in mine either," I said.

"In the back of that truck that took us across Argentina to the ranch, there was a flattened cardboard box taped to the truck's sidewall. The image of a running lion was printed on the box. I assume it was the logo for some Argentinian company. As the truck would hit a bump, that lion would jump, but it was always running right beside us. I know that it sounds silly, but at the time, it meant something to me. It still does."

"I don't remember you ever mentioning that before," I said.

"The stone lion fountain at the pool in North Africa was important for both of us, but the lion that meant the most to me was on a piece of medical equipment standing beside your bed at the medical clinic in Sicily. After you came out of surgery to repair that gunshot in your shoulder, you were still sleeping. As I sat with you, waiting for you to awaken, I noticed the small outline of a lion on the back of the blood pressure meter. When I saw it, I knew that I wasn't alone … that we were not alone."

"We need to go shopping for a lion painting," I said.

Several miles passed before another word was said.

I asked, "Looking back, do you feel that the lion was with you during those months that your wife suffered with cancer?"

"No, I don't. That was a very difficult season. I felt abandoned and angry. I knew the Sunday school answers. I knew what the preacher in me ought to have believed, and I assume now that He was with me, but honestly, I didn't feel His presence at the time," he said.

I could see the pain of those memories in his face. "I know what you went through. When Gary didn't come home, it was like something inside of me was wounded. When the authorities told me they believed that he had been killed, it was like something inside of me died. When all was going well with my life, I spent some time in prayer nearly every day, but after Gary went missing, I found that I just couldn't pray. I didn't even want to pray."

"I understand," he said. "During those seasons, it hurt—and attempting to pray just made it hurt even worse."

"I remember the list you made the first day we were at the cabin as hostages. You were always the list maker, but that list was entitled 'Essentials, things we would die without.' You listed things like food, water, and warm shelter. Then you added prayer. I'll never forget how you worded it. You said, 'I need to start praying, but not like a pastor. Like a man who really needs God.' Do you remember writing that?"

"Yes, I do. It wasn't long after I had written that list that I realized that it's easy to make prayer an attempt to make God listen to us. True prayer is mostly about listening to Him."

Since we still had cell service, I connected with the West Plains National Bank and pulled up Uncle Billy's checking account. "Whose responsibility is it to notify the Social Security Office of a death? They still sent Uncle Billy his monthly check."

"I'm not sure, but I suspect that the government will want it back at some point," he said.

"And I wonder who the KGC thinks they are paying now—and what do they expect to get for their money?" I asked.

"That's another good question. They may want it back too."

As we passed the turn off to the Irish Wilderness, I said, "What's your estimate for the bids?"

"I think eliminating the hundred-foot border may knock out the two big offers. It might get it down to a level where Henry could afford it," he said.

We both glanced at each other.

"That would be fun for Henry to get it," I said.

"I think we will get some phone calls before next Thursday, but I don't plan to answer any of them."

We made it home in good time and picked up Goose from our friend. She was so excited when she saw us.

We spent the next week getting caught up with daily life. One day, I skipped lunch and joined Richard for a visit to his favorite pawnshop. He wanted them to see the fruit of his labor with the metal detector.

They were excited to hear about the old shotgun and the twelve-pound cannonball and wondered if we were interested in selling. Finally, after teasing them, Richard reached into his pocket, pulled out the twenty-dollar Liberty gold piece, and placed it on their counter. That really fired them up.

Roger, the older of the two brothers who ran the pawnshop, managed the old coin section. He quickly took out his monocular and started studying the coin carefully.

The younger brother started flipping through the latest numismatic journals. "An 1870 Carson City twenty-dollar gold piece sold at auction last year for more than three hundred thousand dollars. It wasn't in much better shape than your coin. The record for an 1871 Carson City is eighty-four thousand, but that coin was almost perfect."

Roger said, "Don't get Richard and Rebekah overly excited. This is an 1871 Carson City. It doesn't have any major flaws, but it has been used. Not being in mint condition, you might find a buyer in the ten thousand range, but the shop will offer you $7,500, as is, today."

"We hadn't planned on selling it, at least not yet. We just wanted you to see it, but thanks."

We walked back to the foundation's office with the coin in the protective case that Roger provided. It would go into the foundation's safe for the time being.

—

On Tuesday night, we sat down and crafted our letter to the District National Forest Office of the Mark Twain National Forest, offering the prospect of the back hundred feet. In the back of both of our minds, we wanted to donate the hundred feet, but we both wanted to clarify that prospect after we had reviewed the sealed bids. If we didn't get any bids, we might need to rethink that offer.

As we finished the letter, Richard said, "May I make a suggestion?"

"You certainly may."

"We don't really know what is buried on your uncle's farm. It may be nothing, but we don't know. Why don't we offer to donate the hundred feet under two conditions? First, let's invite the SHSMO organization to come join us for a joint survey of the hundred feet and then split two ways whatever we find. And then, second, we should ask SHSMO to forever waive their hundred-foot claim from the wilderness fence."

"I think that's good, but perhaps we need to add a third," I said.

"What's that?"

"Perhaps we should ask them to waive all claims and legal charges on previous violations of their regulation on the hundred feet," I said with some sarcasm.

"You mean, I would no longer be a felon?" he said with a smile.

We both laughed.

"By the way, I have a question," he said.

"About what?" I asked.

"I've noticed that your purse doesn't seem to be weighted down as much as it was. What did you do with Uncle Billy's Colt revolver?"

"I locked it in his desk's bottom drawer."

"Good idea, but let's remember to bring it home with us. Our friends at the pawnshop would like to see it," he said.

We decided to run the sale of the farm and the donation of the hundred feet through the Polaris Foundation covering. In doing so, the foundation's telephone was listed on the letters, not ours.

Mr. Smith was the first to call—and then Mr. Kirkland called. Mr. Smith called twice more before Mr. Kirkland called his second time. We didn't answer or return any of the calls. The letter clearly spelled out the procedure for delivering the bids and that we had no intention of negotiating with any of the interested parties. Henry never called, though Ozark Realty called three times. To our knowledge, no one directly representing the KGC tried to contact us.

—

The next Monday, we called the law office and asked for Mr. Bright.

He answered and said he was glad to hear from us. When we asked him how many sealed bids had been submitted, he told us that there had been nine so far.

I said, "Is your partner upset with us?"

"He is not upset with you, but maybe with me, but he'll get over it. I assume the person he was secretly representing has submitted a bid, but I really don't know. None of the bids have local return addresses."

We thanked him and confirmed that, as the letter stipulated, we would be in his office at one thirty on Thursday afternoon, October 21, to open the bids.

He agreed.

Richard looked over at me and said, "You once told me that you wanted to see the rivers of the Irish Wilderness. Are you still interested?"

"Yes, I am. What are you thinking?" I asked.

"I've been searching on the internet. There are several river-guiding services on all three of the rivers: the Eleven Point, the Current, and the Jacks Fork. On the Eleven Point, they advertise a three-hour guided trip that's open year-round. I would love to take you down the river."

My face lit up with joy. "That sounds like fun!"

He said, "Weather permitting, we could drive over tomorrow afternoon, spend the night at the river's lodge, canoe the Eleven Point on Wednesday morning, and then spend our last night as owners of the farm. On Thursday, we can be in West Plains in the law office by one thirty. Once the bids are opened, we'll let the lawyer take care of it from there, and we will start back home. Will that work for you?"

"Absolutely! I'm excited."

—

On Tuesday, Richard and I began what might be our last drive to West Plains as landowners. The weather forecast suggested a possible winter storm moving in late Wednesday night, but Wednesday morning was supposed to be clear. After several trips west, the Lexus knew the way on its own, but we did notice that most of the brightly colored leaves were now on the ground. The Mark Twain looked different, naked without its autumn colors.

The river lodge where we stayed was nice. It obviously catered more to spring and summer visitors, but we were told that the Eleven Point was low and clear. After a hearty breakfast, we met our guide and pushed off into the flow. It was fantastic. We could see smallmouth bass and trout darting under the canoe. We stopped twice to look at the massive springs that flowed into the river, and we stopped once to see the twenty-eight-foot paddle wheel that had once turned Turner's Mill. We only signed up for the three-hour guided tour, but we could have spent all day. We loved it.

Richard said, "The blue sky is bouncing off the clear water and reflecting off your blue eyes."

I blushed.

We were disappointed when our three hours were over, and we reluctantly loaded up and turned toward the farm.

As we drove, low-hanging clouds began to move in. The bare trees, the overcast sky, and the falling temperature all served to emphasize that autumn was all but gone, notwithstanding the calendar. It felt and looked like winter was moving in to stay.

The gate into Uncle Billy's was closed, but the lock wasn't on. The chain hung loosely holding the gate closed, but the lock was nowhere to be found. We didn't say anything to each other after Richard swung the gate open, but there was considerable tension inside the car as we drove down the lane.

Once we pulled into the front yard, we both noticed it immediately: the front door was standing open. To my astonishment, Richard opened the center console, extracted his Glock, and loaded it. I didn't even know that he had brought it.

Other than a faint smell of cigarette smoke on the porch, we couldn't find anything missing or out of place. After checking every room downstairs, I started up the stairs, but there was nothing to be seen there either.

With the house secure, we started down the path to the barn and beyond. That's when I first noticed the tracks. A truck and trailer of some type had driven to at least the barn. Another vehicle had driven even farther.

We checked the barn, the log cabin ruins, and then the cave. The tracks veered off out into the grass pasture. They looked to be a couple of days old. We followed them through the wet grass—until we saw the pile of fresh dirt.

A hole had been dug with a backhoe or some other type of digging machine. The hole was about five feet deep and six feet across. Somebody was obviously digging for something. What we didn't know is whether they found it. We stood without speaking, staring into the freshly dug hole. A light drizzle began to fall.

Richard was holding my hand with one hand and the Glock in his coat pocket with the other. "Do you remember the parable of the buried treasure?"

I nodded and said, "Perhaps somebody decided to come retrieve the treasure before the new owners take over."

"Our public invitation about the sealed bids let the whole world know that we weren't going to be in the area until today. Maybe we should have thought about that," he said.

Suddenly, we saw a coyote trotting along the fence line. It stopped and glared at us. We just stood still, but it looked at us as if we didn't belong. The coyote proceeded along its path and disappeared into the misty fog, never even looking our direction again. Perhaps we didn't belong anymore.

On the walk back to the house, I said, "Do you think we should call the sheriff?"

He said, "I thought the same thing, but it's not worth the drive to find cell service, at least not yet."

We were both tired. The canoe trip had taken its toll on us. A light supper, a warm snuggle in front of the fireplace, and an early bedtime were all we had planned.

Richard started picking up some fallen limbs from the timber area for firewood, and we dragged them to the porch. Then he remembered the small pile of wood at the bonfire site. We both walked down and loaded our arms. On the second load, we heard Henry's three-wheeler. Perhaps he had some firewood we could purchase.

I waved at him as we deposited the firewood on the porch. As he pulled up, I said, "Hello, Henry. It looks like we may have some weather this weekend."

"Yes, I think we will. Looks like you two are out of firewood. If I had known, I would have brought some over. I always kept Billy in supply."

"We have enough for tonight," Richard said.

"Tomorrow is the big day. I put in a bid, but it probably will not compete with Billy's high-dollar friends who seem to want it."

"I don't know what's going to happen," I said.

"My wife and I are on our way to Arkansas. Her cousin is getting married to some fellow, and she thinks we should be there. She's probably already packed and sitting in the truck, waiting for me. We'll be back on Sunday unless it gets icy."

"Henry, I know your wife is waiting for you, but did you hear any noises over here this week since we have been gone?" Richard asked.

"No, but my wife and I were gone on Monday and Tuesday. What sort of noises?"

"Don't worry about it. We'll let you know how the bids come out," he said. "Have fun at the wedding."

He rolled his eyes in mock pain and fired up the monster.

Believing that by tomorrow afternoon we would no longer be the owners of Uncle Billy's house and farm, we decided to do a quick survey of the house to see if there was anything of value we would rather not leave. To our amazement, we found nothing, but we did move the Colt revolver from the desk to the car.

Thinking we were finished, I asked Richard about an attic.

We hadn't seen an attic door, so we went looking. In the upstairs sitting room, the ceiling was made of yellow pine slats. If there was an opening, it was well hidden. Richard took a broom handle and started pushing up. In one corner, a section of slats lifted. With a chair, Richard could just barely look in. His flashlight illuminated a pink cardboard box. He handed it down to me.

After cutting the yellowed tape that had it sealed, I could see that it was full of wedding memories. There were a couple of old wedding invitations. There was a guest book. There was a curled photo of the happy couple. And there was a baby shoe.

At the bottom of the box was a yellowed newspaper article from June 1950. It told the tragic story of Mrs. Billy Bowden and her one-year-old boy being killed in a car accident. They were living in Arkansas at the time.

"Uncle Billy was married and had a son," Richard said.

I said, "In his desk, I found an old letter to a real estate lawyer about buying this property in November 1950. After losing his family, I suppose he lived here alone for the rest of his life."

Richard carried down the last few boxes from upstairs and rekindled the fire barrel. The boxes contained nothing of substance, but it felt good to complete the task. After checking the closets of the various bedrooms, Richard made a not-so-silent commitment to never climb the stairs again. He was finished with the upstairs in more ways than one.

Late in the afternoon, we refired the fireplace in Uncle Billy's den and pulled up the only two comfortable chairs in the house.

Richard said, "If we were planning to stay much longer, we would need to secure some more firewood. I haven't seen a chain saw or even a regular bow saw, so I assume Henry was telling the truth about being the main firewood provider."

We sat down and watched the flames begin to take hold. Our feet were interconnected, and we were holding hands, but even with the heater on and the fireplace burning, we could feel a chill creeping into the old house. There was a definite cold front moving in. I suspected that none of the windows were sealed tightly. It was just late afternoon, but the low-lying clouds made it feel much later in the day.

"Do we have enough blankets for the night. It may get extremely cold in here if that front moves in as they are predicting," Richard said.

I took his hand and held it close to my face. "God has hands, doesn't he?"

My question caught him off guard, but he answered, "The Bible talks about God's hands—and his feet, arms, and eyes."

"But somewhere it says that God is spirit, and as spirit, He doesn't have a real body, right? So, which is it?"

He said, "You come up with some of the weirdest questions. Most Bible teachers would say that describing God with hands is the use of anthropomorphism. It's sort of like when we say that 'the trees dance.' We know that trees don't actually dance, but it appears that they have a rhythm when there's a gentle breeze blowing."

"I bet the trees have a real shindig going on right now," I said giggling. We could hear the wind howling.

I got up from the old rocking chair, darted across the cold floor to the bedroom, and grabbed a small dictionary that had been in Uncle Billy's desk. Once back beside Richard, I opened it and read: "Anthropomorphism is a literary device that attributes human characteristics and traits to nonhuman things such as animals, gods, or objects."

"That's right. Webster is always right. Over the years, I've noticed that people are extremely anthropomorphic when it comes to their pets. They freely describe their family dog with human characteristics, but these past few months with Goose have changed my opinion. I think Goose simply has many characteristics of us humans, and she seems to be aware of it."

"I would wager that our dear friend Father Hogan considered his trusted horse, John the Baptist, to have many human traits as well," I said.

"Yes, I suspect he did."

"However, I understand how humans use anthropomorphism when they write to make something more understandable, but did God? If we believe that the Bible is God's Word, and that He inspired the biblical writers, then are we saying that He used anthropomorphism to describe Himself?"

"I've never thought about it that way. You make a good point."

"I personally don't want to limit God to a body, but it makes me feel more comfortable to think of Him with hands that can touch, hold, defend, and bless." I picked up Richard's hand again and held it close to my cheek.

He said, "When I was being unloaded off the oil tanker in North Africa, unsure of what they had done to you, I decided that amid the morning fog, I would just duck and hide into the thick beach grass. I thought I had a chance to not be seen, but just before I was planning to jump down, a hand reached out and touched me on the right shoulder. It was so real that I assumed it was one of the guards or one of the persons in the group behind me, but when I looked, it couldn't have been either. No one was anywhere near close enough to touch me, but I felt all five fingers. What I'm saying is this: Perhaps God is both. Perhaps God is spirit, but He still has hands with five fingers."

"Perhaps that helps explain what it means when it says that humans were made in the image of God. We're both body and spirit."

CHAPTER 13

Timber

It wasn't dark yet, but the low-lying clouds made it gloomy. Partly to clear my mind and partly to stretch my legs, I grabbed my "felony weapon of choice" and stepped into the increasingly chilly outside air. I quickly moved across the front yard and entered the line of trees that separated the yard from the large grass pasture. There was a faint animal trail running through the tree line. Several deer tracks were visible even in the dim light.

Just for fun, I turned on the metal detector and started working my way through the tree line. About halfway toward the barn, I heard a chirp. Out came the shovel, and just a few inches below the grass line, I saw a glass Mason jar on its side. Holding it up to what little light there was, I could tell that it was about halfway full of coins. The tin lid had rusted through, and the coins were mixed with muck and grime. I squeezed it into my coat pocket.

It was one thing to think that a famous outlaw might have been here many years ago, but it was quite another to think that dear old Uncle Billy was a modern-day member of the same secret society. *Were Billy and his friends just playing fantasy games out here at the farm?* Something inside told me that it was more than that, much more. My gut felt that these games involved some serious money. I couldn't imagine what else would make all of this so important to the members. Perhaps we needed to search a bit more before we closed the deal on the sale, but not tonight. It was too dark and too cold.

The northwest wind ushered in a bone-chilling cold. I tried to warm my hands over the fire barrel that was now burning low. I carried in the last armload of broken limbs and found myself backing up to the fireplace to recover the use of my hands and legs. If it wasn't for the bid deadline tomorrow afternoon, I would have suggested that we head home before the winter storm really took hold.

Once I warmed some, I emptied the jar onto the kitchen table with Rebekah looking over my shoulder. The old jar contained several dozen coins of various denominations. Several were probably silver, but none appeared to be gold. One penny that wasn't too corroded was an 1880 Indian head penny. I didn't try to clean the other coins.

We could hear the wind howling outside. It had changed in intensity, and from the sound, it was really starting to blow. We could feel the house slightly sway under its pressure. Watching the light fixture in the kitchen begin to swing back and forth, I said, "Maybe this explains why your Uncle Billy was a hoarder. He was attempting to weigh down the house to keep it from blowing away."

She laughed. "I think we have enough blankets, but we may need to snuggle. At least that is one advantage of this little bed over our California king back at home."

The wind continued blowing with force. It was making the windows rattle, and we checked the Weather Channel again. There was a chance of light snow in northern Missouri, but in the south, the forecast included strong winds until the early-morning hours followed by a heavy frost, but it was going to get cold. I went into the bathroom, grabbed several of Uncle Billy's old towels, rolled them up, and used them to block the draft coming in from under the front and back doors.

After a light supper, I stoked the fireplace, and we both relaxed with our feet toward the fire. The tree limbs burned rather quickly as opposed to the logs, and to keep it burning, a steady diet of broken limbs was needed.

"Do you miss preaching?" she said without looking my direction.

"Yes, I do. I loved preaching. When I 'retired,' it was good. I needed the break, but now I would consider preaching again. You mentioned earlier the truth in Genesis about us being made in God's image. God is the ultimate creative force. Since we are created in his image, we are most at home when our creative juices are allowed to flow. For me, preaching was my creative outlet. I need to either start preaching again or find another creative channel."

"I understand. I need to rediscover my creative outlet. I painted quite a lot before Gary disappeared. Perhaps I should start painting again," said Rebekah.

"I bet you're a good painter," I said.

"I bet you are a good preacher," she responded with a smile.

Either the fire needed more wood, or we needed to go to bed. We decided on the latter.

—

Long before sunrise, I had to get up. I couldn't stay in bed any longer. Billy's worn-out mattress had done a number on my back, so I slipped out and went into the kitchen. After stoking the fireplace, I started some coffee.

On the table, I noticed Billy's Bible still wrapped in the black trash bag. I unwrapped it and thumbed through the pages. There were very few pages that hadn't been marked up with notes and comments, but the beginning of the book of James must have been particularly important to Billy: "My brethren, count it all joy when ye fall into divers temptations, knowing this that the trying of your faith worketh patience" (James 1:2 KJV).

Billy most certainly loved his old King James Bible, but for this verse, he had printed the NIV translation in the column beside it: "Consider it pure joy, my brothers, whenever you face trials of many kinds, because you know that the testing of your faith develops perseverance." I was amused that "divers temptations" apparently was as confusing to Billy as it was to most modern readers.

But I wondered why that meant so much to Billy. Was he facing some trials? Were we? Last year, I could have answered that question quickly, but now I wasn't sure. All things seemed to be going well with us, or were they? I thought about the intruders from almost a month ago. Was that a "trial of many kinds"? It had been a weird month.

Then I thought about Jerry Jives. Was the one who called the foundation office claiming to be an old high school classmate the same Jerry Jives who signed his name in the KGC guest registry? It was such an odd name. It couldn't be just a coincidence. Were the KGC attempting to find us before we even knew about Uncle Billy's death? Did the KGC break into our home and office to locate information on the farm before we ever talked to the lawyer and found out that there was a farm?

In the back of the Bible, there were several handwritten pages of notes. The handwriting wasn't easy to decipher, but I slowly began to realize what they were. The pages contained a pro-slavery sermon series, as if they came from the Deep South prior to the Civil War. I couldn't tell if Billy had taken these notes while listening to someone else or had written them himself to teach others. I wasn't sure I wanted to know.

I continued reading and realized that the first sermon was about the characters in the Bible who were also slave owners, mostly from the Old Testament. I didn't want to read any more, but I sensed that the Knights of the Golden Circle might be more than just an investors' club, and Uncle Billy might have been their chaplain. I tucked the sermon notes back into the old Bible with an unsettled feeling inside. I suddenly realized that even with the possibility of buried treasure, I was ready for Rebekah to sell this place.

As I sat there in the quiet of the morning, the preacher in me took over. I couldn't help myself. My own curiosity led me back to the book, and I pulled out the sermon notes again. The second sermon began with Genesis 9. I knew the story. Following the Great Flood, Noah and his family discovered the "joy" of winemaking. The man of God stumbled under the influence of the new drink, and one thing led to another. Before the sordid story ended, a sober Noah cursed his youngest son, declaring that he and his descendants would forever be slaves. Billy's sermon notes went on to say that the curse on Ham turned his skin pigment black. I knew that such weird beliefs were taught in the South prior to the Civil War, but seeing it in print sent cold chills down my back.

The third sermon used the writings of Paul in 1 Timothy where the apostle said that slaves should not slander God by disrespecting their masters. I thought, *Did Billy really preach this?* As I replaced the old notes and closed the Bible, a KGC pamphlet fell out. In an instant, I understood what the group that met around the bonfire believed. What I did not know was what they were doing based on those beliefs; that remained a mystery.

From the kitchen window, I could tell that the wind had abated some. It was getting lighter, but the low-cast clouds still had us covered. It looked frosty outside, but I decided that I would slip on my coat and try to find more firewood. As I stepped onto the porch, I noticed five deer grazing near the old logging road leading to Henry's place. They saw me before I saw them, but they didn't seem to be alarmed.

Walking out into the grass. I saw the heavy frost on our car's windshield. I tried to scrape some of the frost off, but that wasn't easy. I just happened to glance down the stone-fenced lane. *What is that?* In the predawn gloom, it looked as if something was blocking the lane. I walked toward it and saw that about halfway down the lane, a tree had fallen across the road and blocked it.

I trotted down to it, and at first glance, I thought that I could pick up the tree and move it, but I quickly realized that wasn't going to happen. It would need to be cut into pieces before it was going anywhere. I stood there and looked at it as if somehow it was going to move on its own. *Last night's wind has blocked our only exit from the farm.*

As I walked back toward the house, I thought about the old logging road to Henry's. *His three-wheeler could maneuver it without issue. Could our Lexus?* I walked down the faint path until I could see Henry's house and barn. I knew he wasn't home. We would need to drive slowly over several spots, but I thought the Lexus could make it. Just to be sure, I walked up the driveway to Henry's gate. It was more substantial than Billy's gate, and it had a large padlock on it. We weren't going to be able to get out going that way.

Somewhat frustrated, I turned and started back. As I passed Henry's barn, I noticed an old, rusty wood saw hanging from under the eve of the barn. It was the crosscut logging type that was made for two persons, but I felt certain that I could make it work with just one. I took it down and carried it back to the house.

I found Rebekah at the kitchen table, drinking a cup of coffee, and she was still in her robe and pajamas. "We have a slight problem," I said.

She looked at me with raised eyebrows, and I told her about the fallen tree. "I've borrowed a saw from Henry. I don't think it will be that hard to cut into smaller pieces and get it moved."

"Do you need help?"

"I don't think so. Take your time. It's cold out there. Go ahead and take your shower. I suspect, by the time you're dressed, I'll have the road cleared." I found a pair of leather work gloves in one of the kitchen drawers and started back toward the fallen tree with the old saw.

I had to remove two smaller limbs before I had clear access to where the bigger trunk of the tree needed to be cut. The rusty saw was dull, but it worked well enough for what I needed. After I cut and dragged the two smaller limbs off to the side, I positioned the saw on the cleared trunk. After three or four pushes and pulls, I knew it was going to take more than just a few minutes. Oak was a hard wood. I had to stay committed. The lane had to be cleared sometime this morning, and there wasn't another option.

The sun was nearly up, and even in the frosty air, I was starting to break a sweat. I needed to remove my heavy coat, but I decided I could continue with a few more pulls before stopping. I grunted and groaned as I wrestled with the dull saw moving through the hard wood. I could see my breath in the cold air as I exhaled. I never heard a sound. I never saw it coming. The sister tree that had been standing with the fallen oak, turned loose, and hit me squarely across the back.

At first, I wasn't sure what had happened. All I knew was that I was facedown on the ground in excruciating pain. My left arm was pinned between the tree and the road gravel and was unnaturally twisted. With another limb pressing on my neck, I couldn't get a good look at my arm, but I knew it was broken. The snap of the arm breaking was louder than the tree crashing. My right leg throbbed, but the tree was pressing on it with such force that I couldn't tell if it too was broken. I could taste the saltiness of blood and knew that I was bleeding above one eye.

With my right arm, I tried to push the tree off, but it didn't budge. In those fearful, few moments, I wondered if my insides had also been crushed. I found that if I stayed still, I could almost tolerate the pain. I tried to reach for my phone, but it wasn't in my pocket, and then it dawned on me that I wouldn't have had cell service anyway.

Where is Rebekah? She's probably still taking a shower. All I can do is wait. I could feel the morning frost moving across my body. Not being able to move was a horrible feeling. I felt like such a fool. *How could this have happened?*

Time eluded me as I waited and drifted in and out of consciousness. I don't know how long I was there, but the next thing I remember was Rebekah screaming as she ran down the lane toward me. From what she could see, I was a broken mess. Her vantage point allowed her to see my twisted arm better than I could. Her first instinct was to attempt to lift the tree. She quickly discovered that that wasn't going to happen.

When I finally got her to calm down, I told her to go get her phone, run to the hill a mile past Henry's, and call for help. She tried to argue at first, not wanting to leave me, but then she realized there was no other option. I could hear her footsteps running back to the house. In just a few minutes, she was back holding her phone and a blanket, which she draped over the part of me that the tree was not covering. It didn't really help, but I appreciated the effort. I heard her footsteps sprinting down the lane, and I offered up a short prayer that sounded a lot like, "Hurry! Please hurry!"

I could feel myself nodding off, but something inside kept screaming, "Stay awake!" The fear of falling asleep and never waking up drove me to keep my mind active. I tried again to force the tree up and off, but any movement caused even more pain in both the arm and the leg. I needed to just wait. I had to just wait. I had to keep my mind engaged to make sure that I stayed awake.

In the silence, I thought about that passage in James that I had read in Billy's Bible: "Consider it pure joy, whenever you face various trials." I wanted to tell God that I was sorry, but at that moment, I couldn't find any joy to consider. Patience is easy if you're pinned to the ground and unable to do anything anyway, but joy wasn't anywhere to be found.

Time seemed to stop, but I eventually heard Rebekah's voice. She was out of breath, but she was encouraging me to stay awake. She was trying to be strong for me, but by the look on her face, it was evident that I looked horrible. I knew that the cut over my eye had quit bleeding, but my face was covered in blood and dirt. She sat down and held my one hand that was free. She took off the glove and kissed my hand. I could hear her soft cry. I tried to look at her, but it hurt to move. I said, "It's fine to cry, but I can assure you that I have already cried enough for both of us."

She stayed with me for what seemed to be at least another

hour before we heard the distant sound of emergency vehicles. I was beyond getting cold, but almost immediately after hearing the sirens, I heard multiple footsteps running and loud voices shouting. Lights were flashing all around. Then I heard a chain saw and felt the weight of the tree being lifted off me. There were at least six men in the effort.

Rebekah continued to hold my hand.

Once free from the tree, they carefully rolled me over onto a stretcher. One was putting a neck brace on me, and another was putting a temporary splint on my mangled arm. One handed Rebekah a wet towel, and she started wiping my face free from the drying blood and dirt. A blanket was draped over me, but I needed more. The blanket didn't come close to ridding my body of the deep chill that I felt. Being moved hurt, but it was not as bad as being pinned down and being unable to move.

They carried me to the ambulance and started hooking up an IV. I heard Rebekah declare that she was riding with me, and no one argued. The sound of the chain saw was the last thing I heard as the door closed and we started rolling.

I didn't remember much about the trip to West Plains. That probably had to do with some of the meds flowing through the IV, but I still felt every single bump on the road. In the emergency room, I felt them cutting off my shirt and jeans. A doctor removed the temporary splint from my arm. I heard him tell Rebekah that it would need to be surgically repaired immediately, but they needed to do some X-rays on both the arm and leg, followed by an MRI on my head and back. At that point, I was just along for the ride with the sensation of just floating.

I awoke to the awareness of being washed, clean and warm. A team of nurses was giving me a warm sponge bath mostly to warm my body. My arm was in a cast, having been repaired, and a bandage was wrapped around my head. My leg was sore, but I could move it and wiggle all my toes. I could get up and use the restroom. Rebekah was asking questions of the doctors, but I wasn't paying much attention. They offered me some chicken noodle soup, but I opted to suck on the orange Jell-O instead.

Just after lunchtime, they had me sitting up and then walking. I hurt all over, but apparently only the arm was broken—and there wasn't a concussion. The doctor asked me what I wanted to do, but I didn't know for sure what he meant. He explained that I could be released if I desired. He didn't seem to think there was any reason for me to spend the night at the hospital.

I looked at Rebekah and said, "Let's go get a hotel room. I may be hungry before long, and I know I'm sleepy." I noticed that she had considerable blood on her jacket and shirt. It was my blood.

"I rode with you in the ambulance," she said while examining the bloodstains.

"I know. I wanted you to."

"But that means the Lexus is back at the farm," she said as if she hadn't realized that reality until then. "I need a ride back out there."

The nurse looked somewhat perplexed, thinking Rebekah was asking her to take her, but I said, "Let's call Danny at the garage and see if Dennis and his new Ford might be free for the hire."

A quick call confirmed the plans, and Dennis was on his way.

"I guess we need to let Mr. Bright know that we will not be there this afternoon," said Rebekah.

"He may have already figured that out," I said.

"I'll call him and schedule our bid openings for tomorrow. Do you think you will be up to it by then?" she asked.

I nodded and grinned, but the grin hurt.

When Dennis arrived, Rebekah gave me a quick kiss and said she would be back in an hour or so. I had been sitting in the hospital room, but I walked with her to the front door and watched her climb into the old Ford.

Dennis held the door open for her. His bushy red hair seemed to be standing up even taller. He was excited about getting to use his new vehicle to help someone.

I was amazed at how much the walk to the front door exhausted me. Rather than walking back to the room, I sat in a chair in the lobby. It was late Thursday afternoon. Examining my new cast, I thought, *Today has not gone like we planned.*

I wondered how the bidding had developed. I shifted my weight in the chair, and pain shot through my body. My brain and body competed for attention—and my body won out. The bids were not something I cared about right now.

CHAPTER 14

Patience

The discharge nurse found me sitting in the lobby long after I was ready for her. If Rebekah had already arrived, I would have left without signing the needed paperwork. After asking me to sign several forms that I didn't understand, she explained that I would need to make an appointment with my regular doctor in a couple of weeks to have the arm evaluated.

I nodded in agreement.

"Do you have someone to pick you up?"

I nodded and said, "My wife is on her way."

As she walked away, I noticed the wall clock over the registration desk. It said 4:02 p.m. It had already been a long day. I was wearing a set of purple scrubs as a replacement for my shirt and jeans they had cut off in the emergency room. They had given me a blanket to use as a wrap. I hoped Rebekah would remember to bring me some clothes.

I also hoped she would pick up my phone that I had left charging on the kitchen counter at the farm. It had been the longest I had been without my cell phone in years. I wondered if she would think to get the coins that I left on the kitchen table. It amused me what trivia flooded through my head.

Uncertain of the time Dennis in his "new" Ford left with Rebekah, I still greatly appreciated him willing to take her. It had to have been around three thirty when they left. I wondered how he got out of football practice to run this errand, but I appreciated it. If they did leave around three thirty, the earliest she could be back would be four thirty, but that was doubtful. She would need to get our belongings packed and lock up the place. She would most certainly change clothes since my blood was all over her jacket and shirt. I decided that five o'clock was a realistic expectation for her to return, but it could be fifteen minutes either way. I knew she would come as soon as she could.

From where I was seated in the lobby, I could see the entrance to the hospital's circle driveway. The second she turned in, I could make my way to the sidewalk to greet her. In the landscaped circle, there was a lone tree. I thought it was a birch, but I wasn't certain. From where I was seated, I could see the tree's shadow. It was only a few feet long, and I really didn't consciously notice it at first.

A woman volunteer in a pink smock asked if I needed anything before she left. I had seen her earlier at the registration desk. She explained that most of the volunteer staff had already gone home since it was getting late. Even most of the day-time medical staff and nurses were gone.

I said, "No thank you. My wife will be here shortly."

She didn't ask if I wanted it, but she handed me a bottle of water as she left.

I thanked her. Watching her walk to the parking lot, I noticed the birch tree's shadow. It now stretched out about four feet. The sun was getting slightly lower. The clouds had moved on. I watched several other nurses and orderlies walking to their cars. From the look of their hustle, I could tell that it was still cold, maybe even colder. The clock now said 5:00. I hoped that the Lexus would be the next car to turn into the circle.

Since my legs were getting stiff, I walked from one side of the lobby to the other, stretching my legs and continuing to watch for

Rebekah. Three trips back and forth got the blood flowing, but I was sore. *Tomorrow, I am going to be very sore—and probably black and blue.*

My back and my right leg had just barely escaped being broken. The left arm wasn't so fortunate. The doctor said that they were able to get all the bones aligned, but it was going to be at least six weeks in the cast followed by rehab.

I returned to my chair and carefully sat back down. The doctor had said that the MRI didn't reveal a concussion, but I was still experiencing dizziness off and on. After my "walk," my head was spinning. I had signed the release papers, so I wasn't technically a hospital patient any longer, but I still had to have some patience. It had never dawned on me before why hospitals call their clients "patients."

The shadow from the tree stretched out at least twenty feet now. I couldn't believe that it was accelerating so fast. Several cars passed by on the main road, but not our Lexus. *Rebekah should have been here by now.* The lid to the water bottle was tight, and it took several attempts with my teeth to open it. I thought about all the things that I normally did with both hands. I was going to have to make some adjustments to my daily routines. I was thankful that it was my left arm and not my right.

Walking up to the registration desk, I noticed that there was a phone. A note taped to it said, "For Hospital Staff Only," but I picked it up and dialed Rebekah's number. It had been some time since I had used a rotary phone, and it felt awkward.

Rebekah's phone started ringing, and it kept ringing until her voice mail picked up. If she was still at the farm, she wouldn't have had service, but I really thought that she would be on her way by now. It was possible she had the app turned on that blocked unknown calls, but for whatever reason, I still expected her to answer.

I walked back to the front door and noticed that the lone tree shadow had now stretched across the driveway and into the parking lot. The wall clock was now approaching six o'clock. I had to resist the urge to be angry. *What could she possibly be doing that is important enough to keep me waiting?*

All I had with me was my wallet, but Danny's card was still where I left it. It had an emergency number to call for the garage after hours, so I limped back up to the registration desk and called.

Danny answered, and I said, "Danny, this is Richard Dempsey. As you know, Dennis took Rebekah out to her uncle's farm to get her car. Have you seen or heard from him?"

"Dennis came by the garage just before I closed up about four forty-five. He said that his 'new' pickup drove amazingly well—and that Rebekah wasn't far behind him. She hasn't been to the hospital yet?"

"No. I'm here waiting on her. She probably had to stop for gas. I'm sure she'll be here shortly." I didn't verbalize it to Danny, but I was worried. There is a level of worry that you can swat away like a fly, but there is another level of worry that isn't dismissed so easily. The latter was what I was feeling deep in my gut.

I walked gingerly back to the front door. The lone tree shadow was now gone. The sun had set. The floodlight over the front door fluttered and then came on steady. It was nearly dark anyway, but the floodlight made it appear even darker.

Readjusting the sling holding my cast, I walked back to the registration desk and tried Rebekah's number again. The repeated sound of the phone ringing was a haunting sound. I called two more times. Although it was comforting just to hear her voice on voice mail, the fact that she didn't answer made me sick to my stomach. *Something is wrong.*

An orderly came through the lobby with a broom and asked if I needed anything, but I didn't say what I was thinking. *I need my wife. Where is she?* I sat back down, completely unsure of what I should do next, but then I saw the headlights. I let out a deep breath. I was so relieved. It had to be her.

However, when the vehicle started around the circle, I could see that it wasn't Rebekah— it was Sheriff Nelson's SUV. That was when I nearly lost it. I fought back tears as my mind swirled with possibilities of what could have happened, but I continued to sit watching as the sheriff pulled up to the front door and climbed out.

With his Stetson in hand, he walked inside. He came over to me and sat down facing me. I didn't know what to say. I dreaded what he was going to say. I could see the uneasiness in his face.

"Richard, we found her car," the sheriff said.

"How bad is it? Is she hurt?"

"Richard, we found her car, but we haven't found her—at least not yet."

"Wait, what do you mean?"

"Your Lexus was parked on the grass along the county road about a mile from the state highway, several miles this side of Miller's Orchard. We're not sure how long it had been there, but she hasn't been located."

Not believing what I was saying, I said, "She probably had car trouble and walked up to one of those farmhouses along that stretch. There are at least three houses that you can see from the road."

He nodded and said, "We assumed the same thing. We've already knocked on every door along the county road, and nobody has seen her. We'll keep searching, but now that it's dark, it is difficult."

"Was the car damaged at all?" I asked.

"There was a small dent on the back bumper with a tiny spot of black paint. Was that there earlier?"

"No, there were no dents on it—none at all."

"We could see no sign of a struggle. There was no evidence of blood. The car was just off the road parked in the grass. Is this your cell phone?" He reached into his shirt pocket and produced my phone. "There was a grocery bag of items in the back seat. This phone was on top."

I took the phone and immediately redialed Rebekah, but she still didn't answer. I called it again, but nothing.

"Are these her keys?" He handed me a set of keys. I recognized them and told him so. "They were in the front seat. The car was unlocked."

"I understand that the hospital has already released you. Would you like me to take you to a hotel? We'll resume our search in the morning. We have notified the entire state to be on watch for her, but I don't know what else to tell you."

I followed him out to his SUV and climbed into the passenger seat. Once we started, I asked, "Who found the car? Who reported it?"

"Don Miller's wife called it in. She said that she thought it was your car, and she wondered why it was left alongside the road. She has seen you pass by their orchard several times. We are towing it in as we speak. A suitcase was left in the back."

"Just one suitcase?"

"That's all we found, just one brown leather suitcase. Is that yours?"

I nodded.

"I can bring it by in the morning. They're going through it now," he said. His voice expressed his concern for my situation.

"So, my wife is missing along with her suitcase?"

He cleared his throat, and his voice returned to his official-sounding sheriff's voice. "Mr. Dempsey, have you and your wife been quarreling?"

"What?" I knew where he was going. When a wife disappears, the husband is always the first suspect. "No, we haven't been quarreling."

"Is there any chance that she ran off with a boyfriend?"

"No, there's no chance of that," I said. I was certain of that, but the question itself stung like a dart. "Have you spoken to the kid who drove her out there?"

"No, but I have his number."

"Let me call him," I said. He forwarded the number, and I punched it.

He answered almost immediately.

"Dennis, this is Richard. Did you and Rebekah have any problems going out to the farm?"

"No, sir. We didn't have any problems. That old Ford ran like a top. I'm going to recover the front seat, but the engine runs great. Why are you asking?"

"Rebekah hasn't made it back yet. We're not sure where she went after you dropped her off at the farm."

"Mr. Dempsey, I offered to follow her back to town, but she insisted that she didn't need me to do that. She was planning to change clothes, get packed, and drive into town as soon as possible. She knew you were waiting on her. She is a nice lady. Do you want me to go back out there and look for her?"

"No. Dennis, there's no need for that. Thanks."

The sheriff stopped in front of the Hampton and quickly walked inside without waiting for me. I could see him speak to the front desk clerk, and then he met me at the door. A key card was waiting for me along with a small basket of toiletries.

Rebekah and I had stayed at the Hampton recently, and the receptionist recognized me even with the head bandage and arm cast. Following his computer's lead, he asked, "Will there be just one tonight?"

I nodded, trying not to show any emotion.

"Will you be staying just the one night?"

I honestly couldn't say, so I shook my head, trying to hide my frustration. I feared that I failed miserably.

Both the sheriff and the hotel receptionist walked me down to my room on the first floor. The key worked with the first attempt, and I entered.

The sheriff said, "There is a pharmacy in the grocery store across the street, but it will not be open until the morning. There are several restaurants nearby that will deliver if you're hungry. I will bring your suitcase first thing in the morning."

And with that, I was alone.

I had to try another time. I punched redial. She still didn't answer. The sound of the unanswered ringing was almost more than I could bear. I felt like I needed to pray, but I couldn't find any words. I curled up on top of the bed and just moaned. I cradled my phone like a doll, expecting and hoping that at any moment it would ring with Rebekah explaining what had happened. It never rang. The adrenaline rush of the past twelve hours was beginning to take its toll.

The next morning, I rolled over on the bed. Every inch of my body hurt. The cast-covered arm hurt the least. I shuffled down the hall and ate some scrambled eggs and sausage. The coffee didn't taste good, but I sipped some orange juice. The acid hurt my lip. I hadn't realized that my lip had been busted as well.

As I shuffled back down the hall to my room, my phone rang. It was the sheriff saying he was bringing in my suitcase. I sat on the bed and waited.

Then the phone rang again. It was Melinda at Polaris. She had some information. She didn't know that Rebekah was missing, so I explained our situation to her as best that I could. She listened without responding.

When I finished, she said, "I hope the news I have isn't related to your situation, but I'm afraid that it might be."

A knock on my door followed, and I stood up to open it. With a head nod, I invited the sheriff carrying my suitcase to come inside. I turned on my phone's speaker and motioned the sheriff to have a seat.

"What's your news?" I asked Melinda, after I explained to her that the sheriff was listening in to our call.

She said, "Do you remember the military clinic in Sicily where Rebekah was treated for the gunshot?"

That comment seemed so out of place and unexpected. The sheriff looked at me with a confused expression, but I said, "Yes, it was at the Naval Air Station at Sigonella. They took great care of her. What about them?"

"Several weeks ago, that clinic was broken into. The clinic is not actually on the base, if you'll remember, but someone broke into their records room. At first, they didn't believe that anything was stolen, but after comparing their computer files to their paper files, they discovered something. Rebekah's medical records were missing."

"Rebekah's? Only Rebekah's?"

"As best as they can tell," she said.

"What good would Rebekah's medical records be to anybody?" I asked.

"At this point we can only guess, but her medical records listed her blood type."

"Her blood type? What good would that—" My heart stopped. "When did you say this happened?"

"Sometime early in the morning on September 25, but it wasn't until a few days ago that they discovered that it was Rebekah's file that was missing. They notified me of their findings this morning."

"There's a time change difference, but that's the same time that both our house and office were broken into. I have a sick feeling about this," I said.

"Richard, we are investigating things from our end, and now with Rebekah missing, we'll be calling in the FBI. Polaris will put together an emergency response team. We'll be coming to West Plains as soon as possible. If we discover anything before then, I'll let you know. You do the same."

Out of habit, I glanced over at the sheriff and redialed Rebekah's number, but it was the same as I expected.

"You have quite a story, Mr. Dempsey. I believe that we have much to talk about. Who exactly was that on the phone?"

I said, "That was Melinda Thompson of the Polaris Project. They are an organization that works undercover against human trafficking. They work with UN-GIFT, the United Nations Global Initiative to Fight Human Trafficking, the FBI, Homeland Security, and several other unnamed groups. Most of their operatives are retired Special Forces. They work behind the scenes without having to ask permission or file reports."

"That sounds like the job of most sheriffs, except for the global part. It sounds like you and your wife are involved with some serious organizations, but here we are, just the two of us and a missing wife. I was planning to go out to the location where we found your car and poke around. Would you want to join me?"

Nodding, I pointed to the purple scrubs I was still wearing. Sitting all day in the hotel would have made me even more miserable. Going with the sheriff would at least make me feel like I was doing something to help find Rebekah. He suggested that I should get cleaned up and changed, and he would be back in half an hour.

I knew he was taking me for another purpose. He wanted to be sure that my story stayed consistent. The fact that I was in the hospital at the time of Rebekah's disappearance ruled me off their suspect list, but I was the only one on their list. Crossing me off left it completely blank.

Showering with my cast wrapped in a trash can liner helped keep it dry. I decided that I could wait to shave, but brushing my teeth felt good—even if opening the toothpaste was a hassle with one hand.

My mind was spinning. *They broke into my house, my office, and an overseas military clinic, and the only thing we knew for sure that was missing was Rebekah's medical records.* I knew what the special classification meant for the organization of old, especially when blood types were listed. I never actually saw, faced, or directly dealt with that side of the human trafficking business, but I had seen the paper trails. I couldn't bring myself to voice it as it related to Rebekah. It just couldn't be.

The sheriff's SUV pulled around to the front door, and I started out to join him. He seemed frustrated. He was a man who liked to fix things. He was a sheriff who wanted to solve things. He prided himself in knowing what happened in his county before the event even happened. Our situation had him stumped. He didn't have a clue.

As we started out of town, his phone rang. He answered it, but he never spoke; he just listened and grunted. Finally, he hung up. "The black paint mark on your wife's Lexus was from a late-model

Chevrolet Suburban. There is an APB out for a black Suburban over a ten-state area, but there are a lot of those vehicles. Explain to me how you two got entangled with these government law enforcement groups. What happened to you two?"

I'm not sure why. Perhaps it was the headache, the pain meds, or the sheer fact that I was desperate, but I just started talking. Though I wasn't sure I trusted him, I needed him on my side. I told him most of the details of our year as hostages and the ugly business that we helped bring down. I even outlined the story about the gold that Gary embezzled and that we eventually discovered. He was amazed as he listened carefully. I didn't know whether he believed even half of it, but I didn't care. I needed help, and he was all that I had for the moment.

After he seemed satisfied, I said, "What do you know about the Knights of the Golden Circle?"

He glanced over at me with a peculiar look, and then he said, "The Knights have a long, sordid history, but today, they are only an investment club for the wealthy. They like to meet, sit around a bonfire, and discuss their newest and latest moneymaking schemes. Rebekah's uncle opened his farm to them, but he wasn't really a member. The Knights are big-money people, old money, the kind of money most of us common folks can't even dream about, but they're harmless. I check on them when they're here, but we've never had any problems. Some of them are probably ruthless in the business world, but they're harmless in every other manner. Have they called you about meeting at Billy's?"

"No, we haven't heard from them."

He pulled up to the location where the Lexus had been parked alongside the county road. One of his deputies was already there. All three of us looked around the area on both sides of the road, but we only found an aluminum Coke can and two Budweiser beer cans. The grass was thick and about shin high. So much more could have been hidden.

As I watched the sheriff and his deputy searching along the

fence line, I prayed. I asked the Lord to protect Rebekah and bring her home safely. The cold wind was just as cold, but after the short prayer, I felt warmer inside.

Without explaining my plan, I reached into my pocket and punched redial. The deputy who was closer to the fence started whistling. "Call it again," he yelled. On the third ring, he was holding Rebekah's phone and waving it at me.

Back on the road, he handed it to me. I had mixed emotions. I was glad we had found it, but that meant that she didn't have it. I knew her password and turned it on. The call list showed that some guy named Richard had tried to call her seventeen times since last night. There was an unsent email draft as well. It simply said, "Victor chasing." I had to force myself to take a breath.

The sheriff could read my face and knew that I knew what that meant.

I said, "Victor was our main handler for most of the year we were held hostage. He was killed when Polaris busted up the organization. He couldn't possibly have been raised from the dead, but another 'Victor' could indeed be back in business."

We continued down the county road, driving slowly and watching for any other clues along the roadway. About a mile from where the car had been found, I yelled, "Stop." About twenty feet down the hill, I could see Rebekah's Boston Red Sox cap. It had to be Rebekah's. *Who else around here would have a Boston cap? She must have thrown it from her car before she stopped. The phone was thrown out after she was stopped.*

We continued searching the road until we came to the entrance to Billy's. The gate was locked, but I hobbled out and assumed that Rebekah would use our anniversary date as the combination. I assumed right. We drove down the lane. The emergency crew had cleared both trees, but there were still fresh leaves and chain saw shavings scattered around on the lane.

I spotted the dried blood where I had been pinned down, but I didn't point it out. I was certain that the sheriff had already seen it. We drove down to the house, but I didn't want to get out of the vehicle. Without Rebekah, there was nothing I wanted to see there.

The sheriff and his deputy poked around the house and yard, and I stayed in the SUV. They didn't see anything. On our way out, the sheriff stopped at the scene of my accident. He climbed over the stone fence and examined the logs that had been cut and tossed by the emergency response team.

When he returned, he was shaking his head. and said, "It's hard to tell what made those trees fall like they did. It would have been helpful to have had a chance to examine those stumps before the fire boys got after them. Of course, it would have been better to have seen it before they lifted them off you, but I'm sure you didn't want to stay under them any longer than you did."

"No, I was more than ready to have that tree removed." The memory of my helplessness sent a shiver down my spine.

CHAPTER 15

Trucks and Planes

Richard was anxious to be released from the hospital, and I didn't want to leave him, but I had to get the car. I figured that Dennis could get me to the farm, and I could get back in about an hour. It appeared that Richard was still feeling woozy from the accident and surgery, and he needed some time to just relax.

I was feeling guilty. I should have been out there to help him. I should have found him earlier, but the doctor seemed confident that all was going to be fine. Twice, the doctor had said that Richard was a lucky man, but I didn't really believe that luck had anything to do with it.

Dennis and I had a good visit as we drove to the farm. He was a good driver, and I was glad to have sold him my uncle's pickup. He told me all about their football season and the homecoming game that wasn't at home. He informed me that tomorrow night was a bye game, and that's why they weren't having football practice this afternoon.

He also said he was thinking about taking Holly to the winter dance but hadn't asked her yet. I asked about his family, and he told me that his mom worked in the cafeteria at the local campus of

Missouri State, but he wasn't sure where his dad was. They hadn't heard from him since Dennis was in the sixth grade. He didn't tell me that in anger. He just told it as a matter of fact.

Dennis knew exactly the way to the farm because one of his best friends was Don Miller's middle son. He had been to the orchard many times, sometimes to work and other times to play. After we turned at Billy's lane, I spotted where Richard's accident had happened. I was glad the emergency crew had cleared the road while they had their chain saws running. I needed to remember to give a donation to the West Plains Fireman's Fund this Christmas.

As Dennis coasted up to the front porch, three deer were watching from the barn path. They bolted and ran. I climbed out, and Dennis informed me that he was planning to stay until I was ready, and then he would follow me back to town. I told him that wasn't necessary. I needed to change clothes and pack. I handed him two hundred-dollar bills for bringing me out, and his eyes lit up.

"Thank you, Mrs. Dempsey. Are you sure you don't want me to stay? I don't mind."

I shook my head and said, "You better go home and call Holly."

He smiled as the old Ford rumbled back to life, and he proceeded to guide it back up the lane. It was cold, but the roads were clear of any ice.

As the sound of the truck became too distant to hear, the quietness moved in. Other than the occasional faint chatter from a distant squirrel, silence prevailed. I sat down on the steps and bowed my head. I thanked the Lord that Richard had not been hurt any worse. I thanked the Lord for sparing his life.

Wearing a clean shirt with a sweater, I loaded our things into the Lexus. The last thing I picked up was Richard's phone, which he had left charging on the kitchen counter. With the lights off, I locked the door and started toward the road. Richard had brought a new chain and padlock for the front gate, so I stopped and attached them both on the way out. I used our anniversary date for the lock's combination. It felt good to protect the place.

I turned to the left and checked Billy's mailbox, and then I pulled into Henry's lane to turn around. I thought about the idea of giving the back one hundred feet to the national forest/Irish Wilderness and felt an intense harmony fall over me. It was the right thing to do.

As I entered the big curve just before Miller's Orchard, I realized that a vehicle had pulled onto the road behind me. I hadn't seen it until that moment. It was a black Suburban, but I couldn't see who was driving. I slowed and pulled over onto the shoulder to let them by, but the Suburban didn't attempt to pass. It just proceeded to get closer behind me.

Unsure of what the driver wanted, I sped back up, but the Suburban sped up with me. I slowed, and it slowed. Within a hundred yards of Miller's Orchard, it stopped and pulled to the side of the road. I took a breath and let out a sigh of relief as I started back to full speed. *That was weird. Why would someone be driving like that?*

Another mile farther up, I caught a glimpse of it in my rearview mirror. The black Suburban was charging toward me at a high rate of speed. I moved to the shoulder to allow it to pass, but it pulled up right behind me again before slowing. My heart started pounding, and I got a sick feeling in the pit of my stomach. *What does this person want?*

When the road straightened out, there were three farmhouses visible about a hundred yards off the road. I knew that when I passed the farmhouses, it was only a few more miles to the state highway. I felt like I would be safe once I made it to the state highway. I should have turned into one of those farms, but I didn't consider doing that until I had passed all three. In my panic, I rolled down my window and tossed out my Red Sox cap. It was a silly thought, but for some reason, I thought the Suburban might stop to pick it up, giving me more time to get to the highway.

But the Suburban came up behind me again. I was totally unnerved. I didn't know what to do but keep my eyes on the rearview mirrors. The Suburban would charge right up to my bumper before backing off, over and over. Then suddenly, there was another vehicle right in front of me, a white van. That's when I knew I was in serious trouble.

Without another choice, I pulled off the road and rolled to a stop. The Suburban closed in from behind, and then bumped me sharply. The white van backed up toward me. Just as Richard had been pinned down under the tree, I was now pinned between two vehicles. In my panic, I grabbed my phone and tried to call Richard. His phone rang from the sack in the back seat where I had tossed it.

I started an email as I watched men unload from both vehicles. They all wore tailored suits and looked to be Middle Eastern. I wasn't sure what to say, but I typed a quick message that said, "Victor chasing." That was all the time I had. I rolled down the window and threw the phone out as far as I could. The deep grass swallowed it, I hoped. Either they didn't see me throw it, or they didn't care. I rolled up the window and made sure the doors were all locked.

Two men came up to my side of the car. Both were wearing black driving gloves. One knocked on my window and motioned for me to roll down the glass. I refused. Without a moment of hesitation, he motioned to one of the others, who immediately extracted a sledgehammer from the white van. He positioned himself to swing the giant hammer right into my face. I unlocked the door.

They invited me to step out with hand signals, and the two of them walked me to the black Suburban and seated me in between them. The third climbed into the driver's seat and shifted the Suburban into gear, but before leaving, the rear hatch opened—and something else was loaded into the back. Then we were gone. I never saw the other man or the white van again. I didn't check my watch, but the whole exchange probably took less than three or four minutes.

Throughout the entire event, the three men hardly spoke to each other, and they never spoke to me. The Suburban went south past the state highway, and within an hour, we were stopping at a small roadside park in Arkansas. I watched where we drove and paid attention to every turn. They didn't attempt to block my view. They didn't seem to care whether I could see or not.

There were no other vehicles at the roadside park, but within a few minutes, a large eighteen-wheeler pulled up beside us. I was ushered out and quickly directed to the back end of the shiny black trailer rig. A door opened, and a set of aluminum stairs lowered. The men motioned for me to go up and inside. I was in such shock that I did exactly as they ordered without argument.

It was dark inside the trailer, but it was warm. The two men who had ridden in the seat with me escorted me inside. Once the door closed, the lights inside the trailer came on. It wasn't what I expected.

It was an elaborate gaming room. There were two poker tables, slots, craps, and a roulette wheel. Thick pile carpet covered the floor, and ornate red drapes adorned the walls. There was no one else in the trailer besides the two men who entered with me and the one who acted as our "host."

Toward the front of the trailer, there was a small buffet table. As the truck began to roll, I was invited to help myself to the food. It smelled wonderful, but I was determined not to eat with my captors.

When it became clear I wasn't going to join them, they opened a door behind the food table, and I was directed to enter. I heard the door lock behind me. The room contained a small bed with a bathroom to the side. I could feel the truck build to highway speed, and we were gone. I had no idea where I was being taken.

It was almost dark when I was loaded into the customized big rig, but in the room without windows, my sense of time became very confused. I couldn't imagine how Richard was feeling as he waited back at the hospital. How long would it be before someone found my car? Was my car even still where I left it? I stretched out on the bed. I wanted to cry, but tears wouldn't come. The roar of the truck tires on pavement reminded me where I was but did not hint as to where I was going.

Sometime in the night, I felt the truck slow and turn off the road. I heard voices and other trucks moving about. I assumed we were probably refueling at a truck stop. We weren't stopped for long and promptly resumed our travels.

About the time we had reached full speed, the door opened, and I was invited again to help myself to the food. This time, I decided that, whatever trials were ahead, it would be better for me to have my strength. I took a few shrimp, a couple of meatballs, and some fruit salad, and then I reentered my private coach. There was a bottle of water inside. I snacked some, but I felt sick almost immediately. I didn't want to eat.

I felt like I dozed off several times, but I wasn't sure due to the disorientation caused from being locked inside the room. I had no sense of which direction we were traveling. I kept focusing on my watch, but the hands didn't seem to move. Then I realized the hands weren't moving at all. No wonder they let me keep wearing it. My watch was dead.

Wherever we were, and whatever time it may have been, I felt certain that Richard and the authorities would have found my car by now. Would they find my cell phone? Would they find my Red Sox cap? They had to find it. Richard would know what my message meant, but what could he do about it even if he did?

I noticed that an air conditioner was keeping the room constant in temperature, but suddenly it started blowing slightly more—and the air felt colder. My plan was to pull off the blanket from the bed to fight off the chill, but when I pulled it back, it made more sense to just crawl in under it. I let out a quiet prayer for Richard and slipped away. I was exhausted.

I don't know how long I was asleep. I had no sense of time, but I felt like it was sunny outside now. Why? I wasn't sure, but I could tell that the truck had slowed, turned, and then proceeded down a different type of road surface. Not long after that, it slowed and turned again. Then it came to a stop. I heard its air brakes hiss. I sat up on the side of the bed and faced the door. They would be coming for me.

Hearing the back door to the trailer being opened and the stairs being pulled down, I prepared myself for whatever was coming. There were several additional voices. Then the host opened my door and pointed to the bathroom. I understood, so I went in, used the facilities, and washed my face. When I came out, he was waiting, and he ushered me out and through the traveling casino. The buffet was gone. He guided me to the back door and down the aluminum steps.

The morning sun was so brilliant that I had to shield my eyes. I had been in that truck for at least twelve hours. As they took me to a barn, I could see the landscape around us. It was barren desert. Low-lying mountains were several miles away, and there didn't appear to be much between here and there other than sage and cactus. If I had broken out and started running, it would have taken me days to get anywhere. It wasn't even a temptation.

From the barn, I was led to a small farmhouse that didn't appear to be lived in. It had some furniture, but nothing hung on the walls or filled the bookcases. It was moderately cool, and the window blinds were all closed. They led me to a bedroom and locked the door. I sat down on the bed since there were no chairs. *Where have they taken me?*

The bedside table's first drawer was empty. The second drawer had a map—a well-worn highway road map of Texas. It had not been folded up correctly. I remembered how my dad would howl if my brother or I would try to fold up a road map incorrectly. *Does this mean I am in Texas?*

A few minutes later, someone knocked on the door, the lock opened, and the suitcase that had been in my car was brought inside and given to me. It surprised me to see it. I knew that I heard something being loaded into the rear of the Suburban, but I never dreamed it was my suitcase. I didn't hesitate. I pulled out some clean clothes, jumped into the little shower, and scrubbed off the dust. The water wasn't hot, but neither was it cold. I didn't care. It made me feel better if that was possible. However, I did realize that my Bible and the book I had been reading were missing from my suitcase.

After I was dressed, another knock came on the door. I was given a hamburger with a bottle of water. I ate part of it, but I couldn't eat it all. I heard the truck leave, and several times during the day, I heard footsteps and voices. Peering through the blinds, I couldn't see much. It looked warm outside, but the window glass felt cold. I could see the distant mountains, but they looked farther away than before.

I kept thinking about Richard's accident and surgery. *What a horrible experience to be pinned to the ground by a tree. As bad as that was, it probably didn't compare to the horror of finding my car without me. I hope someone found my car.*

The mostly uneaten hamburger rested on the nightstand on its paper plate. I drank the water, but I couldn't eat the burger. Later in the afternoon, they brought me another plate. This time, it was canned spaghetti. It had been heated, but it wasn't hot. I tried several bites, but the dried-out burger looked more appetizing. The spaghetti plate joined the burger on the nightstand.

Peering through the closed blinds, I checked outside. It was getting late in the day when a knock came at the door. My two regular escorts came in and signaled that it was time to leave. It had been cool and windy when I was transferred from the truck this morning, but now, in the late afternoon, there was even more of a chill in the air.

As I was led from the farmhouse, a van pulled up. One of my handlers tried to wave it back, but the driver didn't respond. I caught a glimpse of eight teenagers being unloaded. My heart dropped. I was watching the group of young teenagers who didn't have a clue as to where their destination would ultimately be. My handlers pretended to not see them and tried to block my view; it was almost as if they were embarrassed.

On a grass strip was an airplane, not a large plane, but it was big enough for four. The pilot was already seated and checking the instrument panel. One of my escorts joined the pilot in the copilot seat. The other escort and I climbed into the back. The back seat was just barely big enough for the two of us, but we squeezed in.

As the pilot fired up the engine, I said, "What's our destination?"

Of the three men, not one of them looked in my direction or seemed even tempted to respond. Being ignored wasn't pleasant.

The plane started rolling, and we were off. It was still barely light outside, but the sun had been down for some time. The first stars were visible. As we continued to climb, the ground became much darker. I thought we had headed toward the mountains I had seen in the distance, but I wasn't sure.

If the truck had brought us to Texas, I was assuming that we were flying south into Mexico. I noticed that the pilot made no contact with any airport or tower. We were flying into the dark, and I was completely in the dark.

I thought about Richard again. I couldn't imagine what he was thinking. I knew he would be assuming that the "company" had me—or some type of similar organization. If law enforcement had found my phone in the deep grass, then they would know for sure. As soon as Richard could, he would call and talk to Melinda at Polaris to get a team to begin the process of finding me. I knew that Melinda and her team would be the best, but deep inside, I tasted only hopelessness.

Out of the window I could see a small village with maybe fifty lighted structures. From the direction of the sunset, I assumed that we were already flying over Mexico. I had vacationed in Cabo San Lucas in the past, and I was familiar with Mexican customs and airport security, but I suspected that we wouldn't be landing at any official airport.

Years ago, I had a friend who had grown up in Lubbock. Her dad was in law enforcement around the Panhandle of Texas—maybe a Texas Ranger—and one of his jobs was to patrol the caprock area for unauthorized aircraft. Late at night, small planes would fly in from Mexico to a predetermined county road, sweep down low, and push out packages of illegal drugs. A car would be waiting and would snatch up the package and be gone within minutes. My friend's dad would go out and watch for the headlights to flash and attempt to chase down the vehicle. I wondered if the same thing was still happening.

After two or three hours, the power was pulled back, and the plane started to descend. The pilot spoke over his radio, but I couldn't understand what he said. Out of my window, I could see nothing but black, yet we continued to descend.

Out of the front window, I caught a glimpse of a row of dim yellow runway lights as we dropped and touched down on a gravel airstrip. Shortly after we came to a stop, the runway lights were switched off. I was directed to disembark, and I did so. I assumed that cooperation would make things go easier unless I saw a clear chance of escape. I was under no illusion that this was ever going to work out for my benefit, but I continued to worry about Richard.

We walked over to a small metal building and went inside. The restroom inside the building was pointed out, and I headed in that direction. I knew that I had better use it while it was available, but it was one of the nastiest "restrooms" I had ever experienced.

Other than the three men traveling with me, I only saw one other person. She was a Mexican woman, up in years, in a big serape and a sombrero hiding her face. She rolled out a barrel with a hand pump and started refueling our plane. One of our men paid her in cash, and we reloaded and prepared to depart.

The men still hardly spoke—even to each other. Not long after we lifted off, I saw the reflection of the moon on a body of water. Was it a lake? Or was it the Gulf of Mexico? Or maybe the Pacific? The water disappeared from my view before I could decide.

About an hour later, we started down again. This time, we banked to line up for an airstrip, and I caught a glimpse of the body of water again. It had to be the Gulf of Mexico. We unloaded, walked over to a row of hangars, and entered the first one.

A group of discarded old chairs and couches was arranged in a circle. I was invited to have a seat. My two handlers sat down near the hangar door and started drinking Tecate beer from long-necked bottles. They seemed to be enjoying the trip more than I was.

Suddenly, the two jumped up and started toward me as they checked their phones. Without any explanation, they led me to the next hangar, and we boarded a different type of plane. Two other men joined us. I didn't know much about small planes, and I certainly didn't know them well enough to know what we had been in or what we were now boarding, but this new plane was definitely larger than the first.

The seats were along the sides rather than lined up facing forward. A large pile of cases and packages was stacked in the back. I assumed the plane was making deliveries—and that I was probably one of those deliveries. The flight wasn't nearly as long as either of the two previous flights, but instead of descending, the men who had joined us started scurrying around and pulling out backpacks.

The two men who had been with me since the abduction in Missouri joined in the activity. One strapped on a pack and attached my suitcase to his chest. The other strapped on a harness of some type. Then they motioned for me to stand up, and one of the harnesses was strapped onto me. The two new men strapped on packs as well, and that's when I realized the packs were actually parachutes. One of the new men motioned for me to turn around, and I could feel him connecting himself to my harness.

We all stood there harnessed together until the pilot leaned back and gave us a thumbs-up. The side door was opened, and cold wind started rushing in. The morning sun wasn't quite up, but it was light enough to see.

My handler had a parachute and my suitcase, and he jumped without any fanfare. The other handler and the man that he was strapped to walked together and just fell out of the door. My expert, at least I hoped he was an expert, and I walked together to the door. In the final two feet, it was as if he picked me up and jumped.

I had always wanted to experience skydiving, but this was not how I imagined it would be. We were falling through the sky. His arms were outstretched, and he seemed to be guiding us, but I was terrified. The wind was blowing my hair into his face, but I couldn't help it, and he didn't seem to care.

I spotted the other two parachutes as they opened below us. Then I felt the jerk of our chute opening, and I could breathe again. It wasn't nearly as cold as it had been when we jumped. I watched the ground coming toward us and braced myself, but just before hitting, we pulled up and floated the final few feet. We were on the ground with ease. I wanted to celebrate, but then I regained my composure and realized there was nothing to celebrate. I had so many questions. *What comes next? Where am I—and what are their plans for me?*

The harness was unstrapped, and one of my handlers whispered in my ear, "Well done." I didn't know how to respond. That was the first time I heard him speak. The parachutes were stuffed into large trash bags as two jeeps rolled up beside us. We boarded, and they took us through a section of thick jungle before we pulled up at a beautiful hacienda set on top of a hill with a breathtaking view. From the porch, I could look out and over what I assumed was the Gulf of Mexico.

Eastern Mexico was my guess, maybe the Yucatan, but I still wasn't sure. I was led to an upstairs bedroom. My suitcase was already on the bed. It was a tropical paradise. My windows overlooked the jungle, and I could see the gulf off in the distance, but I noticed the windows were locked from the outside.

There was a tray next to the bed with fresh squeezed orange juice, sliced pineapple, mango, and a western omelet. A carafe of coffee was on the edge of the large jacuzzi. I knew Richard was worried that I was being tortured or worse. Instead, I was begrudgingly sipping on freshly squeezed orange juice.

Seated in one of the deck chairs, I ate my breakfast. Whoever my captors were, they had hired great cooks. From what I could tell, the villa was vacant except for me. Other than the jungle birds, the house was perfectly quiet. I didn't want to, but I started crying.

I knew that we had given enough information to bring down the "company" that we were entangled with in North Africa, but this villa reminded me of their style. Maybe a new organization had formed, but there was too much that was similar. I knew who had taken me, but I didn't know their purpose or intentions.

This nightmare started on Thursday afternoon. I surmised that all of Thursday night and Friday were spent on trucks and planes, and now it was Saturday morning. Whatever time or day it was, I wasn't worried about that, but I hated what it must be doing to Richard.

CHAPTER 16

Hopelessness

My broken arm was hurting. I had tried to sleep, but I wasn't very successful. I had tossed and turned all night. So far, I had avoided filling the pain prescription I had been given at the hospital, but I glanced out the hotel window and saw the grocery store across the street. *Perhaps I shouldn't try to be the tough guy and go without pain medication.*

There was one clean pair of jeans in my suitcase and one shirt. *What are my plans? I can't leave. I can't go home. I don't even have our car. Would I be able to drive if I did?* A quick shower helped wake me up. Putting on clean clothes felt good, but buttoning and zipping up the jeans with one arm wasn't easy. I decided to stay at the Hampton for at least another night.

I walked down the hall to the hotel lobby. Breakfast was still being served, and I helped myself to some scrambled eggs and sausage. I walked across the street to the grocery store and found their pharmacy. My legs were working, but there was some severe stiffness. The bottle of pain meds came with a cautionary lecture from the pharmacist concerning what side effects to expect. I listened, but I didn't think his advice applied to me. I already had most of those side effects.

After picking up a few groceries, I headed back across the street. In the front parking lot, I saw our Lexus. It was locked, but when I went inside, the hotel clerk handed me the keys and explained that one of the sheriff's deputies had just delivered it. I thanked her and proceeded to my room.

Sitting at the desk, I started making a list of things I needed to do. I didn't get very far before a knock came at my door.

When I answered, a man said, "Are you Richard Dempsey?"

I nodded.

He said, "I'm Paul Williams. Your wife's uncle and I were good friends. I just wanted to come by and visit. Sheriff Nelson told me that your wife has been kidnapped. Would you like someone to talk with?"

Desiring to say no, I found myself saying, "I could use another cup of coffee. The coffee down the hall will grow on you. Come join me."

We walked down to the breakfast nook area and found a table in the corner. The breakfast crowd was gone, and we helped ourselves to the coffee and the few Danishes that remained.

"How did you know Billy?" I asked.

"He came to church from time to time. I was the pastor at a little church across town named Living Waters. I retired several years ago, but Billy and I would still meet to drink coffee once a month or so. I enjoyed our visits together. Did you know Billy?"

"No, I didn't. Rebekah only met him once, and that was ten years ago."

"He had some interesting views about the Bible that produced some lively discussions," Paul said.

"I've thumbed through his old King James Bible. He did have some awkward comments in the margins. I was a pastor until a couple of years ago as well," I said.

"But you're not now?"

"No, my wife developed brain cancer. Before the doctors discovered it, she changed. She started telling people lies about me. It was a weird time in my life. I didn't know how to defend myself, so I decided that for the good of the congregation, I needed to step away, at least for a season. Several weeks later, the cancer was discovered. We spent about four months down in Houston, seeing the best cancer doctors in the world, but it didn't work—and I lost her."

"That would have been hard," he said.

"It was. My life was great. My marriage was great. The church I served was wonderful and growing. And in six months, all I had left was an empty house. To be honest, even my faith teetered. I got angry at God. Nothing seemed just or fair."

"I understand," he said.

"Just before it all came tumbling down, I was preaching through the book of Acts, and I came to the story of Stephen. I knew the story, but this time, it touched me on a deeper level than ever before. As I was working my way through the events of the story, I just started screaming. I was screaming at the young Stephen. 'Stop! You don't have to continue with this. You have already proven your point. Back off! Tell them you're sorry. Tell them that you're still just a kid and don't have it all worked out either. Tell them that they are the real experts of the scriptures.' But Stephen wouldn't listen to me. Even when the Jewish experts started gathering up rocks, he wouldn't stop. He just kept declaring the truth, and it cost him everything. That's when it dawned on me. I would have stopped!"

Paul wasn't expecting such an outburst, and neither was I. The passion deep inside had been building since yesterday when I saw the sheriff's vehicle and not our Lexus pull up to the hospital. Paul wiped away a tear.

"I'm sorry. You came to comfort me, and I vomited all over you," I said as I wiped my nose with a napkin.

"There is no need to apologize. I appreciate your honesty."

"That's what Rebekah said just a few days ago. She said she loved my honesty. Now I don't know where she is. I don't know what is happening to her, and I don't know what I can do about any of it. I do know what kind of people have her. They are professionals, and they are ruthless."

"How do you know who has taken her?" asked Paul.

I gave him a thumbnail outline of our trip to Argentina and our entanglement with the evil organization before our ultimate escape. I told him about the notes we handed over to the authorities that helped bring the organization to its knees. I even shared about the gold that was discovered and how we were using it to continue to fight the horror of the evil organization's business in human trafficking. "But I would give every ounce of gold back to the organization if it would help bring Rebekah home."

"And you're sure it's the same group?" he asked.

"No, it's not the same group, but it may involve some of the same key players—and they're still in the same ugly business." I told him about finding Rebekah's phone and the short email she tried to send. "She knew who was after her. I know who they are, but I don't know why they want her. I can't let my imagination run that direction."

I refilled our coffee cups and told him again that I was sorry for spewing on him, but I appreciated him listening. Most people, especially pastors, wouldn't have been able to handle such raw emotion.

He said, "I know it's hard for you to just sit here and wait. What do you need?"

"All of my clothes are either filthy or cut up into pieces in the hospital's trash. Is there a place in town where I can buy some new clothes?"

He nodded and smiled. "It would be my privilege to drive you there."

As he drove, he told me that there were several nice women's clothing stores in West Plains, but the only men's store had closed about a year ago. We pulled up to the only other option: JC Penney. I was thankful when I found some clothes that fit.

Paul dropped me back at the Hampton, gave me his business card, and offered to help in any way. As I watched him drive off, I thought about the insecurity that Rebekah and I experienced after the intruders broke into our house and office. Compared to where we were now, those feelings were silly.

When I walked into the hotel, I spotted a young fellow wearing a blue sport coat with no tie. He looked so out of place. I walked up to him and said, "I'm Richard Dempsey. Are you looking for me?"

He put down his newspaper and nodded. He showed me his FBI identification, revealing his name to be Doug Douglas, and we moved over to the table next to where Paul and I had just been sitting. He seemed to know all that the sheriff knew, but he asked, "Have you heard from the kidnappers yet?"

"No, I haven't heard from anybody. I don't expect to."

"At the bureau, we have studied kidnapping in detail. We break it down into three types."

I wanted to raise my hand and call time-out, but he just kept talking.

"The first is targeted kidnapping. The kidnappers know who it is they are after, and they know the amount of the proposed ransom based upon the person's family, business, or personal wealth.

"The second type is called 'random kidnapping.' They pick out somebody who maybe looks nice, or is dressed nice, and they propose a ransom amount based on nothing except how the victim acts or what they say."

I remained quiet and decided to just let the young agent run his course.

"The third type is virtual kidnapping. Somebody crosses the border for business or pleasure. Their information is stolen, their family is contacted, and a ransom is demanded. The victim doesn't even know their family has been contacted. They are enjoying their fishing trip or business adventure. Sometimes the ransom money is paid, and the target returns home completely unaware that anything ever happened."

"Okay," I said.

"From what we know thus far, your wife's abduction would fall into the first category. We believe that she was targeted specifically because of her family or business. If this turns out to be correct, you should expect a large ransom demand."

"Your assumption is that this is a kidnapping. What if it's not? What if the captors have taken her for something other than money … I mean … other than ransom money from her family?"

"What other options are there?" he asked.

"What if they captured her in order to sell her for an entirely different purpose?"

That question barely escaped my lips before I saw the hotel's main door open. Melinda Thompson and four others walked through. I enthusiastically waved before she headed to the front counter, and she started toward me. I stood and gave her a hug. I couldn't believe she was already in West Plains.

With us all standing in the lobby, she introduced her team. I recognized Bill Reynolds. He was CIA and had been with us in Sicily and Argentina. He had helped carry PVC pipes filled with gold. I was certain that he was still wearing his Kevlar vest. His presence brought a tone of authority and professionalism.

"This is Vicky Garza, my personal assistant, a lawyer currently on loan to Polaris from the San Joaquin College of Law teaching staff."

I shook her hand. She looked Native American with nearly perfect skin.

"This is Dan Browning, a retired Army Intelligence officer who is on loan from UN-GIFT, as you may remember, that's the United Nations Global Initiative to Fight Human Trafficking. And lastly this is Simon Abel. He too is from UN-GIFT, and he is a lieutenant colonel in the Israeli Defense Force.

I introduced the team to Doug Douglas, FBI, special agent in charge, but Melinda corrected me quickly. Looking directly at Doug, she said, "In this situation, you will not be the agent in charge."

Doug shook her hand and agreed with her correction.

Melinda suggested that we move to the small conference room across from the lobby, but before we could all move, Sheriff Nelson walked through the front door.

In the conference room, everybody introduced themselves to the sheriff. Sheriff Nelson was not one to be easily intimidated or impressed, but this group created a slight nervousness that was evident on his face.

Looking around the table was impressive, but the fact remained that Rebekah was still missing, and the quick assembly of this team showed that we all knew the seriousness of the situation—and how dangerous the force was that we were facing.

Melinda turned directly to Sheriff Nelson and said, "What do we know for sure at this time?"

The sheriff in his best Marlboro Man voice said, "Mrs. Dempsey was abducted off County Road 6, about two miles from State Highway 160, sometime between 4:00 and 5:00 p.m. yesterday. Her car was found and reported by a neighbor not long after the abduction. No one has reported seeing anything out of the ordinary during that period. No neighbors in the area saw or heard anything.

"There were no fingerprints on the car, and the car had no damage except for a tiny dent on the back bumper with a fleck of black paint that matches the paint from late-model Chevrolet Suburbans. No vehicle that matches that has been found yet. Mrs. Dempsey's phone was discovered in the grass about twenty feet from her car. It had an unanswered call to Richard and an unsent email that simply said, 'Victor chasing.' So far that's all we know."

The group asked several questions about why Rebekah was alone, who had taken her to the farm, and if my tree accident had been fully investigated.

Sheriff Nelson answered every question to their satisfaction.

Melinda said, "We have some evidence that a new organization has restructured itself using some of the same operatives from the organization that—with the help of the Dempseys—we brought down not quite a year ago. They call themselves the Order, and currently, we think they are using a Mediterranean cruise line as their headquarters.

"The cruise ship is registered with Windstar Cruise Lines, which is based at the port of Gioia Tauro, Italy. We have observed it moving in and out of the various ports of the Mediterranean, but it hasn't taken on any ticketed passengers in more than nine months. Of course, we are only speculating that the Order is involved with the abduction of Mrs. Dempsey. We are pursuing all leads."

I sat there in silence, attempting to stretch my fingers from under the cast, and I studied each face in the room. I felt assured that each could be trusted, but I remembered that I also trusted Larry who ended up having to be shot by Melinda. Had she not killed him, he would have killed all of us.

I checked my phone and realized it had been almost a full day since Rebekah went missing. In twenty-four hours, she could be almost anywhere. Hopelessness was creeping over me like a dark cloud.

Vicky handed Melinda her phone without explanation.

After reading the message, Melinda said, "We may have gotten a break." She looked at me. "Do you remember Colonel Brighton and the story of his daughter, Norma?"

I nodded, though I didn't remember her name.

"She was abducted from Bolivia while on a mission trip with her church. We have attempted to trace her whereabouts for more than five years now. To be honest, we had little hope left in ever locating her. Where she has been, we don't know, but apparently, almost a year ago, she was traded to an older Arab business tycoon named Shamsheer Al Moopen from Dubai. From what we know now, she became his primary caretaker since he had cancer surgery nine months ago. A few days ago, ninety-two-year-old Shamsheer Al Moopen suffered a heart attack and died. Norma Brighton called the authorities and his family, and then she took the opportunity to disappear. She had passed by the US embassy recently while taking Al Moopen to his doctor, and she knew the directions. She is waiting at the embassy for us to pick her up and bring her back to the States and to her family."

I said quietly, "Five years—and Norma was still alive? That's wonderful."

Melinda said, "From what she has told the US consulate general, she is familiar with the newly formed Order just from overhearing visitors to Al Moopen. She may be able to give us some information about how and where it's operating. We have a team on the way to Dubai as we speak."

With that, all but Melinda and Vicky stood up and left, seemingly knowing their tasks at hand.

As Sheriff Nelson left, he squeezed my shoulder with his giant hand. The sign of support clearly didn't come naturally to the big man.

With only three of us left in the room, I asked, "What could they possibly want Rebekah for? Do you think it's about the money? I have wondered all year who was watching us dig up the PVC pipes full of gold along the river."

Melinda said, "I don't think it's about the money. I think it's about something else. If it is about the gold, someone would be contacting you with a ransom demand."

"Will they sell her into slavery?" I asked.

"We'll find out. You have a broken arm, a bum leg, and a bump on the head, but your thinking is still intact. Trust us. We have the best team that can be put together. I'll keep you informed."

"What should I do? Where should I go?"

Melinda said, "For the next day or so, it would be best if you could stay here in West Plains. Some of us will need to pursue some things around here, and others of us will be global. Has anything else happened with you two concerning the farm or Rebekah's uncle? Has anything weird or unexplained been going on?"

"There have been some unexplained things, but I don't think they could possibly be connected with Rebekah's abduction."

"Such as?"

"We discovered that Uncle Billy has hosted a secret society at his farm for at least twenty years. Everybody here in West Plains seems to know about it, but nobody knows what the secret group does. They gather, pitch some tents, build a bonfire, and sit around and discuss 'things.' Billy's lawyer told us they are simply an investment club, but I'm not so sure."

"Do they have a name?" she asked.

"As a matter of fact, they do. The call themselves the Knights of the Golden Circle."

"Are you serious?"

"Yes, we have discovered literature at Uncle Billy's place that is clearly literature about the KGC."

"I referred to the newly formed human trafficking organization as the 'Order.' They actually call themselves the 'The Order of the Knights of the Golden Circle.'"

My blood ran cold.

"As best as we can figure, the KGC is essentially an investors' club, but we're talking about big money, old money. The Order is a disconnected arm of the KGC that's involved with the human trafficking side of the business. The investors within the KGC may or may not know how the Order is producing such huge profits. Either they don't know, or they don't care—as long as the money is flowing."

"Why can't you stop this?" I asked.

"We can if we get the right information. But there are so many layers to these top-level organizations that makes it hard to track. If you go down the street and buy a pizza, but then you find out that the pizza was poisonous, who is to blame? The kid making ten bucks an hour who throws the ingredients together and sticks it in the oven or the owner of the pizza restaurant who is relaxing on a beach in the Caribbean?"

"I'm at a loss for words," I whispered.

"There are two types of human trafficking organizations. There is a blue-collar level where victims are drugged, beaten, and ripped from the streets. They use threats of violence and torture to demand compliance. Often their organizations are on a small, regional scale with just a few individuals involved. Kids who get nabbed into this type of slavery have a life expectancy of about seven years.

"But then there is the white-collar level. These organizations have recruiters, haulers, and auctioneers. They keep their victims in line with the offers of a better life and a better paycheck. These recruiters sound like they are selling vacation time-shares. The victims never have a clue until their final delivery, and then they discover it was all a lie. The problem is that, at almost every step in the process, no laws are broken until the very end.

"Last year, we discovered a woman in Lagos, Nigeria, who managed a hotel. She was a beautiful lady and was very gifted in management skills and handling personnel. She had no family and just a few friends. She was connected to a church, but her job kept her from attending most of the time. Two European businessmen walked into her hotel one afternoon, and they said they were in Lagos on business and would be there for several days. On their last night in the city, they approached her and bragged about the hotel, its staff, and her management style.

"Then they told her that they represented several large, exclusive hotels in Europe and asked if she would be interested in making a lot more money and living in Europe. She bought into their sales pitch. They bought her a plane ticket and told her someone would be at the airport to pick her up. They were great salesmen. She quit her job, boarded the plane, and disappeared into the dark world of human trafficking. No laws were even broken—until she found herself on the auction block."

"I need another pain med," I said. I couldn't imagine where Rebekah had been taken. I washed the pill down with a can of orange juice. Its foul metallic taste sent me a longing reminder of the amazing fresh orange juice we were served in North Africa. *I wonder what Rebekah is doing. Are they feeding her?*

"I'll meet you back here after I take another med," I said.

"Take your time. I have several calls to make," she said.

Back in my hotel room, I opened my Bible. I recalled what Billy had written concerning the Bible and slavery. Ever since I read through those sermon notes, I kept asking myself, "What does it actually say?"

There was one story in the New Testament that Billy never mentioned. It was the short letter of Paul to a slave owner named Philemon. It told the story of a runaway slave named Onesimus who became a Christian and met up with the apostle Paul. Paul instructed him to return to his master and wrote this letter for him to take back to his master, Philemon. It would have taken great faith and courage for the runaway slave to return to his master. The potential consequences could have been horrible.

But the letter asked the slave owner to receive the runaway back not as a slave but as a son. And then Paul said, "I write to you, knowing that you will do even more than I ask." In other words, Paul was expecting the slave owner's new faith would allow him to honor the new faith of his slave and set him free—and perhaps even adopt him as his own son. Then I realized that was the only way the horror of slavery could be broken: one heart at a time. I wished that I had a chance to visit with Uncle Billy about these things.

In my backpack, I noticed a book that Rebekah had been reading. I thumbed through it and saw a passage she had underlined: "In the hands of a master carpenter, no piece of wood is safe from becoming a masterpiece." My heart paused. *Are Rebekah and I in the hands of the master carpenter now?* I wanted to say yes, but that didn't ease my fears.

CHAPTER 17

Sand Dunes

The obnoxious sound of a jungle bird woke me. I spent most of yesterday in a fog, just staring into the jungle and trying to make sense of everything. I was surprised that I had even slept through the night, but obviously I had.

I found a bathrobe hanging in the closet, and I slipped it on and sat on the balcony deck chair. A morning fog was lifting off the jungle, and the view was breathtaking as the sun rose out over the ocean. It was too bad that I couldn't truly enjoy it. Such beauty was meant to be shared. My heart hurt for Richard.

On the wicker side table was a brief brochure outlining the common jungle birds of the Yucatan Peninsula. The first one pictured was the chachalaca. It simply said that its distinctive call would be heard before it would be seen, but there it was still cackling in the tree nearest where I was seated. It looked more like a sandy brownish gray chicken than a jungle songbird.

The trees below my second-floor balcony were thick, but I could see the road that led up to the villa. Some sort of panel truck had pulled up and was searched at the main gate before being allowed to pass. In less than fifteen minutes, the truck left through the same gate, following the same procedure. It was clear that security was tight.

A soft tap came on my door. I heard the click of the lock, and the door opened. A Hispanic woman brought in a cart loaded with breakfast goods. She was wearing a bright orange sundress and whistling a tune I didn't recognize. After parking the cart, she looked at me and signaled for me to eat. She then left, and I heard the door lock again.

There was a fruit medley, scrambled eggs, bacon, tortillas, and a variety of jellies and jams. There was also freshly squeezed orange juice. I was impressed with the quality and presentation, and it reminded me of the deaf cook at the mansion in North Africa. The memory caused me to shudder, and I wondered what they were going to ask of me.

In Africa, they wanted Richard and me to keep the books for the company. As distasteful as that was, that was how we collected enough information to help bring down the cartel. I couldn't imagine what they were going to ask me to do now.

I had nothing to read or listen to besides the jungle and the distant ocean. Most of the time, I thought about Richard. *I wonder how his arm is feeling. Did they find my phone? Did he get the email I started? Has he talked to Melinda at Polaris?* I wanted to tell him about the parachute jump. I wanted to do it again under different circumstances. In a way, I was in the same position as when we were held in Argentina and North Africa. The only difference was that I was alone.

Another full day passed with only the jungle sounds and regular meals brought to my room. There were at least three other people at the villa, but never once did anyone speak to me. Even the smiling lady who brought in the meals never said a word. I wondered if she even spoke English. Coupled with the lack of conversation from the men who abducted me in Missouri, the lack of dialogue was the most difficult thing I faced.

However, early the next morning, things changed. A woman

who I had not seen before came in and suggested that I get dressed and pack my suitcase. About an hour later, though it was still dark, she came in, picked up my suitcase, and signaled for me to follow.

She led me down to the driveway, and the two of us loaded into the same jeep that carried me from the parachute jump landing zone. We were taken off the compound and down the hill toward the gulf.

In the morning twilight, the jeep pulled up to a large hangar. I was led inside, and we boarded a small jet. An attendant ushered me to a reclining seat and asked me to sit and buckle my seat belt. It was a very nice, well-worn plane. I noticed an imprint on the sliding window cover that said Gulfstream, but that didn't explain anything to me.

The attendant asked what I would like to drink. I asked for a ginger ale. In a few minutes, she returned with my ginger ale. It wasn't a big cup, and I quickly emptied it. About the time I heard the jet engines come to life, I began to feel extraordinarily sleepy. As the plane left the runway, I couldn't keep my eyes open.

The next thing I remembered was a gentle tap on my shoulder. The flight attendant who had given me the ginger ale was attempting to awaken me, "Mrs. Dempsey, Mrs. Dempsey," she kept saying as she continued tapping my shoulder.

The plane was descending rather quickly, and we were banking to the left, apparently lining up for a runway. My window shade was still pulled down, and my mind was amazingly groggy. I tried to keep my eyes open to look for clues to help me remember where I was. The wheels touched down, the engines reversed power, and we were on the ground taxiing.

There were only four of us on the flight, and I didn't recognize any of them. None had been on the plane when I ordered the ginger ale. My head was aching, and my neck was stiff. After the others were gone, the flight attendant came back and helped me stand. The first few steps were awkward, but I was fully awake now. *That was a mighty strong ginger ale*, I thought. She invited me to use the restroom before deboarding.

I was helped down from the plane and then loaded into a black van. In the fifty feet between the plane and the van, I could tell that it was hot, blistering hot. I didn't know where I was, but I knew it wasn't Missouri.

After being walked down to a dock, I was helped into a small fishing boat. Two men who I had not seen before climbed on board with me. They also loaded my suitcase. In a few minutes, we were zipping along the coastline. The cool wind and occasional spray in my face felt good compared to the dry heat of shore.

We traveled a couple miles along the coast before we pulled into a small bay that had a few docks and several cabins. I saw no sign of activity as we tied up to a dock. As was the normal routine, neither of the men spoke directly to me, and they barely spoke to each other. We entered one of the cabins. One of the men offered me a cold Coca-Cola or a cold ginger ale. I chose the Coca-Cola. He grinned and seemed to understand why I didn't take the ginger ale.

The three of us sat in the beach cabin with the evaporative cooler blowing over us for several hours, and then one of their phones buzzed with a text. Apparently following the message, one grabbed my suitcase, and the other took my elbow and led me up a sidewalk to an empty parking lot. Almost immediately, a helicopter descended and landed on the far end of the parking lot.

The three of us jogged toward it, and I was encouraged to board. There were two others already on board plus the pilot. I didn't recognize either of them, but I squeezed into the back seat and was belted in. A mask was placed over my eyes, and the helicopter lifted off the ground. It was the first time in my adventures that I had been forced to wear a mask. It was unnerving to feel the helicopter's movements lift without being able to see. It was impossible to tell which direction we were headed.

It had been so long since I had a phone or a working watch with me that time no longer mattered. Ten minutes could feel like hours, and several hours could be ten minutes. I don't know how long we were flying. I know that we landed once, and I was allowed to get off to use the restroom. I was given a bottle of water, and then I was led back to the helicopter and asked to put the mask back on. I tried my best to see what I could while I was unmasked, but nothing was clear other than it was hot, dry, and dusty.

The next time we slowed and started to descend, I slipped the mask down a sliver, but all I could see were sand dunes. The sun was setting, and as far as I could see was sand. Below us was a fenced-in compound. The buildings looked bright and new, but the landscaping was simply sand and cactus.

The helicopter set down on a landing pad on top of the largest of the buildings. We were unloaded while the blades continued to spin and hustled to a door. Two women in nursing outfits met us at the door and led us down the stairs. I was taken to a very well-furnished hospital room.

I took a seat in a plush leather recliner and tried to relax. I assumed the door had been locked, so I just sat and waited—and waited. I fell asleep in the chair. It wasn't until the next morning that one of the nurses came to check on me. She asked in perfect English why I hadn't come to supper. I didn't know what to say. No one had told me about supper, and I had assumed my door was locked. She invited me to breakfast.

Down the hall was the hospital cafeteria. Breakfast was good, but it was a strange feeling to be alone in a cafeteria that would easily seat twenty-five. Apparently, there wasn't anyone else there but the two nurses, a cook, two gate guards, and my two handlers. The two guards stayed in the guardhouse at the gate. I assumed my two handlers were staying in the other building, adjacent to the clinic, because I only saw them occasionally. They weren't any of the men I had seen before, and apparently the staff ate at a different location or following a different schedule.

After eating breakfast, no one directed me back to my room, so I wandered around. Doors that led to the surgical rooms were locked, but all the rest of the building was open. I even briefly walked around outside, but it was too hot to enjoy it. The two gate guards waved at me to be friendly, but I still had no clue as to why I was there.

The next day, I developed a routine. As soon as I was awake and had taken a shower, I would go up on the rooftop. There were two metal lawn chairs near the helipad, and I discovered that the early-morning desert was beautiful. The dunes would change colors, and the sky would lighten until eventually the sun would rise. The temperature was almost chilly until the sun was fully up, and that hour became my favorite time of the day.

In the coolness of the morning, I rediscovered my ability to pray. I remembered Richard's experience on the ship when he heard a divine whisper, and I remembered when he was on the beach and felt a divine touch. Truthfully, I was envious. God had never touched me or whispered to me, and I wondered why. Maybe Richard was privileged since he had been a pastor or was special in his experiences with God. On the rooftop overlooking the desert dunes, something changed. I can't say that I heard God's voice or felt His touch, but I knew He was with me. I felt His peace wash over me.

After the sunrise, the heat would arrive, and I would go downstairs to eat breakfast alone. From there, I would go to the front lobby. There were several newspapers and magazines on the center table. Everything was in French or Arabic, but it was fun to examine the pictures in the newspapers and attempt to guess what the articles were about. From there, I would walk through the building several times at a rapid pace to get my heart pumping and then show back up for lunch.

The afternoons and evenings were the worst. It was too hot outside, and it was too boring inside. I would nap, or sit, or worry. I knew that it wasn't true, but I felt as if I was unfindable. I felt like even the best team Polaris could put together would never be able to locate me. I could have been on the moon for all I knew, but this I did know, I was on the other side of the world from West Plains, Missouri.

To keep from going bonkers, I started singing to myself. I knew the first part of many songs from almost every genre, but I didn't know all the lyrics to hardly any. But I sang them anyway. I sang worship hymns, Eagles, Moody Blues, Celine Dion, George Strait, Queen, Beatles, James Taylor, Michael Jackson, and many more. When I ran out of the official words, I would just fill in with made-up words. It wasn't a pretty sound being produced, but as far as I knew, no one cared or even heard except for me.

There was another song that I had been listening to while jogging over the past month that a friend had recommended. I liked the song, but the words hadn't meant much to me, and I wondered why my friend wanted me to listen to it. But during those times alone, it began speaking to me. It was sung by a Jewish rap singer named Matisyahu. Like the other songs, I couldn't remember all the words, but the first verse and chorus kept ringing in my ears:

You give your love, and they throw it back
You give your heart, they go on attack
When there's nothing left for you
Only thing that you can do, say

Today, today, live like you wanna
Let yesterday burn and throw in the fire
In the fire, in the fire
Fight like a warrior

As I would sing that song, I could see the trash barrel at Uncle Billy's. There were things in my heart and mind that I needed to throw in the fire. I needed to learn to fight like a warrior.

On the third day, I went into the cafeteria for lunch. There was a dish on the line that I hadn't seen before. It had some type of meat, okra, onions, tomatoes, peppers, and several other unidentifiable ingredients. It looked good, so I started to help myself, but the cook who had not said a word in three days suddenly started waving her hand and mumbling. I tried to understand, but I wasn't getting her message. She put her hand to her throat and started choking herself and then pointed to the new dish. I assumed she was saying it was too hot to eat, and thus I passed it by. She was immensely pleased that I had gotten her message. I really missed communicating with others. I found great joy in this interaction with the cook—even if it was a warning about her own food.

I was still at the cafeteria table when I saw one of the nurses running down the hallway. Another one joined her in a panic. They were extremely excited about something, but since it didn't involve me, I just remained where I was.

From my vantage point, I could see the two guards talking with considerable animation at the main gate, and then I saw a caravan of three Hummers emerge from around a sand dune and approach the gate. The driver in the first one climbed out and entered the guardhouse. He was only in for a few moments before the guard exited and opened the gate. All three of the Hummers entered the compound.

The center Hummer pulled up and stopped at the front door to the clinic. Two armed guards exited the vehicle and helped two females out of the Hummer. The first was an older lady in a golden jilbab and a black hijab. She turned and helped a younger girl dressed in a baby blue jilbab. Both women walked with nearly perfect posture and were ushered into the front door. I didn't know who they were, but it was evident that they were important. I wasn't sure where they went inside the hospital, but I decided I needed to go back to my room.

I went to supper as was my routine, but the cafeteria was just as empty as it had been every other day. The cook nodded at me and signaled that all the food tonight was edible. I smiled, nodded, and filled my plate. I took my usual seat facing the front window and began my meal. As I took my first bite, a pleasant voice behind me said, "May I join you?"

After standing, I turned and faced the young woman who had arrived shortly after lunch. She was no longer wearing her traditional garb. Instead, she was wearing blue jeans and a black Bee Gees T-shirt. She was a beautiful young lady with deep green eyes that seemed to dance. A gold necklace with some type of Arabic gold coin medallion hung from her neck.

"I would be thrilled to have you join me," I said.

She sat down across from me, and the woman who had arrived with her brought her a plate of food. It appeared to be from the same cafeteria line I had gone through, but it was presented on nice gold-trimmed china with silver and crystal. The woman was still wearing her jilbab but had removed her face covering. They spoke for a moment and nodded, and then the older woman left. I assumed she would return with her own plate.

"My name is Amira. What's yours?"

"Rebekah," I said. "Amira is a beautiful name. Will your mother come join us?"

"No, she is not my mom. She is my private nurse. Are you American?"

"Yes, I'm from the United States. I live in Kentucky," I said.

"Kentucky. Isn't that the home of Daniel Boone?"

"Yes, it was, many years ago."

"I like your sweater. I love that color. It accents the color of your blue eyes."

"I liked the clothes you were wearing when you arrived. That was a beautiful blue."

"But you don't like my jeans and the Bee Gees?" she said with a grin.

"That's not what I meant. The Bee Gees look nice too. When do you wear a jilbab, and when do you not?" I asked. I was proud that I remembered the term to describe the traditional clothing.

"When you become a woman, your dad tells you to start covering yourself in public. I don't consider this public." She waved her hand around the empty cafeteria. "Are you a Christian?"

"Yes, I am. I assume you are Muslim."

"I've never met an American Christian."

"I haven't met many Muslims either, especially as lovely as you are."

"What does the name Rebekah mean?" she asked.

"I've been told that it means to be 'tied up or bound.' What does Amira mean?"

"My dad says that my name means 'a princess with a heart of gold.'"

"That's a beautiful name."

"I like the name Rebekah too. I'm glad you're here. I needed a friend. Will I see you at breakfast?"

"Yes, I will be here."

With about half of her meal eaten, she excused herself and scooted back from the table. She waved at me as she exited the cafeteria. She was a remarkable young lady. Her English was nearly perfect with a slight British accent. She carried herself with poise and grace.

I looked forward to breakfast.

CHAPTER 18

Watching

In the early-morning hour, I reached over to touch Rebekah, but she wasn't there. She hadn't been there now for days. My arm hurt almost as much as my heart did. I stayed in bed and tried to imagine where Rebekah was—and what she might be doing. My imagination didn't end well.

While I was eating breakfast at the hotel breakfast nook, Vicky walked in by herself. I waved her over to join me. "Would you like some breakfast?" I asked.

She looked at my half-eaten omelet and decided to pass. "Have you received any phone calls in the past twenty-four hours?"

"No, I haven't, except from Melinda and the sheriff."

"Your phone is now connected to our SKY network. I trust that is acceptable," she said.

"What is the SKY network?"

"Every phone call will be recorded and traced just in case a ransom demand is called in. If that happens, we'll know within seconds where the call originated."

"I didn't think that was legal in the States."

"It's not—except with permission from the phone owner." She pulled out a form and asked me to sign it. "This gives us permission."

"What if it's not a phone call? What if it comes as an email?" I asked as I signed the document.

"SKY will record and trace every phone call, email, and text. China does that with all of its citizens."

"China probably does it with all US citizens, too," I said.

"No, they aren't doing that yet, but they could."

I was being sarcastic with my comment—Vicky wasn't with her response.

"Melinda flew to Germany last night. She is meeting with the colonel's daughter this morning. Norma says that the Order will conduct an online auction this afternoon, and she says she has the code to be able to connect into the online system. Apparently, as Norma has been the primary caregiver for Al Moopen, she has learned much of the organization. If Rebekah is going on the auction block, we may be able to watch her. We may even have a chance to bid on her and buy her back. You and I may be able to watch from here in West Plains, but we're just not sure when this is going to happen."

"They let anybody bid?" I asked.

"Anyone who has the access code, but Norma knows a man who has bought many potential slaves through the system. From what she has told us, several years ago, he had a change of heart, and now he watches and buys as many as he can and then tries to reunite them with their families, but that gets expensive. We have contacted him and have wired him additional funds to increase his bidding power."

"And the Order doesn't care that this happens?"

"As long as his money is green, they don't care who buys."

As I was letting the concept of the auction soak in, my phone rang. Vicky looked at me, but I recognized the number. It was the foundation's number. It was probably Mary Ann.

"Hello, Mary Ann. Is everything all right?"

"Richard, we're praying for both you and Rebekah. I am so sorry."

"Thank you."

"But Richard, in attempting to reorganize the office, I have found something missing. At first, I thought it must have gotten stuffed in one of the boxes, but it's just not here. My written calendar that was in my desk is gone. I've looked everywhere, but it's just not here. It may not be important, but I wanted you to know."

"What kind of reminders did you put on that calendar?"

"Just the major things. Birthdays, trips, vacations … that sort of thing."

"Was our intended trip to Louisville on that calendar?"

"Yes, it was," she said softly.

"Thanks for praying. I'll let you know if anything develops here. Keep the board members updated."

"An office calendar is missing?" asked Vicky.

"Apparently so."

Vicky checked a text and said, "We have been informed that the auction will go live tonight at 9:00 p.m., but that will be at 11:00 a.m. this morning in West Plains. We will need to be ready by then."

"I need to call my daughters and let them know what is happening."

"By all means. Just remember the SKY network, and don't mention the upcoming auction."

As I walked down to my hotel room, I felt unstable. I dreaded these two calls. Micah and Lisa were both so happy with their families. I hated to cast a dark cloud into their lives, but they needed to know. They would want to know, so I made the two phone calls. They both cried, but I tried to convince them that the best team in the world was attempting to track down Rebekah and get her home. I faked a firm assurance, hoping they believed that I was confident.

Waiting for the "auction" time to begin, I noticed Rebekah's phone on the nightstand. I picked it up and glanced at it to somehow feel closer to her. At the bottom was her music app, mostly the songs she listened to on her daily jogs. I tapped on the app, and a song started. I didn't know the song, but I listened to the words: "Today,

today, live like you wanna. Let yesterday burn and throw in the fire, in the fire, in the fire. Fight like a warrior."

—

At ten thirty, I rejoined Vicky in the hotel lobby, but she suggested that we move to the more private conference room. A few minutes before eleven, she loaded her laptop and entered the code she had received from Melinda through Norma. I wasn't sure how I was supposed to feel. I was excited that we might see Rebekah, but what if we did but were unable to buy her? I was as tense as a bowstring.

A masked man came onto the screen and, in French, explained how the bidding would be conducted. Vicky was fluent in several languages, including French, and she translated for me. The first auction was for a sixteen-year-old Brazilian girl. The screen cut away and showed the young girl. She was seated on the foot of a bed in a hotel room. She was obviously afraid and confused—and completely unaware that she was on camera. She stood and walked back and forth, almost like a caged animal pacing across the floor, and the bidding began. The bids flashed at the bottom of the screen. It reflected the amount of the highest bid in euros, US dollars, Russian rubles, and Chinese yuan.

It was fascinating to watch the bids climb—and horrifying to think about what it meant for the young girl. The bidding stopped at ten thousand dollars. It was impossible to tell from the screen who had bought her or where she would be transported.

The next subjects were a brother and sister, ages twelve and ten, from Spain. The thought of the process was nearly overwhelming for me. I had to look away. Then came a twelve-year-old girl from Burma, a fourteen-year-old girl from New Orleans, and then an eighteen-year-old young man from Uganda. The bidding never lasted more than a few minutes, and in an hour, more than thirty individuals or small groups had been sold.

The masked man announced that the next subject would be

the last of the evening. I braced myself, but the subject was a young blonde girl from Denmark. The bidding climbed quickly before topping out at seventy-five thousand dollars. That was the highest sale price of the auction. Then the screen went black. Nearly a million dollars had been exchanged to purchase kids and young adults for slavery. I was relieved that it was over.

Vicky said, “We knew it was a long shot, but we had to be sure.”

I was sick to my stomach. Seeing the actual victims of human trafficking brought it home. Knowing that Rebekah was out there somewhere made it extremely personal.

Vicky’s phone buzzed. She answered and just listened. She looked at me and said, “Melinda wants to speak to both of us.”

I nodded.

She punched the speaker on her phone.

“Richard, we weren’t expecting to see Rebekah go to auction, so I hope you weren’t disappointed.”

I didn’t respond.

“We are putting together some pieces of a giant puzzle that we are now fairly certain involves Rebekah. Shamsheer Al Moopen, the man who recently died—and who Norma Brighton cared for over the past nine months—was the maternal grandfather of Khalid Bin Muthanna. Al Moopen was on the board of Enerflex, one of the largest oil companies in the Middle East. Khalid Bin Muthanna is the director of Mena Properties, one of the largest real estate investment firms in North Africa. He also manages Binghatti Holdings, a massive investment firm. Both Al Moopen and Muthanna would be in the top hundred richest men in the world.”

I looked over at Vicky and rolled my eyes. I was having a hard time keeping up.

Melinda said, “Khalid Bin Muthanna has a daughter named Amira. She was born with a genetic heart defect, and now, at age sixteen, she must have a heart transplant to survive. From what we can gather from our sources, the problem is that she has the rarest of blood types, AB negative, so finding a healthy heart organ that would be a suitable match is almost impossible. However, according to the *Khalleej Times*, a prospective donor may have been located—and the transplant surgery is tentatively set in the upcoming weeks."

I sat in silence and tried to absorb what this meant for Rebekah.

"Richard, the break-in at the medical clinic at the Naval Air Base in Sicily is where Rebekah's medical records were stolen. Apparently, Rebekah has the same rare blood type as the young Amira. As hard as it is to contemplate, we think we now know why Rebekah was taken. Now we must figure out where she is—before that surgery can take place."

"This can't be." I couldn't bring myself to say it. "They took Rebekah for her … this just cannot be."

Melinda said, "There are only a few dozen surgeons in Europe who routinely perform heart transplant surgeries. It requires a skilled team along with an experienced doctor. Bill Reynolds with the CIA has uncovered that Dr. Dominique Leblanc of Beaujon Hospital in Paris has had a recent change in his surgery schedule. Dr. Leblanc studied at Universität Heidelberg and the University of Chicago. He normally schedules two heart transplant surgeries per week. For some unexplained reason, his schedule has been cleared starting Monday of next week for both he and his surgical team.

"Officially, the hospital says that Dr. Leblanc is planning to take his whole surgical team for a much-needed and deserved weeklong luxury vacation to the Steigenberger Resort in Soma Bay, Egypt. So, we think we know who and when—and now we must find the where."

"Do we have a hint? A guess?" I asked.

Melinda said, "Not yet, but trust us, Richard. We have made some big steps in the right direction. I'll let you know."

As her phone went quiet, Vicky said, "Good work is being done. We have a good team in place."

—

As I was attempting to catch my breath, the front desk clerk tapped on the conference room's glass door. "Two lawyers are here to see you Mr. Dempsey: Mr. Smith and Mr. Bright."

Talking about the bids on the farm wasn't my desire at the moment, but I composed myself and invited them into the conference room. I introduced them to Vicky Garza. They expressed their concern for Rebekah. They knew she had been abducted, but they knew nothing else. Had they heard all that we had just heard in the past hour, it would have blown their minds.

"I'm sorry we were not able to be at your office to review the bids on Thursday," I said.

"We understand, but we are curious. Do you have any plans? What should we tell the bidders when they ask?"

"As you know, Rebekah was Uncle Billy's niece. I'm just along for the ride. Until we get Rebekah home, I don't think there is anything we can do with the bids." The "bid" language kept drawing me to the emotional experience I had just witnessed on Vicky's laptop. I couldn't believe I was having this conversation right now.

Mr. Smith said, "I understand completely. Have you proceeded with your plans concerning the back hundred feet?"

"Rebekah and I wrote a letter to the National Forest Service to determine what the process might entail, but we haven't received a response. I understand that your potential buyer may not be interested in the property with that slight adjustment."

The older lawyer said. "I think he is still interested, but maybe not at the same level as before. He didn't tell me what his bid was—or what it might have been before the adjustment—but until Rebekah is back home safe and sound, there's not much any of us can do. Let us know if there is anything we can do for you."

I thanked them both as they left.

Vicky said, "What's the situation with the back hundred feet?"

I explained about the log ruins, the cave, and the history of the disappearance of the Irish community. I even told her about the hundred-foot easement and Billy's attempt to gain permission to excavate. She seemed more interested than I expected, so I even told her about the hole that was dug last week by an unknown party.

"I think we should go out and check on the farm. I would like to see this cave—and perhaps the new hole."

I said, "The problem is that there is no phone service on the farm. If someone needs to contact us, they would be unable to reach us."

"My phone is not dependent upon cell service. It's connected into a satellite system. It should work."

I wanted to go, but I found myself so sore and stiff that the thought of driving or riding didn't sound feasible. I suggested that we go first thing in the morning.

Vicky reluctantly agreed, and we decided to go shortly after breakfast.

—

The next morning, I was still hurting, but I loaded up on pain meds and insisted that Vicky drive.

When we turned onto the county road, I pointed out where Rebekah's Lexus had been parked and where the abduction had occurred.

She got out and looked the area over. "It must have been a quick and efficient transition—and very organized to avoid being seen."

I pointed out Miller's Orchard, where Uncle Billy died, but I still didn't know the exact location.

As we turned into Billy's lane, the gate was closed and locked. I hobbled out and opened it.

Vicky drove us down the narrow lane. She was impressed with the beauty of the place and the old stone fence. "I wonder who built that fence. I've been told that most of the stacked stone fences in Kentucky were built by slaves before the Civil War. I wonder if that applies to Missouri as well."

"From what I've read, the Irish didn't own slaves, but that doesn't mean that somebody else in the area didn't. A fence like that would have taken a lot of manual labor."

The front door of the house was locked, but I knew that the back door often didn't close fully and usually could be pushed open even if locked. I was right, and I walked through and opened the front door for Vicky.

I showed her Billy's Bible, the sermon notes on slavery, and the brochures outlining the KGC material. She thumbed through it all, and then asked, "What's this?"

"We assume it is the guest registry for the KGC meetings," I said.

She sat down at the kitchen table and started reading through the names. "Have you read this?"

"Not really, it's just a list of names."

"In April, about 90 percent of the signees were couples. The five singles all have interesting names. They all have first and last names that start with the letter J: Jamison Jones, Jeremy Johnston, Jeremiah Jensen, Jenny Jefferson, and—"

"I recognize the name that is fourth from the bottom: Jerry Jives." I told her about the phone call to the office and the break-ins that happened early the next morning.

"Melinda doesn't fully agree with me yet, but I think I can prove that the action arm of the KGC, the group that calls themselves the Order, all use stage names or company names. It's as if they take on new identities when they enlist. Famous people do it all the time. Elton John's real name was Reginald Kenneth Dwight. Doesn't flow very well, does it? Alan Alda's real name was Alphonso Joseph D'Abruzzo."

"I think I read somewhere that Ringo Starr's real name was Richard Starkey. I think I get the point, but why do the names all begin with J?"

She said, "Melinda really doesn't buy this either, but she will come around eventually. I think it's because they were fascinated with the old outlaw Jesse James. They desire to relate to his spirit or persona."

"That would explain why they like to come here," I said.

"Why is that?"

"Did I not tell you about the cave?" I realized that I hadn't mentioned the anchor symbol. "Come on. Follow me."

We left the house and started down the path to the barn. As we rounded the corner and saw the cave, I found the flashlight app and showed her the symbol. "Do you know what that is?"

"I assume it's an anchor," she said.

"We did too, but it's more than that. It's the double J brand with the second J reversed. It's the brand of Jesse James."

She looked at me with some suspicion, reached up, and traced it with her finger. Then she took out her phone and snapped a picture. I wasn't sure whether she believed me or not.

We walked down the fence to the hole. "When you said hole, I assumed you meant a shovel hole. I didn't know you meant a giant crater. What were they after?"

"I don't know—and I don't know if they found it."

Vicky's phone rang, and it startled both of us. She was correct; she did have service. She stepped outside of my hearing but just listened to the caller.

When we started back toward the farmhouse, she said, "That was Melinda. Norma knows more than she realized. Less than a year ago, the man she served needed to have a cancer in his throat removed. He was transferred to a small, private surgical clinic out in the middle of the desert in North Africa.

"She wasn't even sure what country they were in, but she was certain that it was about three hours south of Al Alamein, Egypt. We found a medical clinic that matches Norma's description from satellite images. We are watching it closely, but so far, there doesn't seem to be any suspicious activity. It is in Egypt. We might be able to secure legal access if we have time to go through the necessary administrative hoops."

—

As Vicky and I drove back to West Plains, she said, "Richard, are you a Christian?"

"Yes, I am. I was a pastor in a Christian congregation for many years."

"Yes, I saw that in your file, but I'm not sure that all pastors are really Christian believers."

"I understand. I've wondered the same thing. Faith isn't always a constant force. Things happen in life, and if a person is not careful, they can drift away. We can all get angry at God and find ourselves distant from Him. Pastors are not immune. In those seasons, we may or may not know who we really are—or where we stand in our faith."

"Have you ever drifted?" she asked.

"There have been a few times in my life. When my wife died of cancer, I drifted some, but I came back. What about you?"

"I was a Christian when I was in high school, but university and law school tend to beat it out of you—and now I've seen too much. Maybe I still believe a tiny bit, but I don't trust God anymore. I'm sure you remember the story of Joseph and Mary."

"Are you referring to the parents of Jesus?"

"Yes, to avoid Herod's henchmen, an angel came and warned Joseph and Mary to leave town."

"I know the Christmas story," I responded.

"I feel like I'm Joseph and Mary's neighbor, but no angel came and warned me."

I could feel her pain as she said it. "What happened?" I asked.

"I married my high school sweetheart, and in that first year of marriage, we had a baby girl. She was such a sweet baby. When she was five months old, she didn't wake up one morning. The doctors called it SIDS, sudden infant death syndrome. My husband lost it. He said things I know he didn't really mean, but he said them anyway. He blamed me. He said I wasn't a good mom. And then he left. He just packed his junk and left. He didn't even come to our baby's funeral. I haven't heard from him since—except to receive a divorce decree sent by his sleazy lawyer."

"I'm so sorry."

"I don't know if I drifted … or just turned my back and ran. I know too much. I've seen too much."

"I'll pray for you."

"No, you better pray for yourself—and pray for Rebekah. She's going to need it."

I didn't want to argue. The truth was that I agreed with her. Rebekah was going to need it.

As we drove back to West Plains, Vicky's phone rang again. She talked for a few seconds and then handed me her phone. "It's a doctor friend of Melinda's. She asked him to call you."

"Hello?" I said.

"Richard Dempsey, this is Dr. Gilbert Berry from Houston. I understand that you have some questions about heart transplants."

"Yes, I do. Can any heart organ be used for any needy recipient?"

"No, there are two basic requirements for matching. The donor's heart needs to closely match the recipient in physical size, and the blood type must be interchangeable. Some blood types can cross over, and a few cannot. AB blood type needs an AB organ, which is rare."

"How often are heart transplants done?"

"The number is growing worldwide, but in the States, about two thousand are performed per year. However, on any given day, there are about thirty-one hundred individuals waiting to receive a new heart. More than half of them have been waiting six months or longer. The best estimate is that twenty die every day who were on the waiting list in the States. I don't have the worldwide statistics."

I wanted to ask so much more, but I couldn't bring myself to form the words. "Thanks, for calling." I hung up.

Vicky said, "It's hard to wrap your head around, isn't it?"

CHAPTER 19

Dreams

I awoke the next morning with Richard on my mind. I missed his touch, but I went to the rooftop for my usual time alone. The early-morning lighting on the sand was particularly magnificent. My prayers that morning consisted mostly of the discipline of listening. I relaxed my heart and listened. The desert breeze almost had a song to it. I didn't hear God's voice, but I had a strong sense that whatever happened today, I would be in His arms.

When I went down for breakfast, I saw a blood pressure machine parked in the hallway, and I remembered what Richard had said about the blood pressure machine that was beside my hospital bed in Sicily. I turned it around, and sure enough, right on the back corner, there was an impression of a lion walking. The second I saw it, I felt even more at peace.

When I entered the cafeteria, Amira was already at our table. She waved at me and motioned for me to come over. I filled my breakfast plate and joined her. She clearly had something on her mind.

"Tell me about what it means to be a Christian," she blurted out with considerable excitement.

"For me, the Bible tells me that something was deeply wrong

between my heart and God's. So, He sent His Son, Jesus, who was crucified on a cross, but He didn't stay in the grave. He came back to life. His death and His resurrection opened the door for me to experience God's love and forgiveness. He did all of this for me because he loved me." I tried to keep it simple.

"We believe that Allah loves us too, but that's not discussed very often. We're told that Allah wants us to submit to him. He wants us to apologize to him when we fail, but forgiveness is never mentioned. I don't think Allah forgives."

"How are you to submit to Allah? Is there some special way to do it?" I asked.

"Yes, the five pillars. First is the testimony where we declare that there is no god but Allah—and Muhammad is his messenger. That's our testimony. We are supposed to recite it over and over.

"Then there's prayer. Five times a day, we are called to kneel and face the Kaaba. It's best to have the Quran read over you during this time if possible. Then there is the giving of alms, where you give to your mosque and to the poor. Then fasting during Ramadan. And lastly the hajj, or the pilgrimage. Those are the five pillars."

"I've never heard of the Kaaba. What is that?"

"I haven't been there yet. My dad said he would take me some time, but it's a big black box at a mosque in Mecca. It's a great honor to touch it, but mostly just men get to do that."

"It's a big black box?" I asked.

"My dad said that a long time ago, before Muhammad came, the desert peoples had three hundred and sixty different gods, but when Muhammad came, he told the people that this was wrong. He said that there was only one god, and all the other gods were just man-made idols, so they were all destroyed. Now there is just the one god, Allah, but he lives in a black box in Mecca."

"Allah lives in the black box?"

"I don't know for sure because we're told that Allah lives everywhere, but I guess the black box is his special home. I've only seen pictures of it.

"I've heard the Quran being read from a minaret at a mosque, but I can't understand it. I asked a Muslim friend of mine what it meant, and she said, 'It's better to not understand. You should just relax and allow the words to wash over you. It's not about understanding; it's about submitting to the words and sound.' I didn't understand what she meant.

"I asked my dad once what the imam was saying, and he told me not to try to understand, just bow to it. A friend of mine, the daughter of a mosque leader, told me that the key was to bow your head and your body. After that, it was fine to think about whatever else you wanted."

It took me a while to process all that we had talked about. That was a deep breakfast conversation.

—

At lunch, she joined me again and was eager to resume the conversation. "I hope you don't mind me asking my questions. I've never had this chance before," she said as she took her usual seat. "I've been thinking. We're taught that Jesus was a prophet like Muhammad, but Allah saved him from the cross and took him straight to heaven. Jesus' name is mentioned 187 times in the Quran, so he is important. He is called the great Muslim and the prophet who introduced the way for Muhammad to come. But he's not alive now. He died and went to heaven just like Muhammad died and went to heaven. Now our calling is to submit to Muhammad. The meaning of *Muslim* is to submit or bow."

"In the United States, we don't have the opportunity to meet Muslims like you," I said.

"What do you mean?"

"Our view of Islam is tainted by radicals who hijacked airplanes and crashed them into buildings to kill as many as possible. Or by those who strap on bombs and try to blow up as many innocent people as they can."

"I know. I'm sorry. On the day that the airplanes crashed, I was just a little girl, but Muslims all over our city were dancing and celebrating because so many Americans died. I asked my dad, who did not celebrate, why everybody was having a party. He told me that many believe America is our enemy, but he didn't believe that. He is in business with many Americans, but Americans confuse me."

"America sometimes confuses me too."

"We are taught that America is a Christian nation, but most American television can't be watched in the Muslim world because so much of it is immoral and impure. My dad doesn't want me to watch any of it, but sometimes when I'm in a hotel alone, I've watched some. Men say horrible things and women dress with no thought of modesty. My dad loves American football, but he refuses to watch it because on the sidelines are beautiful women dancing with hardly any clothes."

"I agree. American television is confusing. America was built upon Christian principles, but not all Americans are Christian."

She responded with her teenage innocence, "Americans can choose to not be Christians?"

I nodded.

"In most Muslim countries, if you choose not to be a Muslim you could be punished or worse."

"There are different types of Muslims aren't there?" I asked.

"Yes, but basically just two. There are the Shi'a and the Sunni. We are Sunni, but I don't really know the difference. My dad says it's like going into an ice-cream shop. Some people prefer chocolate, and others prefer pistachio. It's still ice cream, but they don't taste the same. Aren't there different flavors of Christianity?"

"Yes, there are. There are many."

"There are two kinds of Muslims because when Muhammad died, he didn't tell anybody who was in charge, and the two sides started arguing. I don't understand that. Maybe I'm too young. Muslims believe that Allah is in absolute control, so I don't understand why we don't just let Allah be in charge. Don't Christians believe that your God is in absolute control?"

"Some do; some don't. Most believe that God gave us free will to make choices for ourselves."

"Is that what you believe?"

"I believe that God has a beautiful plan for me. If I choose to follow His plan, my life will be fulfilled. If I don't, then I will bring misery upon myself. Jesus talked about two doors."

"Allah says there is only one door, his door. Everything that happens to me is Allah's will. I just need to submit to his way, and I will find peace. In the end, Allah will look at the scales. My good deeds will be on one side, and my bad deeds will be on the other. Whichever weighs the most sends me to heaven or hell."

"What are good deeds?"

"Doing the five pillars."

As I listened to her, I realized that she was very interested in the things of faith, but her understanding of her Muslim faith was very simplistic. Most of what she knew came directly from her father. I wondered what he would say if he found out about these conversations and her questions about Christianity.

"Rebekah, why are you here?"

"I'm not sure. No one has told me why I'm here. Why are you here?"

"Because I'm going to die if I don't get a new heart. My dad said that I've had a bad heart since I was born, but now I'm old enough to handle the surgery. The doctors said that I needed to be at least sixteen years old. My dad said that I would be here until a heart has been found for me."

As the words came from her innocent lips, I suddenly knew. I knew what the plan for me included. I knew that in the human trafficking world, I had a special code. I wanted to run. I wanted to hide. But when I looked at Amira, I knew she didn't know. She didn't know what I knew.

"I have to go," I said, and I left the cafeteria, trying not to break out into a run or fall apart in tears. I went straight to the rooftop. The initial heat was almost overpowering, but I scooted one of the chairs to the small area of shade behind the staircase entrance. I sat down and began to cry. *How can this be?* But the longer I cried, the more I kept thinking about Amira. *She is a special young lady—with a special purpose in life. She is not far from the kingdom, and I have grown to love her.*

Then I thought about Stephen. He was stoned to death, but another young man was watching his execution from the sidelines. His name was Saul, who later became Paul, and he became one of the greatest apostles in the church. Stephen's death touched the next generation. How would my death influence the next generation? I didn't know. But if this was God's plan, then I was ready. I was ready—or was I?

I had no appetite for supper. I just didn't want to look Amira in the eyes. I stayed in my room and just sat and watched the wind begin to blow outside. The sand was starting to move. It was moving in sheets as the winds increased. It looked nasty. It felt nauseating even from the protection of my room.

Before it got dark, one of the nurses came in. It wasn't the usual nurse who checked on me. In fact, this was the first time this nurse had ever spoken to me. She wanted to know if I was feeling well and why I hadn't come for supper. She took my blood pressure and then drew a blood sample. I asked her why she needed blood, but she really didn't give a clear answer. I knew why. Their plans needed me to be healthy. I noticed that she avoided making eye contact, but she asked if I desired to have a meal brought to the room. I declined.

Sleep wouldn't come. The wind continued to blow. Even in the dark, I couldn't see the lighted main gate due to the blowing sand. The yard light over the guardhouse was just a dim red orb, just barely visible. Even inside, I could feel it in my lungs.

At about eleven o'clock that night, the nurse returned and handed me a breathing mask to wear. She pointed to the window and the blowing sand. She said for me to wear it until it quit blowing.

Sometime in the early morning, it finally did ease, but dust was still hanging in the air. My rooftop devotional hour wasn't possible, so I stayed in my room. When it came time for breakfast, I had to force myself to go down the hall to the cafeteria.

The cook waved her hands as if to slap the dust out of the air. She was attempting to be humorous. Lids covered the food entrees, but the cook walked down the line, opening each dish and allowing me to help myself.

I smiled and thanked her.

After I found my seat, I prepared myself for Amira. I was watching for her, but when I saw her, I knew she had been crying. Her face was red, and her eyes were swollen. Her eyes reflected a pain deeper than the blowing sand. I knew that she knew.

She came in and sat down in her usual spot without speaking. We didn't speak until her plate was delivered—and we were alone. She opened her mouth as if she was going to say something several times, but each time, she choked it back. After she finally composed herself, she said, "Have you ever had a dream?"

I nearly fell backward. That was not what I was expecting to hear, but I said, "Yes, I have."

"Have you had lots of dreams?" she asked.

"Yes, but most of them I can't remember."

"Have you ever had a dream that you knew you would never forget?" she asked.

I nodded and thought about my cave dream, but before I could speak, she said, "I can't tell anyone about this but you. I'm afraid to tell anyone but you. I had a dream last night." She choked up again and fought back the tears.

It was agonizing, but I had to wait.

"In a dream last night, I met Jesus. He was holding a little lamb and brushing dried mud off its feet. Then Jesus saw me, and He put the little lamb down, patted it on the head, and reached over and picked me up, just as He had the lamb.

"He started washing the dirt off my feet. He was crying, and He was using his tears to wash my hands and arms. He said that He loved me, and that I was a princess with a heart of gold." She started crying again, harder than before.

I walked around the table and put my arms around her. As I held her, I glanced around to see who was watching, but no one was in the room but us.

Eventually, she took a napkin and wiped her face. "Excuse me. I'll be right back."

When she came back, her face was still flushed, but she was more in control. "I don't know why I was crying so hard. It wasn't fearful. It was the most wonderful experience of my life. I feel special. I feel wonderful. What am I supposed to do now?"

"What do you want to do?" I asked.

"I want to give my heart to Jesus, but can I? I'm a Muslim. Allah will be angry. My father will be furious. Jesus can't receive my heart because it's broken. It's been broken since I was a baby!"

"I wish I had a Bible. Then I could read it to you. But in Jeremiah, God promised that He will give us a new heart."

"A new heart? I need a new heart," she said with firmness.

"A friend of mine was talking to a friend of hers who had visited Jericho in Israel. She was told that several Muslims in Jericho have been having dreams, dreams like yours, dreams about Jesus. She said that groups of Muslims are now becoming Christians because of those dreams. They're meeting in their homes and reading their Bibles together. She also said that she had heard that the same thing has been happening in Damascus and Beirut."

"So, I'm not the only Muslim having dreams about Jesus?"

"No, you're not."

"But even if I was the only Muslim in the entire world who has had this dream, it wouldn't matter. I met Jesus. He came to me. He held me like a little lamb. He washed my feet, He washed my hands, and He cried tears over me. Allah never cries. Jesus cried for me. I will never be a good Muslim again. I can't."

I held her hand across the table.

She took both of my hands and said, "Help me. I don't know what to do now."

"Just tell Jesus what's in your heart."

"And Jesus will listen to me? He will hear me?"

"Yes."

She said, "Jesus … thank You for picking me up and holding me. Thank You for telling me You love me. Thank You for crying over me. I want to love You forever. I want to belong to You forever. I want to be a Christian." Then she looked up at me. "Is that good enough?"

"Oh my, yes! That was beautiful," I said.

We both stood and met at the end of the table. We hugged, and we both wept. I thought I had already used up all the tears I had, but I found a whole new bucketload. Before this moment, I looked into Amira's eyes and saw poise and grace—almost royalty. Now I looked and saw a joy deeper than any joy I had ever seen. And I was filled with her joy.

CHAPTER 20

Parched Land

Vicky dropped me off at the Hampton. As I walked into the lobby, Sheriff Nelson was reading a newspaper on a couch. He stood and walked toward me. We went into the conference room and closed the door.

"I received a phone call this morning. It was from a member of the KGC."

"What did he want?" I asked.

"The gentleman told me that since Billy is no longer available, they have canceled October's outing. The farm is a special place for them, and they hoped that, at some time, they will be able to return for their biannual meetings, but for now, they needed to cancel. He told me to convey his concern for Rebekah."

"Thanks for letting me know, but how did he know about Rebekah's abduction?"

"Now that you mention it, he didn't say," said the sheriff.

"May I ask you something?"

He nodded. His face didn't seem to reflect that same harshness as it did the first time we met at Lucille's.

"When Rebekah and I first met you, you strongly suggested that we sell the farm to the potential buyer who Mr. Smith represented. Why? Why did you care what we did with the farm?"

"I still think that would have made life easier for you two, but I was pleased when I heard of your plan to receive bids and give others a chance to purchase it. I started to put in a bid myself. I have gotten to know several of the KGC members over the years. I think they would have taken good care of it, and I thought they should be able to buy it."

"So, you believe the KGC is a good organization?" I asked.

"Mostly … there are a few individuals who show up that I have questions about, but the group itself is decent. They discuss how to turn their millions into additional millions. I wish I had a million to try to double. I assume you haven't examined the bids that have come in."

"No, Rebekah is the owner. Until I get her back, I'm not sure what to do."

"Have you learned anything else about Rebekah?" he asked.

"It's complicated, maybe, but nothing for sure yet. I'm waiting to hear what is next."

"It's a difficult situation. I wish I could be of more help. The abductors were really organized. They probably had her out of state before we ever discovered her parked car," he said.

"Probably so, but I have another question. While we were home in Kentucky, somebody came onto Uncle Billy's farm with a backhoe. They dug a hole along that back fence, a big hole. Do you know anything about that?"

"A big hole, like somebody was digging up something?" he asked.

"Yes," I said.

"There have always been rumors floating around about a treasure buried out there somewhere, a treasure from the loot of Jesse James, but as far as I know, nothing has ever been found. Billy never found anything except nails and a few coins. I think the state pestered him about that, but why didn't you call me about this?"

"Nothing else was damaged. They cut the lock off the gate, hauled in a big backhoe on a trailer, and then dug their hole. Apparently, they knew where to dig. Rebekah and I discussed calling you, but since we discovered the hole, we both have been somewhat busy."

"I understand. I can snoop around. There aren't that many backhoes available in Howell County for hire. If one of our local contractors rented one out, I think I can track down who it might have been. I'll let you know."

—

After Sheriff Nelson left, I went to my room and stretched out on the bed. I ordered a pizza to be delivered from the same place Rebekah and I had eaten. After it arrived, I only ate a few slices. It wasn't as appetizing without Rebekah to enjoy it with. It just reminded me of her.

On Monday morning, I heated some of the leftover pizza in the microwave and turned on the TV. I usually liked to catch up on the major news events each day, but I hadn't watched much television since Rebekah and I watched the Jesse James documentary together, unless the Weather Channel counted. Frustrated that nothing new was on the news, I shut it off and opened my Bible.

I had been reading the psalms for several weeks before the tree fell on me and Rebekah disappeared, so I opened to where I had left off: Psalm 143. My mind was so unfocused that I didn't fully catch what the psalm of David was trying to say, but several phrases jumped off the page: "Lord, hear my prayer, listen to my cry, come to my relief, my soul thirsts for you like a parched land, answer me quickly, do not hide your face, and let the morning bring me word." Those phrases pounded like a kettledrum upon my heart. The phrase about a "parched land" seemed to be especially important, but I didn't know why. *Was Egypt a parched land?*

I realized there was no reason to stay in West Plains. *My*

current world revolves around answering my phone. I can do that from anywhere. I need to make an appointment with my doctor to examine my arm. The foundation will run for a short time without me, and I have nothing to do here living in a hotel. I was ready to go home, but I hated the thought of driving home to an empty house. As I pondered the question of what I should do, there was a tap on my door. It was Henry.

"The sheriff told me what happened to you and Rebekah. I am so sorry. I wanted to come by and see you."

"Thanks, Henry. How was the wedding in Arkansas?"

"It was just a wedding. Families are weird. While I tried to stay out of the way, I thought about an old Red Skelton story he once told about a farmer who had two daughters. A young man came one day and said he was there to see one of his daughters. The farmer said, 'Which one? Lassie or Mildred?' The young man was confused and said, 'Lassie is a dog,' but the farmer responded, 'Wait till you see Mildred.'"

"So, your wife's cousin was Mildred?" I asked.

"No, she looked more like Lassie," he said snickering.

"That's terrible, Henry."

"I know. I just heard about all that's happened to you while I was gone, and I thought you needed a laugh. How's the arm?"

"Broken."

"And there is no word about Rebekah? She is such a sweet lady."

"Not yet," I said.

"Is there anything I can do to help? Sheriff Nelson told me that, due to the circumstances, the bids haven't been opened yet."

"No, without Rebekah, I'm unsure as to what to do."

"I understand. Are you planning to stay out at the farm while you wait?"

"No, without phone service, I can't afford to be out there. I'm actually thinking about going home to Lexington."

"If you would like, I'll check on the place from time to time," Henry said.

"I would appreciate that."

"I guess Billy's special friends will not be coming this year," he said.

"No, I don't think so."

—

I walked Henry out to the parking lot, and I saw the Lexus. I hadn't been in it since before Rebekah's disappearance. I checked the dent on the back bumper. *That must have been terrifying for Rebekah. I wonder how they got her to stop.*

In the back seat, I noticed the sack where the sheriff said he had found my phone. The door unlocked with the touch of my hand since the keys were in my pocket, and I leaned in to see what else was in the sack. It was the walnut fruit bowl that Rebekah had bought at the Downtown Antique Mall. I slipped it from the sack and examined it. It had been hand-carved, not turned on a lathe. A closer examination revealed the faint carving marks. It was indeed a unique item. *I wonder if Rebekah has a spot for it at home or whether she was planning to take it to the shop to resell. I miss her.*

As I put the bowl back into the sack, I noticed that the bottom of the sack contained a bloodstained jacket and shirt. *Those are the clothes Rebekah was wearing in the ambulance with me.* In my mind, I could still hear her screams when she found me under the tree.

After returning everything to the sack, I thought about what I ought to do. First, I needed to call Melinda at Polaris and ask if there was any reason I shouldn't drive home. *Can I even drive?* I stretched my leg. It was still sore, but I thought I could probably drive. As an experiment, I took off walking at a fast pace around the block. By the time I made the full circle around the hotel, my hip was seriously hurting. *At least I made it. Perhaps I should try again later in the afternoon.*

It was approaching lunchtime, and I wanted to see how it felt to drive. I eased myself behind the wheel and tapped the brake. I knew I could drive; I just hoped that no one pulled too quickly out in front of me.

As I drove toward the center of town, I saw a dry cleaner. The sight of the establishment triggered a plan, and I turned in. I removed Rebekah's jacket and shirt from the sack and carried them inside. The sweet lady inside assured me that she could remove the stains and would continue to pray for both of us. Having her clothes cleaned was an offensive action that told my heart she would be coming home.

I drove to town and saw a parking spot across from Lucille's. *Why not?* I parked and shuffled across the street to the famed café. As I opened the front door the usual café chatter almost immediately grew silent. Stepping inside, I realized that every eye in the place was directed at me. Then it started. They started clapping, and then it got louder. Then they all stood and applauded with cheers and whistles. The waitress met me and led me to the only empty table as they continued to applaud. *West Plains is truly a unique community.*

As I ordered and ate, nearly half the folks stopped by my table before leaving with words of encouragement and promises to pray. So many came by that I found it hard to eat my lunch, but eventually it slowed, and I was able to finish.

The waitress refilled my drink, leaned over, and said, "Your lunch is on the house today. We're all praying for you and Rebekah."

I left a healthy tip and walked out a bit straighter and perhaps taller.

—

As I drove back to the Hampton, my phone rang. It was Micah, my daughter. She wanted me to hear her baby laughing. I think she really was just checking to see how I was doing and wondering if we have heard anything. I brought her up to date and thanked her for calling.

Walking down the quiet Hampton hallway, I felt overwhelmed.

I wanted a change of scenery. I decided to relax this afternoon and get up and start driving east in the morning. I called Sheriff Nelson and told him my plan. He didn't argue. I would call Melinda from the road if she hadn't called me by then.

Sleep was hard to find, and before sunrise, I crawled behind the Lexus's wheel and pointed it east. My plan was to stop whenever I needed to. I had no schedule to maintain. The forest looked barren as I drove. I missed the leaves. I missed Rebekah's excitement about the beautiful fall leaves. I called Melinda and left a message concerning my decision.

I wasn't planning to, but I turned toward the Irish Wilderness's main entrance. There wasn't a single car in the parking lot. I found my winter coat and started limping into the wilderness. The sign said that Brawley Pond was less than half a mile away. The more I walked, the better my back and hip felt. I found a comfortable stop to relax at the pond and watched as fish were dimpling during a morning hatch.

Wanting to stay longer, I noticed that my phone didn't have service, so I started back reluctantly. The short hike had my blood flowing, and I felt better. I drove for some time. Without tracking my progress, I found myself crossing the Mississippi River in the early afternoon.

Rebekah wouldn't have approved, but I stopped at Kentucky Hillbilly BBQ and had a plate of ribs. The food was good, but I realized that I was subconsciously dragging my feet in more ways than one. I wasn't sure how I would feel about the empty house. To be safe, I stopped at a Holiday Inn in Paducah. The next morning, I got on the interstate and continued to Lexington. I never heard back from Melinda. In my mind, I didn't want to disturb her important business. *If there is anything new, she will call me.*

I stopped and picked up Goose before pulling into our driveway. She was full of energy and zeal. I threw the ball for her to retrieve several times, and then I finally entered the quiet house. I turned on the TV and cranked up the volume. I wasn't watching anything, but I needed the noise.

Goose couldn't bring herself to leave my side. She knew my heart was heavy, but even with her "human traits," she couldn't understand why Rebekah wasn't at home with us. The few times she left me, she simply went and checked on Rebekah's favorite chair in the den.

I spent most of the night in my recliner. When I turned off the TV sometime in the early morning, the house became quiet. My phone was quiet.

On Thursday and Friday, I piddled around the house, organized the garage, and played with Goose. I called Mary Ann and let her know that I was in town, but I wasn't sure when or if I would come into the office. She insisted that nothing demanded my attention and encouraged me to take it easy. Not being able to do anything but wait was painful.

Two of the foundation's board members brought me supper on Friday evening. It surprised me and I expressed my appreciation, but after they left, I put it all in the refrigerator. *Maybe I will be hungry tomorrow.*

On Saturday morning, my phone rang. It was Melinda.

"We think we have been watching Rebekah," she said.

"What? Where?" My heart started thumping wildly.

"Bill with the CIA has connected us with their eyes from space. The surgical clinic where Norma said she and her master stayed while he had surgery last year has been located. It's out in the middle of the Egyptian desert, and we have started watching it very closely. We believe that she was delivered by helicopter late Tuesday afternoon her time. Satellite images can't confirm facial features, but this morning, a woman went to the rooftop of the clinic and sat for about an hour before sunrise. Does that sound like something Rebekah would do?"

"Yes, it does. That sounds exactly like something Rebekah would do. And no one is guarding her?"

"The clinic is located within a fenced compound. There are guards at the main gate, and there are several medical staff present, but there doesn't seem to be much else to protect the compound. We are already talking with Egyptian authorities about the situation and what the various options might be."

Aren't the United States and Egypt on friendly terms?" I asked.

"Officially, yes, but unofficially, there are some issues. In 2011, there was a 'peaceful' revolution that ousted President Mubarak. The new regime claims to be a 'US-friendly' one, but in reality, they operate in fear of several terrorist organizations. The government's primary goal is not to aggravate the numerous splinter groups of the now-defunct Muslim Brotherhood."

"Sounds complicated," I said.

"It is extremely complicated. Egypt is controlled by the uber wealthy. Most of the general population lives in stark poverty, but the wealthy control the media, and they portray to the world that all is well in Egypt, when it is not. Al-Mulathameen, a terrorist group, is also known as the Brigade of the Masked Ones. They are supported by the Egyptian poor, and they keep the Egyptian government on edge."

"What can we do?" I asked.

"We are currently negotiating with the Egyptian authorities, but we must be careful and not reveal too much of our intelligence capacity. Dan Browning is leading our negotiating team. He has had past connections with Egypt, and I believe he will get us in. The Egyptian government denies that anything of this kind could be happening within their borders, and so far, they have refused to allow us to enter. We will continue to seek diplomatic channels, but we will be ready to go in if we must. If all the key players arrive, we will no longer have time to negotiate. We will go in immediately.

"The clinic's location may allow us to slip through the back door by way of Libya. If so, we could be in and out before either Libya or Egypt are aware of our presence. I don't ask this very often, but I suggest that you pray. This is going to be a difficult rescue mission if that's our only choice."

"I understand," I said, but I really didn't. My guts were flipping upside down.

"Richard, Bill is calling in. I'll let you know if something else of importance develops." Her phone went dead.

After lunch, I cleaned up my cooking mess. As I stepped into the den, the phone rang. It was Dr. Jeff Billingsly with the Mark Twain National Forest Regional office. He said, "I'm sorry to call your private number, but your assistant at the Polaris Foundation said that you would like to speak to me personally and gave me your number."

"I'm glad you called, but since my wife and I mailed that letter, there have been some developments. Rebekah has been abducted and is being held hostage."

"Oh my, that's horrible," he said.

"I'm sorry. I don't know how else to inform people. I'm still in shock myself. We really do want to talk to you, but until we get her home, there's not much I can do since she is the legal heir. I will call you when things are resolved."

"I'm so sorry. You can call whenever. I hope she is returned home quickly."

"Thank you."

Goose and I went for a walk in the late afternoon. When we returned, I took a pain med. I didn't take any during the drive from Missouri, but I needed one now. I was trying to remember the list of side effects the pharmacist had warned me about. With that in mind, I called my doctor and made a follow-up appointment in two weeks. I trusted that the arm was healing well. While I was still holding the phone, it rang again.

It was a friend from church. They wanted to bring me another meal. I agreed without telling them that I had an untouched meal in the refrigerator. I supposed the whole church knew about Rebekah by now, although I hadn't heard from the pastor yet. *He may not know I'm home. Everyone assumes the pastor already knows everything when, in all actuality, he might be the very last to be told.* I thought about calling him, but it was getting late on Saturday afternoon. *I'll call him after church in the morning.*

About the time Goose was fully asleep, the phone rang again. It was Melinda.

"Richard, yesterday afternoon, we watched, by satellite, a caravan of three Hummers. The three vehicles arrived at the clinic, and two women were unloaded. We can't be certain, but it appears that the two women consisted of Khalid Bin Muthanna's daughter and her private nurse. The pieces are coming together. All they need now is the surgeon and his medical team. When they arrive, we will only have a few hours to respond."

She continued without allowing me to react. "According to the Beaujon Hospital in Paris, Dr. Dominique Leblanc has canceled his appointments and surgeries beginning next Monday. The official hospital statement is that Dr. Leblanc is taking his surgical team on a week's vacation. We're planning to stop him at the airport, but we may not be able to do anything except slow down his travel plans."

"Melinda, what should I do? I drove home to Lexington this week. Should I stay here and just wait?"

"I was going to suggest that you catch a flight into Tel Aviv and join the team in the Mediterranean off the coast of Egypt. I can't take you with us on the extraction mission, if that is what ends up happening, but I can't imagine Rebekah wouldn't like to see your smiling face first and foremost when she is safe. Are you up to travel?"

"I think so. I will figure out travel details and let you know my ETA."

"Richard, there are still several major hurdles for us to jump, but the organization has no way of knowing that we have already located where Rebekah is being held. We believe that we have the surprise factor on our side. Norma has been a tremendous asset, and because of that, our chances look good. I'm firmly convinced that we're going to be able to bring Rebekah home safely."

"Thank you, Melinda. I hope we get to meet Norma sometime and thank her in person," I said.

"That is certainly our goal."

CHAPTER 21

Shouts

It was lunchtime, but I wasn't hungry. With all my heart, I didn't want to look Amira in the eyes, but I was torn. I wanted to see her. I wanted to hug her, but I just didn't want her to know what I knew. At last, I decided to go. The cafeteria was quiet. My friend, the cook, was busy in the back, so I helped myself without her. I sat down facing the cafeteria door, instead of toward the window and main gate, but Amira didn't show. I waited. I ate a few bites, but mostly I just watched for her. She didn't come.

No one explained anything. The cook stayed busy. The two nurses were nowhere to be seen, so I walked back to my room. I sat in the recliner and just relaxed, if indeed that was possible. I prayed for Richard. I prayed for Amira. I prayed for myself.

In the middle of the afternoon, one of the nurses came in and pretended to check my vitals. She never spoke and never looked me directly in the eyes. When she was finished, she closed the curtains, causing the room to become dark. She knew. She also probably knew that I knew. I felt for her.

About an hour later, I heard a vehicle pull up to the main gate. I lifted the corner of the curtain and peeped out. It was a large recreational vehicle in a deep gold color. It had stopped at the main gate, but then it moved on through and pulled into the corner of the compound and parked.

The door opened, and out poured the travelers. There were at least eight, plus the driver, and all were wearing medical smocks of various pastel colors. Several large trunks of equipment were also unloaded and carried inside the clinic. All eight of them seemed to be in great spirits. I knew what they were here for. Watching them laugh and tease each other was painful.

A few minutes before supper, Amira knocked on my door. She was wearing her traditional garb in dark green. It was obvious that she had been crying. Her usual bright and joyful face had disappeared. We hugged each other until she stopped crying.

I sat back down in the recliner, and she sat down on the foot of the bed. *This is not going to be an easy conversation.*

"Do you feel well?" she asked.

"Yes," I responded.

"I heard two of the new nurses talking. I know. You don't have to hide it anymore," she said as she wiped away another tear.

I handed her a tissue from the side table.

"How long have you known that you have cancer?" she asked. It seemed painful for her to utter those words.

I didn't answer her question. I was at a loss for words.

"My dad just called, and he told me that it was true. He said you were dying, and after ..." She choked back more tears.

I had the strangest mix of emotions. There was anger, white-hot anger that they were planning to do this horrible deed and were lying about it to Amira and apparently to some of the staff. There was fear. I wasn't afraid of death, but dying like this? How were they planning to do it? But there was also grief. *Can one grieve for themselves? I hurt for Richard.*

"My dad is planning to come sometime tomorrow," she said.

She meant it with innocence, but for me, I heard the alarm clock set. The tick of the countdown clock began.

"You have never mentioned your mom. Is she coming too?" I asked.

"No, my mom died when I was a little girl. I think she had cancer too, but my dad never wanted to talk about it. I don't really remember her, but I would like to think that she was a lot like you." She reached over and took my hand.

"How long have you had cancer?" she asked again.

My mind was still reeling, but I suddenly realized that she deserved to know the truth. If I didn't tell her now, she would never know. I tried to form the words to spill the information, but just as I opened my mouth, the door to my hospital room burst open.

Amira's personal nurse entered and started shouting at her. Amira stood and shouted back. The two of them shouted back and forth as if I wasn't even in the room. They finally left together, still snapping at each other with serious anger. I could hear the Arabic word battle until it finally faded down the hallway. It appeared that the nanny didn't think Amira should be in my room talking with me. I was numb. I was completely drained.

In a few minutes, a nurse brought me a plate with supper. It was the same nurse who had been in earlier to close the curtain. She still didn't speak, and she still avoided any eye contact. When she left, she locked my door with a key from the hallway. I was locked up. I could hear the ticking clock growing louder.

My mind continued to race. *What kind of doctor would do this? How will he do it? Will it hurt? Will Amira ever know? Will Richard find out the truth? What will they do with me after they take what they want?* The room felt cold. I felt cold. I peered out at the sand dunes. *Are those dunes going to be my grave?*

All night long, I thought I could hear footsteps outside my room, but no one ever came. I was sleepy, but my eyes stayed wide-open. I thought I could hear a wind starting to howl outside, but what difference did that make? I stayed in the recliner all night and used the bedspread to defend myself from the chill.

I left the curtain closed just as the nurse had left it, but I regularly looked outside. *Is the wind still blowing? Is the sun starting to rise?* I wanted to spend some time on the rooftop, but with my door locked, that obviously wasn't allowed.

Close to what I thought to be breakfast time, I heard the faint sound of footsteps. They stopped at my door. My heart stopped beating. The lock turned. The door was pushed open. It was the nurse. She was carrying a breakfast tray. She looked at me with curiosity that I wasn't in bed, but she didn't say anything.

As she poured the orange juice, I heard a shout. It was more like a scream. Footsteps came running down the hall.

There were other shouts back and forth. An alarm went off. The nurse pouring the orange juice turned and ran, spilling most of the juice. Her face had turned almost white. She didn't lock my door. She didn't even close it.

A medical alarm continued sounding. Shouts continued. It was originating from down the other hallway, Amira's hallway. I eased out of the recliner and walked down the hall to the corner. I peered around the corner looking. Nurses were running back and forth, in and out of Amira's room.

Two of the new nurses stopped without looking in my direction. They were closer to the corner than the others. In English, one of them said to the other, "How did she find those pills? Do we even know what kind of pills they were?"

The other nurse said, "They're pumping her stomach right now, but it's probably too late. She has already slipped into a coma. She probably will not wake up."

"Poor child, she was such a sweet young lady. I think her dad was planning to come today. I don't want to be around when he gets here."

I couldn't listen anymore. *Did Amira really do this? I didn't even tell her the truth. Did she find out some other way?* I walked back to my room and closed my door. I wanted to lock it myself; instead, I opened the curtain.

The colors of the morning sun shimmered over the sand dunes. I drank the partial cup of orange juice. I wiped away a tear. I thought of slipping up the stairs to the rooftop, but the blowing wind changed my mind. I sat down to wait, and I felt the Lord's presence enter the room. I had nothing to say, but I could feel the warmth of His breath on the back of my neck.

By midmorning, the hospital had grown quiet. I didn't hear any more running footsteps or harsh words. It was eerily quiet. I had been praying for my friend, but I wanted to know what had happened. *Did she really overdose on meds? Was she still in a coma? Would she survive?* Twice, I started to walk down the hall to find out, but both times, I backed out. It wasn't my business—or was it?

At the usual lunchtime, the nurse invited me to follow her. I hadn't showered or dressed, but I put on my robe and slippers and followed her anyway. She led me to the cafeteria. It was empty. She motioned for me to help myself, and then she turned and left. I helped myself. I even took some of the hot peppered dish that the cook had warned me of before. It was hot, but it was not as hot as some things I had eaten in my life.

I went back toward my room, pausing at the corner, and I listened. I couldn't hear anything. It was as quiet as a graveyard. I wanted to cry, but I couldn't. Back in my room, I took a much-needed shower and dressed. *What comes next for me? It's clear that I was taken so that Amira could have my heart. Now what will they do with me?* It was horrifying to think that I was going to be used according to their plans. It was equally horrifying to think that I was of no use to them at all now.

Supper was identical. The cafeteria was empty except for me. I still didn't know what had happened. As I sat in my usual seat, facing the outside window, I saw the medical team carrying their suitcases and gear to the golden RV. They were quiet and businesslike. Their spirits were down.

The bus driver started the engine to get it warmed up. In a few minutes, the entire team loaded up, and then the RV pulled out of the compound. It disappeared behind the sand dunes almost immediately, but its dust plume could be seen for several miles. I hated to admit it, but I was glad to see them go.

Back in my room, I sat down in the recliner. I hadn't been there long when I heard the distinctive chop of a helicopter. It was louder from inside than I had imagined. It was obviously landing on the clinic's helipad. I could hear the slowing of the rotors and the door to the stairs opening.

As far as I knew, the only one they had been expecting was Amira's father. There were at least five men dressed in white Muslim garb who passed by my window without looking inside.

I remembered what I heard the nurse say about not wanting to be there when Amira's father arrived. I assumed she got her wish, thinking about the timing of the RV's departure.

Nearly an hour passed without a sound coming from down the hallway, but then I heard it. Footsteps—at least two sets, perhaps more.

My door slowly opened, and the nurse entered. Her face was ashen and expressionless. She looked me square in the eye and said, "Rebekah, this is Khalid Bin Muthanna, Amira's father." With that introduction, she stepped out of the room.

I stood, and Amira's father entered. He was dressed in a white robe with a black shirt. His head was covered in a white headscarf with a black band holding it in place. His skin was dark, and his black beard was neatly trimmed. His presence was striking.

I didn't know what to say.

But he knew what he wanted to say. His eyes were on fire. He was in control of himself, but I could feel his red-hot anger from across the room. "You tricked my Amira. You told her lies!"

I shook my head. "I never told your daughter a lie. Never!"

"How do you explain this?" he said as he held up a letter-sized handwritten note.

"I don't know what that is."

"It's my daughter's suicide letter. In it, she told me that she would rather die and be with *Jesus* than live in my world." He spoke the word "Jesus" as if he had a bitter taste in his mouth.

"Your daughter came to me with questions. I answered her questions, but then she came to me and told me that she had a dream that Jesus came and picked her up and held her."

His face tightened even more, and he took a step toward me.

I was afraid I had said too much. I understood why Amira loved him—and also why she was terrified of him. He might have been the most formidable man I had ever faced.

His right hand made a fist, but it stayed by his side. Then he said, "You killed her. Your lies took her life from me."

"I'm so sorry. No one told me that she died. She was my friend. I am so sorry for your loss."

If the nurse had not been standing just outside the door, I'm not sure what he would have done next. From the look in his eyes, I knew what he wanted to do. He continued to glare at me with a pure fiery hatred, but I refused to look away. I think that made him angrier. Then, without another word, he dropped the crumbled letter and turned and walked out of my room. In less than five minutes, I heard the helicopter fire up on the rooftop. A few minutes later, I heard it lift off.

The nurse stepped inside my room, looking somewhat fearful but relieved, and looked at me with her eyes wide-open. "That was terrifying. Nobody stands up to Khalid Bin Muthanna. Nobody looks him in the eye, especially not a woman—and an American woman at that." Her body was trembling. "I haven't told anyone else this. Amira took the pills from my locker. It was my fault. I don't know how my locker was left unlocked."

"Her father said she was dead. Is she? Please tell me. She was my friend."

"She is dead to her father. He declared her '*murtad*.' He disowned her, but—medically speaking—she is still in a coma. It appears that her organs are shutting down. We tried to pump her stomach, but

I'm afraid we were too late. Please don't tell anybody about the pills." She wiped away multiple tears.

I nodded, but I wanted to cry.

Just as she left my room, I heard footsteps and a man shouting in English. It was an order for her to get down on the floor. No shots were fired, but she dropped to the floor. I could see her feet in front of my door.

CHAPTER 22

Tears

I was able to secure a flight from Lexington to Tel Aviv by way of Newark for the next evening. My back and leg both ached, and I dreaded the flight. However, the thought of not going to join the team never crossed my mind. I wanted to be there. I had to be there.

The flight from Lexington was uneventful, but I had an hour layover in Newark. As I was waiting the El Al flight, Melinda called and said, "Our team has stopped Dr. Leblanc at the Paris Charles de Gaulle Airport. They are interviewing him now, but they don't think they can hold him. He claims that he doesn't know where the heart organ for the transplant will be coming from and that he rarely knows that personal information for any of his transplant surgeries. He claims that the source of the organs is neither his business nor his responsibility. There are organizations that seek to match the organs with the transplant recipients. They are the groups that are responsible. Most of the time, they do a great job. He says that every transplant surgeon must learn to trust this supply line.

"When we told him about Rebekah, he flat-out refused to believe us. He hasn't broken any laws at this point, but in checking his credentials, we think we have delayed him long enough to miss his flight. The surgeon is the one missing piece. We must get there before he does. Egypt is still refusing to cooperate. They haven't closed the door completely, but we are running out of time. We're preparing for a rescue mission that will be ready as soon as the need demands. Time will be of the essence. We're going to secure Rebekah. Trust us, Richard. Have a good flight."

I told her about my ETA for Tel Aviv, and she told me that one of the team members would meet me at Ben Gurion.

Watching the El Al representative watch me hobble toward him, I wondered if he was even going to allow me to board; instead, he asked me what had happened. I gave him a brief account of my mishap with the tree and told him that I needed to meet my wife who would be waiting on me in Tel Aviv. He didn't ask any other questions, but he explained that the flight had a canceled seat in business class, and due to my situation, they would upgrade me.

I didn't argue, and I thanked him.

El Al's business class had reclining seats that laid completely back. Once we were in the air, I took a pain med and took advantage of the special seating. Twice, I got up and stretched, but for most of the flight, I was quite relaxed and comfortable.

According to the interactive flight map, we were less than twenty minutes from touchdown. The flight had been smooth, but I was anxious about what was next. Thumbing through the in-flight magazine, I stopped on an ad from the Israeli Tourism Board. Centered on the page was a lion image. That image brought peace to my nervous heart.

I saw Vicky waving at me as I stood at passport control, and since I hadn't brought any checked luggage, the two of us walked out of the airport rather quickly. A cab took us down to Joppa, and we boarded what appeared to be a commercial fishing yacht. On topside, there were the usual tools of the fishing trade, but once Vicky and I went below deck, I realized that not much fishing happened on this vessel.

There were satellite screens, computers, and various other

pieces of surveillance equipment that I didn't recognize, and then I saw Doug Douglas, the young FBI agent. He was dressed like a fisherman, but it was good to see him.

As we shook hands, he leaned over and said, "This hasn't been your typical kidnapping."

I nodded.

Vicky handed me her phone and said, "Melinda wants to talk to you."

"Did you have a good flight with the bum leg and the cast and all?" she asked.

"Yes, all went well. What happened with the Paris surgeon?" I asked.

"We delayed him long enough to make him angry, but he caught the next flight anyway. He's already in Cairo, waiting to be transferred to the clinic, but we think he just discovered that his surgical team has already left the clinic for some reason. We do not know why."

"What do you mean? What happened?" My mind was racing into panic mode.

"Something has certainly happened at the clinic that has changed the plans. We cannot tell what it is, but we need to get in and get Rebekah out as soon as possible. We have a team of five standing ready at El Alamein. I'm here with Bill Reynolds, along with three other very capable operatives, and we're waiting for a sandstorm to blow over. The plan is to fly low along the Egyptian and Libyan border. That way, we'll have a good chance of avoiding detection from either country. However, flying in the blowing sand is too risky."

"What is the forecast?"

"The wind should cease by morning. Our plans were to go in during the early morning darkness and wait about a mile from the clinic. We can cross the dunes by foot and catch the clinic totally by surprise. Once Rebekah is secured, the chopper can fly in and out in a matter of minutes. Unfortunately, the blowing sand has delayed our mission until daylight, but it is still workable."

"What do you mean that something has happened at the clinic?" I asked.

"We don't know. There was considerable activity this morning. They acted like it was a medical emergency, but we haven't been able to figure out what it has entailed. Rebekah missed her usual rooftop devotional time, but we don't know why. Perhaps it was just too windy, but it appears she is still in her room.

"A helicopter flew in and out about noon. We thought it might be our doctor coming in from Cairo, but it only stayed about forty-five minutes and left with all the individuals who arrived on it. It makes no sense. We still believe that we have the element of surprise on our side—unless the Egyptian government has tipped them off."

Our "fishing yacht" was traveling at full speed across the choppy Mediterranean Sea. Several dolphins were attempting to keep up with us, but they soon lost interest. The dark sky was clear, and the stars were bright. The only other vessel visible was a large oil freighter heading to ports unknown.

Our boat moved a mile off the coast of northern Egypt and proceeded to act like a charter fishing vessel. I watched the crew, but it was obvious that they weren't expecting to catch any fish unless one jumped on board by itself. It appeared that Doug Douglas knew his way around a charter fishing craft.

Vicky and I began watching the satellite screen. She pointed out what we were seeing, but it didn't make much sense to me. A voice over the radio informed us that the wind had abated enough to attempt the mission. I watched the helicopter lift off and move down the coastline to the Libyan border. We had no additional radio contact, and we lost satellite vision. Vicky explained that we would pick it back up before they arrived at their destination.

When the satellite came back online, we could see that the team was only a mile from the clinic where it set down in the sand. We saw the six team members moving quickly through the sand dunes and approaching the clinic. The air wasn't completely clear, but the wind had calmed.

The two main gate guards were caught unaware and were incapacitated without a shot being fired. Two other team members crossed the compound and climbed to the rooftop where the stair entrance opened near the helipad. The door was unlocked, and they entered. They were in the hallway next to Rebekah's room. A person, probably a nurse, went down in the middle of the hallway, but as best as we could tell, the person had not been shot.

The other two members of the rescue team entered the adjacent building. The two "company" men opened fire on the team members, but they were eliminated promptly.

Vicky was standing beside me and said, "Unless there is a secret defense force that we don't know about, it appears to be over. They have Rebekah. She is safe. They are probably calling for their helicopter now and will be on their return trip shortly. You will be seeing your wife in less than two hours. That was a clean mission."

Just as she said this, the radio crackled. "Rebekah is refusing to leave. It has something to do with the young girl. Melinda is saying that we may create a major international incident if we take the girl with us."

—

When Bill Reynolds stuck his face through my hospital room door, he said partly to his radio and partly to me, "We're secure and healthy. The helicopter is on its way. Get your stuff together."

I couldn't believe it. It never crossed my mind that I could be located out here in the middle of the desert, but there he was in full battle garb. I recognized his face. His other team member was standing over the nurse who was facedown on the floor. I stepped out into the hallway, helped the nurse to her feet, and said, "We can trust her, Bill." I turned to the nurse and said, "Take me to Amira."

Without hesitating, she led me down the hall to Amira's room.

Bill tried to argue, but I refused to listen to him. He followed but looked confused.

At the nurse's lead, I walked in and took Amira's hand. She was warm and clammy, but she felt completely lifeless. I spoke to her, but there was no response.

Amira's personal nurse was seated in the corner and started to rise, but the nurse told her in Arabic to remain where she was. The nurse looked at me and said, "She is in a coma. She can't hear you."

"Will she wake up?" I asked.

"Probably not. We did what we could, but it may not have been soon enough. I know that you two were friends. I'm sorry."

"What happened when her dad came in?" I asked.

"Amira was already in a coma. She didn't hear what he said," she explained.

Melinda stepped inside the room and said, "We must leave now. We need to board the helicopter immediately."

"No. Not yet," I said. "What did her father say?"

The nurse shook her head, obviously not wanting to repeat the event.

"Do you read Arabic?" I asked.

She nodded.

I reached into my pocket and pulled out the letter that Amira's father had dropped in my room. "Read this to me." I handed it to her.

She unfolded it and tried to smooth out the wrinkles:

> Father,
> I'm sorry for what I have done to dishonor you, but I could not allow you to complete the mission you had laid out. I would rather be dead than to live with the heart of my friend, but do not worry. I had a dream. Jesus came and held me like a little lamb. I have given my broken heart to Jesus. I will be with Him forever.
> Signed with love,
> Amira, your daughter

The nurse gently folded the letter, handed it back to me, and wiped away a tear. I slid it back into my pocket. My mind was racing. *How did she figure it out? I was going to share with her what I knew, but I didn't get a chance. She found out and chose to die instead.* As I held her hand, I thought I could feel her life slipping away. "How did her father respond after he read that letter?"

The nurse said, "He screamed at her, and then he declared that she was dead to him. I thought he was going to slap her, but he seemed to reconsider since she was wearing an oxygen mask. Then he turned and left the room. That's when he demanded that I take him to you."

Melinda was still standing in the doorway.

I said, "Melinda, Amira needs help. We're taking her with us."

As I said that, Amira coughed slightly under her mask and moved the hand I was holding. Her eyes didn't open, but she was trying to move.

The nurse immediately started checking her vitals. "She needs more than we can provide."

Melinda was attempting to argue with me but didn't speak. I could read her face. *Taking the girl could cause an international incident. Leaving her would kill her. She may not survive, but it was clear that we were her only chance.*

The nurse said, "We can air-flight her to the hospital at El Alamein. The emergency service will take about two hours to get here. I'm willing to stay with her here and go with her on the flight. I hope her young body can hang on that long."

"What then?" I asked. "Do you think her dad will change his mind?"

"About the suicide attempt? Maybe. About the letter concerning becoming a Christian? Probably never."

"I could feel his anger in my room," I said.

"I doubt that any woman has stood up to Khalid Bin Muthanna as you did. I thought he might strike you."

Melinda stepped down the hall and spoke on her phone. When she rejoined us, she said, "There are two Egyptian military helicopters about twenty minutes out. We must get out of here—now!" She turned to Bill. "How many people can we load onto the chopper?"

"Eight men, perhaps ten total if some are women and children," he said.

Melinda looked at the nurse. "Do you want to come with us?"

She nodded.

"Ask the personal nurse. There's room for her if she wants to come."

The nurse spoke to the personal nurse in Arabic, but she immediately refused. Her face reflected a mixture of fear and terror. She knew she had failed in her duties.

"Then let's go. Is there a stretcher we can move Amira onto? We can carry her, leaving the IV hooked up."

In just a few minutes, the nine of us and the pilot were loaded. The beating of the rotors sounded unbelievable.

—

Vicky and I had been attempting to decipher what we had been seeing on the satellite screen from the boat. It wasn't easy to determine, but the loading of the helicopter and the liftoff was certainly evident. We assumed the person on the stretcher was Amari, but we still didn't know why. All I knew for sure was that one of the females who boarded was Rebekah.

The two Egyptian aircraft were ten minutes away from the clinic. I wondered what they would find. I climbed up to the deck, looked out across the gentle waves of the Mediterranean, and thanked the Lord. *Rebekah is safe.*

Vicky came up and joined me. "Perhaps I should have accepted your offer to pray for me. It appears your prayers have some power."

I didn't respond as the cool sea air blew into my face.

Her phone buzzed, and she answered but didn't speak. When she put her phone down, she motioned to the captain to start us up. "Head to Tel Aviv!"

I looked at her confused.

"Our people have been keeping tabs for any unusual activity at El Alamein. There are at least twenty Egyptian armed militia waiting to arrest our team and Rebekah the second they touch down. Our team stopped at the Siwa Oasis and were able to refuel. Due to the medical needs of the young girl, they are now going straight to Tel Aviv. Thanks to Colonel Simon Abel, the chopper will be allowed to transfer Amira directly to a hospital. They will probably be there before we will."

—

The Mercedes cab pulled up to the front door of Sourasky Medical Center. Melinda was waiting for us in the foyer. After a quick elevator ride, we stepped into the ICU unit and into a room. Rebekah was in a chair, holding the young lady's hand, and medical machines and pumps were casting their sounds around the room.

I stepped up behind Rebekah, and we embraced.

Rebekah turned back toward the bed and took my hand. "Richard, I want you to meet someone. This is Amira—she's our new daughter."

"What?" I swallowed hard.

"Amira, this is your new dad."

A doctor and nurse came in and asked us all to step out for a moment.

"A daughter?" I said as I looked at the most beautiful lady in the world smiling bigger than the sky. "Have you asked her? Have you asked if she wants to be our daughter?"

"Not yet, but her father disowned her. She has nowhere else to go. She has no other family. I think that her dad doesn't even know that she is still alive."

"Is she going to live? What are the doctors saying?"

"They are encouraging, but not really. She took a whole bottle of sedatives and half a bottle of blood pressure meds. The doctor said she was lucky to be still breathing. Having her stomach pumped helped, but she still absorbed a lethal dose of both. They are having a difficult time believing that she is still alive. She is a very special young lady."

The doctor came out and said, "Are you two her parents?"

Rebekah grabbed my hand and said, "Yes, we are."

"She is a remarkable young woman. I understand from her nurse that she has had a genetic heart defect since birth."

We both nodded.

"I can hear a slight heart murmur, very slight, but if her nurse hadn't told me about the heart situation, I wouldn't have known. Her heart sounds strong to me. The drugs are working their way through her system. We are going to need to watch her carefully for the next twenty-four hours. If she makes it through the night, I think she has a chance. However, I do need to ask this question. Do you know why she tried to end her own life?"

Rebekah looked at the doctor and said, "She didn't want to undergo the heart transplant surgery that was scheduled."

He said, "I understand. Her heart will need to be checked out if she comes through this, but right now, it appears strong. We'll keep watch on her tonight. You two look like you have been through some tough times yourself. Does that arm need to be examined?"

I was so used to carrying around the cast that I had forgotten I still had it on.

"No, I have an appointment with my doctor back home. Thanks for taking care of our daughter."

The Egyptian nurse came out and joined us. "What did the doctor say?"

We told her and then invited her to join us in the cafeteria. It was getting late. None of us had any other plans but to stay, and all three of us needed a snack.

As we sat down, Rebekah turned to the nurse. "I'm sorry. I don't even know your name."

"I'm Jomana Akila."

"You're a great nurse. Thanks for coming with us and helping care for Amira on the flight."

"I'm not actually a nurse. I'm a PA. I went to school in North Carolina," she said.

"Really? So, you are a part of the Tar Heels?" I asked.

"No, bite your tongue. I'm a Blue Devil. I'm a Duke Blue Devil."

All three of laughed together. Laughter had been a rare commodity over the past several hours.

She said, "As far as coming with you to help, I was honored—but I didn't have much of a choice. I would have been in a lot of trouble if I had stayed. I may still be. I'm not sure what to do now."

I said, "Come back to the States with us. My personal doctor is trying to hire a PA. I'll give him a call if you're interested."

Jomana said that she was interested. "I'll go check on our young lady." She stood up and started to walk away.

Rebekah said, "Jomana, are you feeling well?"

"My blood pressure is probably high, but I'm good." She winked at Rebekah and continued to walk away from the food court.

I took Rebekah's hand. "I've missed you."

"I'm so sorry. There was nothing I could do. I couldn't believe that they transferred me from Missouri to Egypt so quickly. I assume you found my phone and knew what my message meant."

"Yes, your phone rang in the grass when I called it. Melinda had a Polaris team implemented in less than twenty-four hours. It's been amazing to watch them in action."

"How did they track me down to a desert in Egypt? In my mind, I didn't think there was any way for you to find me."

"That's a long and amazing story. I'll tell you when we have more time. Tell me about Amira. Is she still going to need a heart transplant?"

"I assume so, but the doctor's words make me wonder now."

"We'll get her to a doctor as soon as we get home."

We both stood, and Rebekah started crying. The tension of the day broke over her.

I held her tightly and whispered, "Father, thank you for bringing my Rebekah home. Heal Amira's heart."

Several Jewish medical staff were staring at us, so we started back to the ICU.

Halfway to the room, one of the ICU nurses approached us. She had been in and out of the room several times, but we hadn't heard her speak English. She looked around to see who might be listening and said, "You two need to read this." She handed us a computer printout and walked on without explanation.

It was a news release from Dubai with an English translation at the bottom:

> The family of Khalid Bin Muthanna has announced the death of their daughter Amira. After a long illness since birth, her heart finally gave way days before a matching transplant organ had been located. The family asks that you respect their grief.

The announcement was postdated less than an hour ago.

Rebekah said, "I didn't think anybody here at the hospital knew who Amari actually was, but her dad has let the world know that his daughter is gone."

"Amari means a lot to you, doesn't she?" I asked.

"She is an amazing young lady. Wait until she tells you about her dream," she said with a look of pure joy on her face.

"I think I'm missing part of the story, but I can wait. You look amazing," I said.

As we walked down the hall, Rebekah said, "Did you examine the bids on Uncle Billy's farm?"

"No, I wasn't even tempted without you with me."

She squeezed my hand, and we reentered the ICU area. Amira was still asleep. Jomana and Rebekah sat down together, facing Amira's bed, and I sat down next to Amira. I studied her face. Even with the oxygen mask on, I could tell she was beautiful. Her skin had a deep golden tone. Then I studied her hand. It was so delicate but strong. I wanted to meet her. I glanced at my watch. It was early in the morning, but with the jet lag, the boat experience, and now the hospital, I wasn't even sure what day it was.

Jomana looked at Rebekah and said, "I'm guessing that you aren't really as sick as we were told."

"No, I'm healthy, at least I think."

"I knew you didn't appear to be one who was suffering with cancer, but …"

"It's okay, I don't blame you."

Jomana pointed at me. "What happened to his arm?"

"A tree fell on him and broke it," said Rebekah.

While I continued to hold Amira's hand, a soft voice said, "Who are you?" At the same time, her hand squeezed mine.

"I'm Richard."

Rebekah and Jomana both jumped up and joined me beside her bed.

"Where am I?"

Rebekah said, "You're in a hospital in Israel." She seemed to be trying to process that answer as she continued to study my face.

After what seemed like forever, she moved her neck and looked at Rebekah. "I know you. You're my friend."

Two ICU nurses rushed in. Her movement must have triggered an alarm at the nurse's station.

One nurse said, "I'll get the doctor."

The other nurse began to check her vitals. "This is a miracle. This is an amazing miracle."

I looked at Rebekah, but words weren't enough.

CHAPTER 23

Snow

Rebekah and I were seated on an outdoor bench in downtown Lexington. It was Christmas Eve, and the streets were decorated with beautiful white Christmas lights. It didn't feel very cold, but a light snow was falling. I was holding a cuddled-up cute little "chunk" of a grandson who was fast asleep.

"That was quite a Christmas gift the doctors at the University of Kentucky Medical Center gave Amira. She will need to be checked out every six months, but she may have outgrown the need for a transplant," I said. "The doctor said that it happens, not often, but it has happened where a person outgrows the problem. Of course, he kept asking why we didn't have her complete medical history."

"She claims it's a healing from our prayers," Rebekah said.

"I'm not going to argue with her, are you?" I asked.

"No, I'm not," she said.

"Neither am I. You are home, Amira is healthy, my arm is out of the cast, and our grandbaby is beautiful," I said.

Rebekah pulled up the baby's quilt to protect him from the light snow. The girls were shopping together down the street.

"I have forgotten something," I said.

"What?" she asked.

"Your shirt and jacket are still at the dry cleaners in West Plains."

She started laughing. "What a tragedy."

A family walked by being pulled by a large dog on a leash.

I said, "I can't believe how Amira and Goose have teamed up. She told me that her dad never let her have a dog."

"They are fun to watch together. When do you start your physical therapy for your arm?" Rebekah asked.

"The doctor said I can wait until after Christmas."

She said, "And speaking of things to be thankful for, I love the way Uncle Billy's farm sale worked out."

"We need to thank our two West Plains lawyers for that. When we told them to open the bids, they discovered that the two KGC potential buyers didn't know the other was bidding. They decided to buy it as a team and were fine with the hundred-foot adjustment. They were even agreed to involve Henry to care for the place in exchange for the same income Billy had been receiving. That worked out great."

"I can't believe you talked the KGC guys into joining us in building an Irish Wilderness museum and ranger station," I added.

"They didn't even argue. The Forest Service agreed to staff it, and SHSMO is setting up a joint survey of the hundred feet with at least a dozen metal detectors and historians. They want to wait until spring when it's warmer."

I said, "Henry and Sheriff Nelson agreed to help oversee the project."

"That will be fun. Perhaps we should feed them when they are all there. Does Lucile's cater? Who knows what will be found with a systematic search of the area?"

"That's a great idea," I said. "Privately, the two KGC men buying the farm told me they have broken off all relations with the Order. They said that they didn't know what the Order was involved with. Maybe they didn't. Perhaps, as a form of restitution, they both made big donations to Polaris and the new museum. I think they felt guilty about the fact that they should have known."

She said, "I'm glad we disrupted the KGC's relationship with the Order, but I wish we could have done more damage to the new human trafficking organization."

"I understand. Melinda says that they have identified the mastermind who was behind organizing the French doctor, Amari's father, the Egyptian clinic, and—"

"And me. I was the key link to that plan," she said as the snow continued to fall.

"He's been identified, but not located. At least not yet. As you know, the cruise ship was empty when Melinda's team boarded, but Melinda believes they will locate him. Her team is quite effective in locating an individual," I said.

"Yes, they are. They are very good." She squeezed my leg.

"Melinda told me that this spring she wants to have a get-together and bring Norma so we can meet her," I said.

"Without Norma, things would not have worked out as well as they did. I really want to thank her," she said.

"I'm still haunted from watching the online auction. Perhaps, with the help of the foundation, Melinda and her team will be able to slow down that horror," I said.

We both knew that we lived in a fallen world and that evil will not be stopped until Jesus returns. Our grandkid stretched out his little hands into the falling snow as if to proclaim, "Hallelujah."

"There has been so much going on that I forgot to mention that the sheriff discovered the hole-digging culprit. One of Dennis's classmates went on a spree while his dad was out of town. The lure of Jesse James's treasure was more than a teenage spirit could handle. He took their new backhoe to demonstrate to another friend that he knew how to use it. He told the sheriff that they didn't find anything, but the sheriff made the boy go back out and fill in the hole. I told the sheriff we didn't want to press charges."

"I've been thinking about one other possibility. Let's set up a college scholarship fund in honor of Billy. I even know who the first recipient should be," she said.

"Does he drive an old blue-green Ford?" I asked.

She grinned at me.

We continued to sit there, holding our new grandchild and watching the soft snow fall, as couples and families passed us on the sidewalk. None of them could be as happy as we were.

"Are you good?" I asked.

"I think so. I spent a lot of time in trucks, planes, and desert hospital rooms. I tried to make sense of what was happening, but it was never enough. It wasn't my mind that was really suffering; it was my soul. I think that is why God didn't send us a book of answers. He sent us a Savior."

Without realizing it, I noticed that she reached up and felt for the bullet hole scar in her shoulder. I think it was more of a reminder to be thankful than anything else.

The snow started falling heavier. Against the Christmas lights, it was an amazing sight.

"Did Bill Jackson call you this morning," she asked.

"Yes, he did," I said. "I'm still thinking about what he said."

"What? What did he say?"

"Our pastor told the elders last week that his parents in Vermont are not doing well. He thinks he needs to move up there to take care of them. Bill asked me if I was interested in coming back as their pastor."

"Are you interested?"

"I'm praying about it."

She grabbed my hand and squeezed with a smile that was big enough to melt the falling snow.

We heard the laughter of our three daughters, "There you are!" they yelled. Micah, Lisa, and their new little sister, Amira, were briskly walking toward us.

Micah said, "We have something we want to show you. Get up, you two world travelers."

They led us down the street to a small art shop and ushered us inside.

Amari led the way to the back of the shop, but Micah was the spokesman, and she said, "The three of us want to buy you a Christmas gift—and there it is." She pointed to an amazing painting of an African lion standing on a rock cleft. It was a marvelous painting.

I whispered, "I can almost hear his roar."

Rebekah leaned in close and whispered, "So can I."

AUTHOR'S NOTE

This novel is a work of fiction. The characters are fictional, but most of the place names are real. However, liberty was taken in describing the various places. For example, there really is a West Plains, Missouri, but as far as I know, there is no Lucile's Café. There really is an Irish Wilderness and a Mark Twain National Forest, and I plan to hike the eighteen-mile White Creek Trail someday. There really was a Father Hogan and a Jesse James, though the latter may have never entered the Irish Wilderness.

The two actual truths within this fictional story are reflected within the purpose of its writing. Beyond an interesting story, there is a description of true Christian faith that honestly struggles within the lives of the characters. Faith is a battle, and I trust reading this story has increased your desire to discover "the warrior within."

The other truth revealed is the tragedy of modern-day human trafficking. Writing the description of the human auction left me with a heavy heart for several days. I so wanted to end the story with the destruction of the human trafficking organization, but that would not have been honest. This evil exists in our world and brings terror to many here and around the world. Writing about the experience of the new faith of a young Muslim girl lifted my heart with an unspeakable joy. I trust that you, as a reader, will realize the depth of this evil while experiencing the power of this joy.

I wrote my first book, *Lost Under the Lion's Shadow*, with a good story in my heart, but I lacked the tools to do it justice. After attending the Novel Writing Intensive with Steven James and Robert Dugoni, I realized the feebleness of my writing ability. Both men challenged me to learn the tools of the trade. About halfway through the intensive experience, Steven James asked me how I was handling the intensive situation. I told him that I felt like I showed up at a Harley-Davidson convention while riding a tricycle. I thank both Steven and Bob for the challenge.

I also greatly appreciate two friends of mine who graciously helped me edit the rough draft. Randa Upp and Mike Davis both greatly contributed making the story more readable. I hope you have enjoyed reading as much as I have enjoyed writing.

—Dr. David Ray

Printed in the United States
by Baker & Taylor Publisher Services